MW01093375

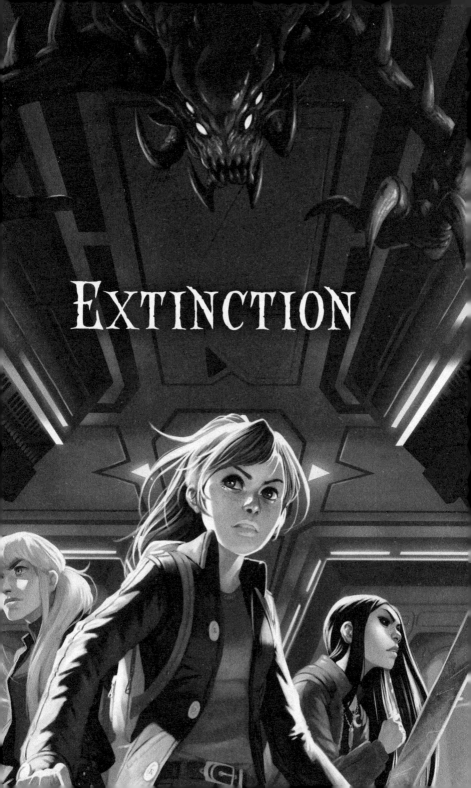

EXTINCTION

ALSO BY

HEIDI LANG & KATI BARTKOWSKI

Whispering Pines Series:
Whispering Pines
Infestation
Reckoning
Extinction

The Mystic Cooking Chronicles:
A Dash of Dragon
A Hint of Hydra
A Pinch of Phoenix

WHISPERING PINES
EXTINCTION

Heidi Lang & Kati Bartkowski

MARGARET K. McELDERRY BOOKS
NEW YORK LONDON TORONTO SYDNEY NEW DELHI

MARGARET K. McELDERRY BOOKS
An imprint of Simon & Schuster Children's Publishing Division
1230 Avenue of the Americas, New York, New York 10020

Text © 2023 by Heidi Lang and Kati Bartkowski
Jacket illustration © 2023 by Xavier Collette
Jacket design by Tiara Iandiorio © 2023 by Simon & Schuster, Inc.
For information about special discounts for bulk purchases, please contact
Simon & Schuster Special Sales at 1-866-506-1949 or business@simonandschuster.com.
The Simon & Schuster Speakers Bureau can bring authors to your live event.
For more information or to book an event, contact the Simon & Schuster Speakers
Bureau at 1-866-248-3049 or visit our website at www.simonspeakers.com.
Interior design by Michael Rosamilia
The text for this book was set in Adobe Caslon Pro.
Manufactured in the United States of America
0823 FFG
First Edition
2 4 6 8 10 9 7 5 3 1
CIP data for this book is available from the Library of Congress.
ISBN 9781665921916
ISBN 9781665921923 (ebook)

For Lillie, Bridget, and Maya. You were such a large part
of our childhood that there's a little bit of all of you
in every middle-grade story we write.

PROLOGUE

Blake shifted on the hard cot, the Green On! jumpsuit they'd given him scratchy against his skin. He wasn't sure how long he'd been in here, unconscious. He was dimly aware of drifting in and out, of several people checking his wounds, replacing his bandages, adjusting his IV, but it all seemed fuzzy and dreamlike, the people evaporating like smoke the moment he tried to focus on them.

He'd only become fully awake recently. A day ago? Two? It was impossible to tell down here, where there were no clocks and no windows.

His room was small enough to walk across in three big strides, with four walls made of a thick glass that sent his distorted reflection back at him and a single door set into one of the walls. That door was kept locked at all times; he'd checked. Repeatedly. A toilet and sink sat in a small alcove in one corner, and a cot with one thin blanket was set in the middle, and that was it for comforts.

Since he'd woken up, his only visitor had been a quiet man with pale eyes and graying hair who refused to answer any of his questions. At first, Blake had tried asking if he could talk to his parents, his friends, even Patrick. Anyone who'd be able to tell him what was going on. But the man never responded. He would just set down a tray of food and water and then change Blake's bandages, as if Blake were nothing more than another piece of lab equipment, before leaving again as silently as he entered.

So Blake gave up trying. Now he just lay on the cot listening to the overhead light buzzing and the increasingly dark spiral of his thoughts.

He'd *seen* the scientists remove the bugs, had watched as they slit open his stomach and carefully removed the two dark, glistening bodies. He'd been awake through it all. Horribly, terribly awake, since there hadn't been time to put him under; as they'd rushed him to the lab, his stomach had already been bulging and shifting, the bugs clawing and digging from the inside. It was only afterwards that he'd been able to escape into unconsciousness.

So why was Green On! still keeping him hidden down here if their surgery had been successful? Why not let him recover in a hospital, or at the very least see his parents? There had to be a reason. But the only ones he could think of were sinister. Maybe Green On! planned to keep him down here until everyone on the surface had forgotten about him. And then . . . what?

He couldn't help thinking of all the kids who had gone missing from his school. One or two every year, at least. What if all those missing children were here? Deep in the bowels of Green On!, hidden away in a lab that no one knew about, being used in unspeakable experiments . . .

Blake tried pushing those thoughts away, but the truth was, he'd known something was wrong with this place. Known it the moment he was approached by Patrick Smith, the senior consultant to Green On!, a surprisingly young man with the kind of wide, easy smile his Uncle Gary had taught him never to trust. Blake didn't always listen to his uncle—the man preferred goats over people, after all—but when he'd gazed into Patrick's blue eyes, it was like looking into a pond and realizing it was only a shallow puddle; there wasn't any depth there. No spark of humanity.

Somehow Patrick had known about the impossibly giant bugs Blake had seen in the woods. And in exchange for more details, Patrick had offered him an internship position with Green On!. Blake had accepted despite his misgivings, especially after Patrick promised he would use all the resources at his disposal to find those bugs.

And maybe he'd kept that promise; Blake had no idea. All he knew was that the very monsters he'd left the woods to escape had gotten him anyhow, dragging him deep underground. And even though he'd supposedly been rescued, he hadn't seen daylight since and was beginning to wonder if he ever would again.

"Beep! Beep! Beep! Shutdown procedures commencing immediately. This is not a drill."

Blake froze, terror cascading over him in an icy wave. The overhead light flickered like a candle in an open window, making mysterious shadows sway and dance throughout the room as the alarm blared on.

"Beep! Beep! Beep! Everyone to your designated safe rooms. You have fifteen minutes. Countdown begins . . . now."

The overhead light flickered one last time, then went out, plunging the room into darkness just as the alarm fell silent.

Blake lay there, his ears full of the sound of his own breathing, harsh and fast, and the rapid pounding of his heart. He'd been here once before when an alarm had gone off. That time, it had ended up being a false nuclear meltdown. He doubted Green On! would make the same mistake again.

Something was wrong. Horribly, terribly, truly wrong.

There was a soft *click* and a red light filtered down from the ceiling, filling the room with its pulsing bloody glow. Blake pushed himself up to sitting, his head spinning with the movement. He ignored it and the rush of weakness as he yanked the IV from his hand. He had to get out of this place. Now. Or he was certain he would die down here.

He eased himself off the cot, waiting a second for the strength to return to his legs, then stumbled over to the door.

Locked. Of course it was still locked. He was trapped here.

"Beep! Beep! Beep! Fourteen minutes remaining. This is not a drill. Shutdown procedures commencing."

Frantic now, Blake began pounding on the door, shouting, "Someone? Anyone? Help me! Please!" again and again until his throat ached and his hand went numb and he was forced to stop, panting and terrified and sick with the knowledge that he'd survived having alien bugs crammed down his throat only to die here now, in this place.

"Please," he whispered, his voice breaking. He leaned his forehead against the cool glass of the door and closed his eyes, the emergency lights painting the backs of his eyelids in vivid red.

The door whooshed open so abruptly he almost fell. He staggered back, staring at the figure framed in the hallway, and for a second his mind went blank and he was back in the caves again, trapped in a giant egg sac.

It oozed around him, warm and sticky, clinging to his chest, his legs, his arms, sliding under his clothes and seeping into his skin, the rancid burning-tire smell of it filling his nostrils. And inside that ooze, the feeling of thousands of tiny bodies wriggling against him, waiting for their kin to burst from his body so they could feed on his guts.

And then *she* was there, clinging to the rock like some kind of superhero, firelight glinting in her dark eyes, her mouth bared to reveal all of her small sharp teeth as she cut him free with a ferocity he never would have guessed she possessed.

Vivienne Matsuoka, who had saved him. Who was here now, ready to save him again.

Maybe he'd never left the cave, and all of this—the scientists, the lab, the alarm—was just a dream his mind had spun out to fill the short time he had left. And Vivienne was nothing more than a mirage. A last, desperate hope for a savior from somewhere deep inside his soul.

"What are you *doing*?" Vivienne snapped at him. "Don't just stand there!"

He blinked, and reality crashed back into him. It *wasn't* Vivienne. This woman was much older, her black hair streaked with white, wrinkles fanning out from the corners of her eyes and mouth. Vivienne's *mom*, who worked here as the head of the nuclear division. The red lights reflected strangely in her dark eyes and painted her face a garish color, but he still recognized her.

"Wh-what's going on?" he stammered, his tongue thick in his dry mouth.

"The end of everything," she said grimly. "Including us, if we don't get out before shutdown."

As if on cue, the alarm blared again. *Beep! Beep! Beep! Thirteen minutes remaining. Report to your designated safe rooms immediately.*

"Come on!" she yelled, turning away from him and hurrying down the hall.

Blake forced himself to follow after her. Each step sent pain shooting through his abdomen, but he didn't slow, didn't stop. He kept his gaze focused on the back of Mrs. Matsuoka's lab coat, now noticing the blood smeared in patches across it, the way she held her left arm as she ran, how she was limping slightly.

This, whatever it was, didn't seem to be a nuclear emergency. So what was it? What could have injured her like that?

He noticed rooms to the left and right of him as he ran. They were made of glass too, and he caught glimpses of other people moving inside them, their arms up, mouths opening and closing soundlessly as they yelled for help. People, trapped the way he had been trapped.

"What about them?" Blake panted.

Mrs. Matsuoka spared one quick glance at the closest room, the corners of her mouth turning down. "I can't do anything for them. Not right now."

"But we can't just leave them—"

Mrs. Matsuoka whirled, grabbing him by the front of the shirt and yanking his face close to hers so abruptly he gasped.

"This is a lockdown," she hissed. "Once it's complete, no one gets in, and *nothing* gets out. I couldn't just leave you here after what Vivi went through to save you, but there's no time for me to help anyone else. So either follow me to safety now, or stay and die with the others." She released him and he stumbled back, crashing against the wall.

Blake rubbed his chest as Mrs. Matsuoka limped away down the hall, not waiting to see what he'd do. He glanced once more into the room behind him and the doomed man inside, and guilt squeezed his heart. That could have been him. He hesitated, not feeling right about just leaving, whatever Mrs. Matsuoka said.

And then from somewhere behind him came an earsplitting scream, long and high and terrified.

Blake froze, every muscle in his body tense as that sound went on and on. He'd heard a scream like that before. Once. His uncle's goats, at the start of the infestation. Only this was no goat.

The scream cut off in a loud, horrible gurgle.

Fear took over Blake's body, and suddenly he was running, sprinting after Mrs. Matsuoka. Any guilt dropped immediately from his mind, the pain in his stomach barely registering as he tried to outrun whatever might have caused that sound.

He caught up with Mrs. Matsuoka as she turned the corner, leading him down another hallway. As she ran, she spoke into something. "Where are you?"

A burst of static. Some answer Blake couldn't decipher.

"We're on our way," Mrs. Matsuoka said. "Wait for us."

Another burst of static, but this time Blake heard the words "closing the gates."

Mrs. Matsuoka swore and picked up her pace, Blake struggling to match her. He'd never run so fast in his life, the walls to either side a blur, and still he could swear he heard something gaining on him, the click-click of talons as it got closer, closer . . .

They turned another corner, and Blake stumbled, tripping over a pile of clothing someone had left behind. He caught his balance on the wall, and then realized it wasn't clothing at all. It was a leg. The *entire* leg, as if something had just torn it free as easily as his little sister pulled the legs off her Barbies.

There was no sign of the rest of the body.

"Oh, God," Blake whispered, clapping a hand over his mouth. He was going to be sick. He was going—

A shriek behind him, a sense of movement from the corner of his eye, and he was running again. Dimly he noticed the blood pooling on the floor. The other pieces of what had once been at least two more people. The gore spattered against the walls. But mostly he thrust all that out of his mind, not allowing himself to *really* see it. He couldn't, or he'd freeze up again. And to stop now was to die. Horribly.

Don't think too hard, just run became his motto. *Just run. Just survive.*

He was so caught up in that mantra that he almost crashed into Mrs. Matsuoka's back when she skidded to a halt in front of a large metal door. He staggered to a stop behind her, breathing heavily, heart pounding as she swiped the keycard that hung around her neck over a sensor set next to the door.

Nothing happened.

Frowning, she swiped it again. Still nothing.

Blake looked back the way they had come. The emergency lights flashed red and awful, turning the hallway behind him into a mass of moving shadows.

He blinked, and the shadows were still there. Except they weren't shadows at all but monsters. The one in front looked at him through four narrowed glowing eyes, its snakelike head thrust forward, short arms tucked against its chest. Its lips peeled back in a wide smile, revealing rows of long, needle-sharp teeth, before it threw its head back and shrieked.

All the moisture seemed to evaporate from Blake's mouth, his entire body went numb. The creature was so close he could see the bloodstains on its teeth, the breath puffing from its slitted nose, the way its muscles rippled like water as it moved. It made a soft noise in the back of its throat. A sort of *click-click-grrr.*

Blake wanted to run. *Needed* to run. But he couldn't get his feet to move. They felt like they belonged to someone else. Like his body wasn't his own anymore.

And then, from his other side, he heard it. *Click-click-grrr.*

Slowly, very slowly, he turned his head.

Another one of those creatures was oozing toward him from the opposite end of the hall. Its lips curled back in a mockery of a smile, its four glowing eyes curved into narrow, satisfied slits. *Click-click-grrr.* It slid forward, its mouth opening wider, revealing a piece of bright green cloth snagged around one needle-sharp tooth, and a long, snakelike tongue that wriggled in anticipation. It didn't run; there was no need. Blake and Mrs. Matsuoka were trapped.

"Mrs. Matsuoka?" he whimpered, clutching at the back of her lab coat.

"A little. Busy. Here," she muttered, her words clipped, her fingers racing across a keypad that had been hidden behind the door sensor.

The creatures slid closer. He could smell the blood on them, its scent sharp and metallic, could feel the air whispering as they moved through it. They'd be on them in five seconds. Four. Three.

The door popped open.

Blake stared at it for half a second, surprised, before Mrs. Matsuoka grabbed him by the front of his jumpsuit and yanked him through after her.

"The door! Shut the door!" she screamed, and he scrambled forward, finding the handle and tugging it closed.

Too late.

A long, curved talon caught the edge of the door just before it shut, pulling it back outward; a head thrust its way into the open space, teeth snapping. Blake yanked on the handle with every ounce of strength he possessed, trying to squash the thing's face, but he wasn't strong enough. A second talon joined the first, and the door began opening wider.

"Let go!" a man's voice boomed behind him.

Let go? Blake held on tighter, gritting his teeth.

"Now!"

Tears streamed down his cheeks, but he kept his grip until his hands cramped and his fingers were too weak to hang on any longer. The handle slid from his grasp.

The door banged open.

The monster on the other side reared back, its long neck stretching up, up, towering over Blake, filling the doorway. It had the elongated face of an eel, its head and neck forming one continuous line. That face lowered down, the lips drawing back, mouth opening. Blake closed his eyes, his whole body tensed, and prayed it wouldn't hurt too much.

Blam!

His eyes flew open. The monster lurched back, greenish blood oozing from a hole in its chest.

"What the—" Blake whispered, just as a second *blam!* echoed through his ears. This time he saw something shoot past him, the heat of it sizzling as it missed his face by inches, slicing into the monster's neck. The monster staggered, then toppled sideways.

"*Now* shut the door!" the man yelled.

Blake felt as if he were watching himself from somewhere outside his body as he stepped forward and slammed the door shut. It made a satisfying *click* just before a second monster crashed into it, shrieking. The door wobbled, the metal in the middle denting slightly, but held as the monster slammed into it again and again. After its third attempt, it stopped.

Blake waited, hardly daring to breathe, listening with every fiber of his being. He could hear it snuffling on the other side. Then another shriek, and footsteps, and it was gone.

He sagged back against the door, then turned to face the room.

A man stood just behind him. He had a wide squashed nose, an unruly beard, and a truly terrifying scowl. But despite that, there was something comforting about him. Maybe it was the giant weapon held in his hands, or the way he stood with his legs spread, shoulders wide as if ready for anything. He looked like the kind of person who could deal with a situation like this.

"Thank you," Blake whispered.

The man nodded, then turned away. "Where's everyone else? We need to move."

As if on cue, the alarm blared, *Beep! Beep! Beep! Eight minutes remaining until complete lockdown. Beep! Beep! Beep!"*

Blake gazed out across the small room. It looked a lot like one of his school's science labs, with tables set in front of desks, glass vials lining the walls, and a sink in the corner. There were about a dozen people clustered in the middle, all adults, half of them wearing modified hazmat suits and holding weapons. The other half were dressed like Mrs. Matsuoka in simple lab coats.

Another woman with short curly hair spoke into a walkie-talkie, then waited, her lips pressed together in a tight line. No one answered. She spoke again and waited. Then she looked up. "I think this is everyone who made it."

The air seemed to leak out of the room, and Blake wondered how many people they'd been expecting. He decided not to ask. He'd rather not know.

"Don't look so scared, boy," the man with the laser told him. "You made it here. You're safe now with us."

"But who *are* you?" Blake asked.

The stranger grinned, his teeth flashing white and sudden against the darkness of his beard. "We're from Green On!'s experimental and research department. And we've been preparing for an event like this for years."

"What event is that?"

The smile dropped away. "An invasion, boy. A hostile alien take-over. What did you think was happening?"

"But . . . but why? What do they *want*?"

"Isn't it obvious? Our extinction." The man turned away, following the rest of the group through a small door in the back. Blake hurried after them and down a narrow corridor, all his questions dying as he struggled to keep up with the others. His stomach burned as he ran, and he worried his stitches might burst. But there was nothing he could do about that now.

Mrs. Matsuoka stopped them all at another door. She swiped her keycard, then punched in a code. There was a beep, and she pulled the door open to reveal a steep metal stairway lit by the same familiar flashing red emergency lighting.

Everyone filed past her until it was just her and Blake.

"Go on," she told him. "The exit out is at the top of the stairs."

Something about her voice made him hesitate and really look

at her. She looked . . . sad. It was her eyes, the way they shone like she was holding back tears. "Aren't you coming too?" he asked.

"Not yet. There's one more thing I still have to do." She put a hand on his shoulder. "Find Vivi for me, would you? And tell her . . ." She paused, took a deep breath. "Tell her I'll see her as soon as I can, okay?" Her voice broke on the last word, and she let him go. "Hurry now," she whispered. "The others won't wait for you."

Blake nodded.

He left her standing there. Alone. A few steps up and he heard the door slam shut behind him. He flinched but kept going, already knowing he'd never be able to explain to Vivienne that her mother had saved his life, and then he'd left her behind.

As he climbed, he noticed the way the front of his jumpsuit had begun to stick to him. Tentatively he pressed a hand against it. It came away bloody, and he wiped his hand on his pants and tried not to picture his guts spilling out of the open wound. Wrapping one arm around his stomach, he moved faster up the stairs. Only now he could feel his blood trickling out and knew he must be leaving a trail behind. One that anything could be following . . .

He tried not to think about that either, but it was harder to push it from his mind. Especially in here, where the air felt hot and still and smelled unpleasantly musky, like the den of some animal. Various noises echoed strangely around him: the clanging of metal, the echo of a scream, ominous-sounding whispers. It was impossible to tell where any of it was coming from.

Blake finally caught up to the others near the top of the stairwell just as the alarm announced the two-minute warning. He could feel the breeze from outside, could smell the crisp autumn air, and his heart beat faster.

They were leaving through the open door ahead one-by-one, like a trail of slow-moving ants, each person looking around before darting outside. Blake fought down the sudden urge to shove everyone out of his way and dive through the door as he slowly climbed the remaining stairs until he reached the small, cramped landing. Just three people ahead of him. Then two. Then one, a woman in a lab coat with tightly braided blond hair.

She poked her head out the door before rearing back, almost running into Blake.

"Frank!" she gasped, catching her balance as someone blocked the doorway in front of her. "What are you *doing*?"

Blake recognized the thick beard and squashed nose of his earlier savior. But the expression on the man's face was all wrong. His eyes were wide and bloodshot, his lips pulled back in a strange rictus of a grin. Huge fat beads of sweat rolled down his forehead.

"Frank?" the woman said again.

Blake had a sudden terrible feeling in the pit of his stomach. He opened his mouth, but his warning died as Frank's hand shot out, grabbing the woman by the neck.

She made a strangled sound as he lifted her off her feet, her legs kicking, hands scrabbling at his fingers as he brought her face close to his own. He opened his mouth impossibly wide, ropy saliva dripping from his teeth. It was like he'd been possessed and was going to eat her face right there on the stairs.

Instead, he made a horrible gurgling in the back of his throat and spat a thick glob of yellowish-green mucus right into the woman's eye. Then he dropped her.

She fell to her knees on the landing, gasping for breath, one hand desperately wiping at her face. "That," she gasped, "was the grossest thing I've ever experienced." She wiped harder as Blake stood frozen behind her. Unable to help. Unable to *move*.

She turned and looked at him, her eyes wide. The one Frank had spat in was changing, blood vessels bursting, turning it a bloody, irritated red. "What's . . . happening?" she slurred, her lips getting stuck on her teeth on the last word. No, not stuck. They were pulling back, the way Frank's had, turning her face into an inhuman mask.

Blake's heart hammered, and he looked from her to Frank to the open door. He backed up, his heel sliding off the edge of the landing behind him.

"Beep! Beep! Beep! Ten seconds remaining until complete lockdown," the alarm blared.

The noise seemed to confuse Frank; he spun around, searching for it.

"Ten . . . nine . . . eight . . ."

But the woman was still staring straight at Blake, and now both of her eyes were bloodshot, sweat beading on her forehead and upper lip.

"Five . . . four . . . three . . ."

The door made an angry buzzing noise.

"Run," the woman whispered. And she lunged at Frank, yanking him against the wall and clearing the doorway for one precious second.

That was all Blake needed; he threw himself out the door, sliding across the ground on his stomach. Pain erupted through his entire body, so intense he almost blacked out.

"One."

The door slammed shut behind him, locking Frank and the woman inside.

Blake clung to consciousness, taking shallow breaths, then pushed himself up to his hands and knees and looked around.

The sky was just starting to lighten, highlighting individual trees in the surrounding mass, turning them from black to green. The nearest tree soaked up that light, practically glowing. Blake stared at it, noticing the weird fungus growing along its bark in thick ropy tendrils, reminding him unpleasantly of Frank's saliva. Several knobs the size of his fist protruded from those tendrils, each of them pulsating like an infected wound.

Blake scrambled to his feet and moved instinctively away, one arm clutched tightly around his stomach. Beyond the tree stood a handful of people in bright green suits and lab coats. He took a step toward them, then stopped as one-by-one, they all turned to face him.

At first he thought they were grinning at him. And then he noticed the way their lips were pulled back too tightly. And as they lurched closer, their eyes bloody, he knew that Frank had been dead wrong.

No one was prepared for this.

1.
RAE

Rae watched the trees blowing outside the car window. Their naked branches were moving so fast in the wind that they almost looked like the tentacled plants of the Other Place. She closed her eyes a second, opened them again, and they were just trees.

That seemed to be happening to her a lot lately. Ever since she'd gotten out of that awful alternate dimension, she'd felt as if a part of her were still there, still trapped. Or like she'd brought that place with her.

"So . . ." Ava began, the word heavy with meaning. And then she just stopped there, waiting. She had agreed to drive Rae to the café across the street from her school this morning so Rae could meet her friends there before class started. Supposedly it was a nice gesture, but really Rae figured her older sister just wanted the chance to yell at her. Rae had gone into the Other Place and then followed a man she knew to be dangerous inside a secret spaceship, all without first telling anyone.

Doctor Nguyen had come to their house yesterday and filled Ava and their mom in about the spaceship and about Patrick. How he was really an alien, and how he'd used Rae's desire to find her dad as a way to trap her. She'd suggested that their mom tell Ava and Rae the truth.

Their mom had told them some of it. Like the fact that the *real* reason they'd moved here was because their dad was somewhere in this town. Only, some kind of secret organization that worked at Green On! wasn't letting him contact them. Apparently they were still mad he'd released Patrick—the alien—a year ago. Even though he'd had no idea the alien was evil. He'd just been trying to help.

After that bombshell, Rae had told her sister about the Other Place. How she and her friends had been sent into it, and how Caden and Aiden had somehow destroyed it. So now there was no Other Place. Instead, they had a forest here full of monsters just waiting to descend on the town. The only thing stopping them was the magical barrier Caden's parents had created around the Watchful Woods.

Her sister had listened to her story, thanked her for *finally* telling her something true, and then hadn't said much more than a word to her since. Obviously she was angry.

Rae turned away from the window and the darkening storm clouds racing across the sky. Might as well get this lecture over with. It wasn't as if she didn't deserve it. "So," she said, watching her sister's profile. Everyone said they looked alike. Same big brown eyes, similarly colored brown hair. But where Rae's jaw was square, her chin prominent, her sister was all soft lines and rounded features. It made her seem more vulnerable, even though she was four years older.

Maybe that was why Rae was so reluctant to tell her everything. She wanted to protect her from some of the nightmares she'd had to face herself.

Ava's gaze flicked to her, then back to the road. And in that moment, Rae remembered that Ava had faced her own share of nightmares recently. She'd faced them, and they hadn't broken her.

"I'm sorry I haven't been good about keeping you informed," Rae said. "I should have told you I was going into the Other Place, but it all happened so fast. And . . . I didn't want you to try to stop me."

Ava nodded but said nothing.

"And the spaceship," Rae continued. "I should have told you about that, too. But again, so fast. And . . ."

"And you didn't want me to try to stop you," Ava repeated, her voice flat. "I get it, Rae. I do. But the whole point of our deal was that we were in this thing together. You promised, but you keep leaving me behind anyhow. How am I supposed to help find Dad if I don't even know what's going on?"

Rae looked down at her lap. "*I* don't know what's going on either," she said quietly.

"But you have some ideas."

"Not really." She took a deep breath. "But I know someone who does. We both do." She glanced at her sister, waiting.

After a second, Ava's eyebrows lifted. "Doctor Nguyen."

Rae nodded. She had been Patrick's right-hand woman, helping him with all his plans, up until the end when she'd decided to help Rae instead. And she'd known their dad was somewhere in Whispering Pines. There had to be a lot more that she knew. But after yesterday, Rae couldn't shake the sense that, despite all her secret knowledge, the scientist was in over her head.

"You think we should talk to her?" Ava turned onto the road that led toward Rae's school.

"Well, I was thinking . . ." Rae paused as the outline of Dana S. Middle School came into view. The red bricks of the outside looked especially dramatic today against the coal-black of the sky, and the nearby trees whipping frantically in the wind. Several teachers hurried in through the front doors clutching their hats and scarves, as if afraid the sky would open up on them at any moment.

Ava drove past the school, pulling into the parking lot of Kat's Café across the street. "You want to go see her," she said as she parked.

"Yes."

Ava sighed. "When?"

"Honestly? Now."

Ava frowned. "What about your little party?"

Rae had told her friends she wanted to meet this morning to celebrate surviving the world's worst internship. But that wasn't really why she wanted to see them now. Or at least, it wasn't the full reason. If all went according to her plan, she and Ava wouldn't be going to see Doctor Nguyen alone. "Fine. After the celebration."

"I can't let you skip school. Mom would kill me if she found out."

"I know." But the thought of sitting there another day, pretending she cared about her classes, all the while knowing that her dad—her *dad!*—was somewhere close by, felt almost impossible.

"How about right after school?" Ava said. "I'll pick you up, and we'll go straight there."

"Really?" Rae looked at her sister.

"Really." Ava smiled. "You and me."

Rae smiled back, relief making her eyes watery. "Let's do it."

"Don't sneak off without me now, okay?"

"I won't," Rae promised. She wrestled the door open and got out of the car, the wind howling around her. Waving, she managed to get the door shut again and then sprinted toward the café as the pressure of the storm built around her. Crossing the street to her school would be fun in this weather. She'd never experienced a storm quite like this one in California.

It felt a little better inside, away from that wind. Still, there was a strange energy crackling through the café. People huddled around their drinks and breakfast sandwiches, talking softly as they glanced uneasily at the trees whipping about outside the window. It reminded Rae of animals in the wild. How they'd all go to ground whenever a big storm was coming.

They know, she realized. Something was coming. Something bigger than this storm. Then she wondered where that thought had come from.

2.
CADEN

Caden paced across an overgrown yard, kicking at piles of dead leaves and scowling at the ragged rosebushes beside him. They were a stark contrast to the cheerful blue of the house, which had been carefully painted and maintained. A house he had once helped Rae break into, mere weeks ago. Weeks that felt like months.

He and Rae had believed the occupant of the house—Doctor Anderson—had been the Unseeing, a monster that stole the eyes from children. After they'd discovered their schoolmate Jeremy Bentley chained up in the basement, his eyes gone, his mind destroyed, Green On! had hauled Doctor Anderson away.

According to Rae, Green On! had him stashed away inside an alien pod on their secret buried spaceship. Even though it turned out he'd been innocent all along. The psychiatrist *had* been snooping around Green On!'s property, trying to expose whatever dirty secrets they might have. Maybe he'd found something.

Caden felt a tiny flicker of guilt, but he couldn't do anything for Doctor Anderson right now. Apparently, he couldn't do anything for anyone.

His mood darkened, and he wrapped his arms around himself as wind howled around him, the sunrise hidden behind a sheet of deep, foreboding gray clouds. The air felt heavy with the pressure of a building storm. Caden welcomed it. At least it would distract him from his thoughts.

"Wake up, Caden," his brother had said earlier that morning, shaking him. "Get dressed. We have to meet Mom and Dad. They need our help." Aiden had refused to answer any questions, only telling him that something major had happened, and the spell his mother had cast to contain the monsters of the Other Place inside the Watchful Woods was now unstable.

They'd driven through the predawn gloom to Doctor Anderson's house—the place his parents had turned into their headquarters— and been greeted at the door by a short redheaded woman wearing a flowing purple dress and matching glasses. Caden had recognized her as part of the local coven of witches that lived in Whispering Pines. There were six of them, four women and two men. Caden had met them briefly before; his mother didn't like to work with anyone outside the family for her own magic, but occasionally she would assist in someone else's spellwork. The fact that they were here now meant things must be dire.

"It's about time," the woman had said, ushering Aiden in. When Caden tried to follow, she'd stopped him. "Just the older Price boy."

"But I can help," Caden had said, trying to get past her. He'd managed to get one foot in the door before his mom was there, her expression grim.

"Wait outside," she'd said.

"But—"

"We'll call if we need you." And then she'd firmly shut the door in his face. As if he were a little kid and would just be in the way.

That had been almost an hour ago, and since then, nothing.

Caden's scowl deepened. Hadn't he proven himself to his parents yet? His mom had told him that he was the heir to the family business, Paranormal Price. He'd be the one taking over her duties, protecting the town of Whispering Pines from the supernatural. And yet now, when things were bad, who did she turn to?

Aiden. Always, always Aiden.

The familiar well of resentment and jealousy swirled around him, threatening to suck him under. For as long as he could remember, he'd always been torn between the strong desire to be just like his powerful older brother, and an equally strong terror that one day, he really *would* become exactly like Aiden.

Aiden wasn't a nice person. He made bad things happen to people who angered him, and he was arrogant and selfish in his quest for more power. It was his decision to tear a rift into the Other Place ten months ago that had started everything: he'd released the Unseeing into their town, and the energy signature had attracted Patrick's attention, ultimately bringing him to Whispering Pines.

Everything else—Patrick's determination to get into the Other Place so he could use it to power up the spaceship, the demon that had almost destroyed all of them, the current infestation of their woods with creatures that belonged on another planet—could also be traced back to Aiden's reckless act.

His brother would never apologize. In his mind, he'd suffered most of all, having endured nine months of torture inside the Other Place. He didn't care about the eight kids who'd had their eyes removed, or about Rae's sister, whose soul had almost been devoured, or about the damage to their town. He only cared about himself.

Caden took a deep breath, trying to loosen the web of negative emotions binding him. His mom must have her reasons for wanting Aiden in on the spell—and not wanting *him*—and he had to respect that. Whether he liked it or not.

He reached the picket fence and paused, gazing out at the Watchful Woods beyond. The trees seemed to gaze back, their branches eerily still despite the wind howling around him, as if whatever storm was building out here stopped at the forest's edge.

Below the trees, a stone wall formed a solid moss-covered line that snaked out in either direction as far as he could see, encircling everything. The air above the wall shimmered, rippling like the waters of a lake, and Caden thought he heard the echo of a cry—the shriek of some creature that did not belong in their world—before it was abruptly covered in a cocoon of silence.

His remaining anger and hurt pride dissipated, washed away in a sudden icy burst of fear as he stared out into that darkness, his eyes straining for movement, his senses open. The spell around the woods pulsed like a bad strobe light, its magic fading in and out. If it failed, then all the horrors of the Other Place would spill out into the town. The Devourers, the Unseeing, the Ravenous. Things with tentacles and talons and too many teeth. *Hungry* things.

He felt another pulse of magic as the spell in the house reached its crescendo. The air above the wall seemed to thicken until it formed glowing lines crisscrossing all the way up, curving above the trees into a giant domed cage. The lines shimmered, then faded, but he could still feel them there, the magic no longer flickering, but stable.

He squinted, even though the lines were invisible now. There was something about them that bothered him. They didn't quite feel like his mother's magic, but instead like . . .

His mind scrambled to find the right description when he caught a whiff of rotting odor, like eggs left out in the sun.

Demon.

Caden froze, the hairs on the back of his neck rising. But there was no mistaking it. That was what he'd sensed, woven into the magic of his mother's spell: demonic residue.

At least now he knew why his mother had needed Aiden's help on the spell.

Two nights ago, his brother had done something that should have been impossible: he had somehow absorbed a demon. He hadn't seemed like he was possessed by the thing, but rather had trapped its spirit inside him. It gave him powers Caden could only guess at, since Aiden hadn't shared the details of his arrangement, but that kind of magic always came with a cost.

If Aiden was drawing on that demonic power now in order to stabilize the sealing spell, what did that mean? And, more importantly, what had he promised the demon in return for that power?

"Caden?"

He turned slowly away from the woods. His mother stood framed in the doorway of Doctor Anderson's house, her face pale, long hair tumbling loose around her shoulders. Even from here he could see new streaks of white mixing with the once dark strands, as if she'd poured her own essence into the spell.

"Is it done?" Caden asked.

She nodded and took a shaky step from the house, one hand gripping the railing beside her for balance as she navigated the porch. His father appeared in the doorway behind her, looking almost as drained, his skin grayish, his hair sticking up in sweaty clumps.

Caden walked toward them, trying to ignore the feeling of the Watchful Woods at his back, encased in its shell of demonic energy. He wanted to ask his mom about it, but as he drew closer, he saw the blood oozing from her nose, the way her eyes kept wanting to flutter shut, and so instead he just put his arms around her and his dad, wordlessly giving them strength.

Caden didn't need any of his special abilities to sense their fear. It was all in the way they hugged him back so tightly, as if he were their only anchor.

As if they'd thought they might never see him again.

He pushed that thought away immediately. His mom was one of the strongest people he knew, and while his dad's magic wasn't at the same level, he'd always been good at spellwork. Especially the protective side of it. His parents would be fine.

"Isn't this a touching scene?" Aiden asked.

Caden pulled away. His brother stood leaning against the house. And while their parents seemed like washed-out versions of themselves, Aiden was extra vibrant, his dark eyes gleaming, skin flushed and rosy, lips red. He looked as if he'd just eaten a very satisfying meal.

He caught Caden's eye and smiled, a slow, lazy smile that sent chills racing up Caden's spine.

"What happened?" Caden asked, looking from Aiden to his parents.

His mother sank down to sit on the porch. "Green On! wasn't contained within the original spell," she said, her voice soft. "And since it sits at the northernmost border of the Watchful Woods, that meant there was a thin stretch of forest that also wasn't contained. A small hole."

"How small are we talking here?" Caden asked, alarmed.

"Not small enough," his dad said grimly.

"Did anything get out?" Caden asked.

"We don't think so," his mom said. "But . . . I felt something early this morning. A pressure coming from Green On!, as if a tide of creatures had flooded through the labs and were pushing at our boundary, searching for that escape."

Caden thought of Green On!, and the spaceship hidden below it. The one Rae had claimed was full of pods, each one containing another alien species. "Did something happen at the lab?"

His parents exchanged a look. "We're not sure . . ." his mom said at last, but she said it in such a way that Caden knew it wasn't true. "But we were able to expand the spell to contain Green On! within its boundaries. So now there's no way out."

"Wait, what?" Caden stared at his parents, then at Aiden. "What about the people inside Green On!? Are they trapped now?"

"Oh, brother dear," Aiden said, shaking his head sadly. "Anyone who was still inside Green On! is already dead."

3.
RAE

R ae hovered near the wall, watching the people enter and leave the café. None of her friends were there. As she retrieved her croissant and mocha from the counter, she began to worry that none of them would show up.

"That looks good," a girl said.

Rae looked up, relieved to see Becka and Matt. "You made it!"

Becka smiled, her teeth flashing white against the vivid red of her lipstick. "An excuse for a mocha? I'm always up for that."

Matt mumbled something sleepily, then followed Becka over to the counter to order something.

Rae grabbed the largest available table next to some men hanging up a SEEKING SAMANTHA banner and a lady adjusting a pair of large box speakers. Rae vaguely remembered hearing something about Seeking Samantha, a local band that a lot of kids at her school were into, but she had never heard any music by them.

Nate entered the café with a blast of cold air. The rain must have started to come down outside; some of it sparkled in his curly brown hair and beaded on his glasses. He saw her and gave a half-hearted wave before joining Becka in line. Rae didn't take it personally. Nate had been the one to complain the most when she had suggested the morning meeting, saying that no rational human would ever get up earlier than was necessary on a school day. They had finished their conversation with him muttering "serial killer" under his breath as she hung up. Still, he came.

Rae grinned and took a sip of her mocha, then waved as Vivienne and Alyssa strolled in.

"I thought we'd at least beat Nate here," Vivienne said, waving back. "Ooh, chocolate cherry mochas?"

"Caffeine stunts your growth, you know," Alyssa said.

"Eh, it's too late for that." Vivienne was the shortest of their group, but it didn't seem to slow her down; she had also been the fastest runner on their school's cross-country team back before their coach had been eaten by giant alien centipedes.

Rae took a bite of her croissant—warm and flaky—as she waited for her friends to get their food and drinks and join her. Vivienne squeezed into the seat next to her, with Alyssa on her other side, while Nate, Matt, and Becka sat down across from them.

"Hey, everyone," Rae said. "Thanks for coming."

"Why are we here again?" Alyssa asked, throwing her long blond hair over her shoulder.

Rae bit back her reply because it wouldn't have been nice, and these days she was trying to be kinder to Alyssa. The two of them had gotten off to a rocky start, partly because Rae and Vivienne had hit it off so quickly and Alyssa was jealous. But also, if Rae were honest, because *she* hadn't liked the tall blond girl either; Alyssa had reminded her too much of her ex-best friend. Eventually, though, Rae realized she was being unfair. Alyssa could be kind of mean at times, but she was a loyal friend. The opposite of Taylor.

And these days, Rae felt nothing but sympathy for the other girl. Alyssa's mother, the vice principal of their school, had been sealed away in an alien pod, along with Rae's old therapist, Doctor Anderson. Even in the dim café lighting, she could tell that Alyssa's eyes were puffy from crying, and her normally glossy hair hung in limp strands.

"To celebrate, obviously," Nate said. "I hereby declare the 'we survived the world's worst internship' party officially begun." He held up his drink as everyone cheered.

"And here I thought you claimed this was a ridiculous hour for a party," Rae said.

"Oh, it is. But now that I'm awake and well-sugared," he nodded at his giant peanut butter cookie and cup of hot chocolate, "I'm much more in favor of it."

Rae grinned. "I thought it was worth celebrating." She hesitated. Should she tell everyone the *real* reason she wanted to meet today? Everyone except Alyssa looked so happy, eating their pastries and drinking their beverages, relaxed in their wooden chairs. Grateful to be alive. She wasn't sure she wanted to ruin that yet.

"What is it?" Vivienne asked.

"Caden hasn't gotten here yet," Rae said, stalling. She glanced over at the café door, a little surprised that he was so late.

"Maybe he forgot?" Alyssa said. "Anyhow, whatever it is you *really* wanted to say to us, you might as well get it over with. We have to leave soon, or we'll be late for school."

Rae frowned, but it was true. She could always fill Caden in later. "It's just, I was thinking . . ."

"Yes?" Alyssa raised her eyebrows.

"Well, I was wondering if we should start planning our next mission."

Matt dropped his fork on the ground, his eyes wide. "The internship is over," he said quickly. He was one of the biggest kids in their school, but in that moment he looked small. Small and frightened.

"This wouldn't have anything to do with the internship," Rae said. "It would be something different. A mission for us."

"What kind of mission?" Vivienne asked.

"A rescue mission." Rae waited a moment, but no one said anything, the silence around her congealing faster than the grease on Matt's bacon sandwich. "Look, we know there are people trapped on that spaceship. And we know where the spaceship is. We should go help them."

"We should enjoy being alive," Nate said, pushing the bridge of his glasses up higher on his nose.

Becka set her cup down on the table. "Nate's right." Everyone turned to look at her. She had been on the other team of interns, and she was older—an eighth grader like Matt and Nate. She radiated so much confidence and competency, she was a little intimidating.

"I am?" Nate said, sounding more surprised than anyone.

"Yes." Becka smiled at him. "We all survived. Barely. So now we should celebrate, not throw ourselves back into danger."

"Easy for you to say," Alyssa snapped. "Your mom isn't trapped."

"No, my mom's dead."

Alyssa opened her mouth, then shut it again, her cheeks going pink. "I'm sorry."

Becka shrugged. "It was a long time ago. But it means my dad and my little brothers need me to stick around, not die on some alien spaceship in a failed rescue attempt. Besides, didn't Doctor Nguyen already say she was working on it?"

"She did," Rae admitted. The scientist had told her she was going straight over to the spaceship to open the pods after she left Rae's house last night. "But she hasn't been in contact since." No text, no missed calls, nothing from Doctor Nguyen at all. And Rae couldn't assume that she'd hear anything from her today, or ever. She was part of the organization that was keeping Rae's dad from her, after all.

Becka sighed and put down her napkin. "I'm sure popping open an alien pod is not like opening a car door. Give her time."

"I don't trust her," Alyssa said.

"Why not?" Becka asked.

"Well, she did send us to a hellish dimension," Nate pointed out.

Rae turned, shocked at hearing those words come from him. He had all but worshipped Doctor Nguyen throughout their entire internship.

"I thought that was all Patrick's idea," Matt mumbled around a mouthful of bread.

"Eat first, then talk," Nate said, looking sick.

Matt swallowed down his food, then said, "Patrick was the one who sent us out there, not Doctor Nguyen."

Rae shrugged. "Six of that, a half dozen of another."

"What?" Matt looked at her blankly.

"She means that *both* Doctor Nguyen and Patrick are guilty of sending a bunch of kids to a hellish dimension," Nate explained.

Silence fell around the table again, and Rae was sure everyone was remembering their time in the Other Place. A dimension full of yellowish-green fog and flesh-eating tentacled plants and monsters. So many monsters.

"I vote we give her a week," Becka said at last, breaking the silence. "If she doesn't contact you by then, then we organize a mission."

"A week?" Alyssa shoved her plate away. "Seriously?"

"That would actually give us time to plan," Vivienne said. "If we're going into hostile territory again, it would be nice to be prepared for once."

Rae's heart sank as she looked around the table. Everyone seemed to be in agreement. Everyone except her and Alyssa. "I just . . . I feel like something must be wrong," Rae said, trying one last attempt to convince everyone. "Doctor Nguyen should have made some progress by now."

"Maybe she did, but she just didn't share it with you," Becka pointed out.

Rae frowned. That was a good point. She was sure there was a lot Doctor Nguyen was keeping secret. Including the fact that Patrick, Alyssa's mom, and Doctor Anderson weren't the only living things sealed away in pods inside the spaceship buried deep below the lab. There were also hundreds, perhaps thousands of alien creatures.

"Fine," Rae said at last, although she had no intention of waiting a week. She'd still go with Ava today. It might actually be better with just the two of them for once.

Alyssa sniffed but didn't argue.

Rae took another bite of her croissant, only now she couldn't stop thinking about the aliens on the ship. For the first time she pictured Doctor Nguyen down there, trying to open a single pod among all those others. What if something really *had* gone wrong? Abruptly her annoyance with the scientist dropped, replaced by fear.

4.
CADEN

Caden watched the scenery out the window as his brother drove him to school, his mind racing. Something terrible had happened at the lab. Did Rae know? He didn't think so. He glanced at his cell phone, but there was no reception.

"Yeah, cell service is probably going to be down for at least a day," Aiden said. "Too much magical interference."

Caden slid his phone back into his pocket, trying to ignore his growing sense of unease. He'd see Rae at school; he could tell her about it then. He glanced at the clock, and his heart sank. He'd already missed Rae's celebratory breakfast at Kat's Café, and would be late to school, too, skating in just after homeroom, which meant he wouldn't see Rae until the afternoon. They didn't share any classes today, but they still usually ate lunch together.

He glanced over at Aiden. His brother's earlier smug look had vanished, replaced by an expression Caden almost never saw on his face: worry.

Caden's stomach clenched with nerves. "What is it?" he asked.

"It's . . . well. The spell didn't go exactly how Mom hoped."

Caden wanted to ask about the demonic residue but was a little afraid of what Aiden would say. "How so?" he asked instead.

"It's not a complete seal; anything currently inside the Watchful Woods can't escape. But there's nothing stopping anything—or anyone—from waltzing *into* the woods from this side."

Caden thought about that. "Isn't that a little dangerous?"

Aiden shrugged. "People should know better by now than to enter the woods. But . . . Mom doesn't like it. And Dad *really* doesn't like it. They wanted to fix it, but they're both bordering on magical burnout. You remember what that's like?"

Caden had done a very powerful spell in order to pull Ava back from the edge, and it had used up his magic for several days. He remembered that feeling of reaching for power that wasn't there all too well. Until that moment, he hadn't realized how much he depended on his supernatural abilities.

"What happens if they burn out?" he asked.

"Then the whole spell will collapse. If we're lucky, that just means the things contained in the woods will be free. If we're not? Well, remember what happened when Alice's spell collapsed?"

Their ancestor had created the Other Place as a magical prison, using a team of witches in a complicated ritual to seal away all the alien energy and creatures in an alternate dimension. It hadn't gone too well for the others involved in her spell. "Everyone died," Caden whispered.

"Pretty much. It's why Mom refused to tie *you* to the spell."

Caden stared at his brother. "*That's* why? To protect me?" He felt his heart lifting, and he remembered how his mom had actually agreed to open a rift into the Other Place so his brother could bring *him* out when she'd refused to do the same for Aiden.

She always did love you best.

Aiden had told him that, but Caden hadn't believed it. He'd spent too many years watching the way his mother would light up when Aiden was near, how proud she was of his growing magical talent. How devastated she'd been when he disappeared. But maybe—

"Look at you, getting all sappy." Aiden laughed. "I mean, you can tell yourself Mom is just trying to protect you if it makes you feel good. But it's not the truth. Not the whole truth, anyhow."

"Then what's the real reason?" Caden asked.

"Simple. If we all die, someone still needs to be around to clean up this mess." Aiden flashed another of his quick smiles. "That someone is you, dear brother. Fun, right? You'd get to deal with monsters running rampant through the town and a bunch of dead witches."

"And how could *I* possibly deal with that?"

"Simple. First you'd have to bind the town, containing everyone and everything within its borders. And then . . ."

"And then?" Caden demanded.

"You'd have to destroy it."

Caden frowned. "Destroy . . . the town?"

Aiden nodded.

"Like, all of it?"

"No brick unturned, no tree unburned, no street unharmed." Aiden's eyes glittered, and for a second Caden could see a deep crimson red burning beneath the familiar brown. *Demon.* The word flashed through his mind. Then the red was gone, and it was just his brother, looking more serious than normal. "But that's just a worst-case scenario. I'm pretty sure it won't come to that." He paused, then added, "Probably."

Caden wasn't sure what to say, so he turned away from his brother and kept his gaze firmly fixed out the window the rest of the drive.

5.
RAE

Somehow, Rae had almost made it through the day. She'd tuned out through most of her classes and spent her lunch period researching in the library—they had all the old Whispering Pines newspapers saved, and she'd hoped one of them would give her a clue as to her father's exact whereabouts. But no such luck.

Now, as she settled into a seat near the back of her social studies classroom, she mentally prepared herself for one more hour of torture. Just one last class and she'd be free. This was her least favorite class, mostly because her teacher seemed to care so little for the subject. Also because she didn't share it with either Vivienne or Caden.

Alyssa shared this class with her, though, and she and Alyssa were friends now, for the most part. So when the other girl walked into the room, she waved and indicated the empty desk next to her.

Alyssa didn't wave back, but she did walk over and sit down, dropping her books and notebooks on her desk with a loud *thump*. She looked different from the girl Rae had met on her first day of school. She still wore her long blond hair in its trademark high ponytail, but the lines of her face seemed to have shifted, her cheeks thinner, her lips a hard line. It made her face look older, and much more like her mother's.

"What?" Alyssa demanded, turning to face her.

"Nothing," Rae said quickly.

"I know I look awful, okay? You don't need to say anything."

"I didn't. I mean, you don't," Rae said hurriedly.

Alyssa narrowed her eyes, then huffed and turned away. "Whatever," she muttered.

Rae reminded herself that Alyssa was going through a lot right now. And really, she wasn't so bad. But she still wasn't someone Rae would have chosen to spend a ton of time with. Other than their friendship with Vivienne and running, they really didn't share much in common. And she could tell Alyssa felt the same way about her, even if they had reached a sort of truce. It was almost a relief when class started.

"Today," Ms. Wallace said, "we'll be discussing the tools of the ancient world." From anyone else, that might have sounded like an exciting topic, but Ms. Wallace announced it the same way someone else might have said they would be discussing the best way to properly clean and organize a closet.

There was a collective groan from the class. A few kids put their heads down on their desks.

Ms. Wallace narrowed her eyes. "Open your notebooks and make a list of all the tools you noticed in last night's reading."

Rae hadn't done the reading. She hadn't even known there *was* reading to be done since she had missed class yesterday due to her internship and being locked on a spaceship. Maybe she could sneak a quick peek at it now.

"No textbooks!" Ms. Wallace snapped.

Sighing, Rae flipped open her notebook. No choice but to wing it.

The lights overhead flickered, then went out.

Rae sat there, frozen. It felt as if the school itself were holding its breath, everything so still, so silent. Even the wind outside wasn't howling, although the sky remained that deep charcoal gray. Barely any light filtered in, turning the room into a gloomy cavern of deep shadows.

A few whispers started.

"Quiet," Ms. Wallace ordered. "Just wait. The generator should come on in a second."

But a second passed, and then another one. And Rae felt it again: that certainty that something terrible was about to happen. Was *already* happening.

"What are you doing?" Alyssa hissed.

Rae realized she was standing. She looked out at Ms. Wallace, who was now arguing with a kid in the front of the class, and at the other dim shadows all around. "I can't stay here," she said. "I just . . . I need to go. I need to go now." And she slipped along the side of the room and darted out the door.

6.
CADEN

aden doodled on the edge of his paper as Mr. Henry droned on and on about the symbolism in the story they were supposed to have read. Caden hadn't even cracked the cover. Worse, he couldn't even remember which book it was.

He should really be listening now, since he knew Mr. Henry was planning a pop quiz at the end of class; he recognized the sizzle of apprehensive excitement his English teacher always got when he was hoping to get one over on his students. But on a day like today, with the pressure of that eerie storm building outside and the knowledge of what lurked within the nearby Watchful Woods, he couldn't bring himself to care about his grades.

If we all die, someone still needs to be around to clean up this mess.

Caden shivered, his thoughts circling back to that disturbing conversation with Aiden. The one that had been weighing on him all day. Between that and Aiden's declaration that anyone still at Green On! was already dead, Caden found he couldn't really focus on anything else.

He blinked, then scribbled out the picture he'd been drawing. It looked too much like a creature with large fangs and soulless eyes.

Vivienne gasped, and he turned to see her sitting bolt upright in her chair next to him, her eyes wide.

"What?" he whispered.

She looked at him. "It's starting."

"What is?" Caden asked, his heart hammering.

The lights went out.

For a second no one moved, the room full of the sounds of their breathing, their panic building around Caden in a suffocating wave before finally flaring outward in sharp yellow spikes. And with that, the questions came pouring forth.

"What's going on?"

"Is it from the storm?"

"Where are the emergency lights?"

"Quiet, everyone, please," Mr. Henry called. "The generator should be kicking on any second now. This is hardly our first storm." He laughed, but it sounded fake, the noise echoing strangely.

Caden glanced toward the window. Even though the sky was dark with threatening clouds, there was no sign of lightning. And while it had certainly been windy that morning, now the air outside seemed almost unnaturally still, the nearby trees not moving at all. This storm wasn't bad enough to cause a power outage. Something else must have done it.

The last power outage he'd experienced had been at Rae's house, when the Devourers were hunting for him. He could still picture their long snouts, scythe-like claws, and the eerie way they moved as they circled his house. It was too easy to imagine them oozing around the school now.

He watched outside for any sign of unnatural movement, but it all looked calm. Too calm?

He turned away from the window and found Vivienne watching him intently. It was so dark he could barely make out her face, just a pale oval in the gloom of the classroom, her eyes unreadable. But he could feel the intensity behind her gaze and knew it wasn't just Vivienne looking out at him. A shadow lurked in the background, observing everything. Waiting for its chance.

Vivienne and her mother had been spelunking in the tunnels below Whispering Pines months ago when one of those tunnels had collapsed, sending Vivienne into a mysterious cavern. She'd found a strange column there, one that called to her, but the moment she'd touched it, she'd begun changing. Some of the changes were good—increased speed and strength, and the ability to see in the dark. Others, like her sudden desire for blood, were less ideal.

Over the summer, her mother had gone to Caden's mother for help. And when the protective amulet Vivienne had been given had stopped working, she'd turned to Patrick next. His elixir had seemed to be effective, but then he'd begun withholding it. And now, of course, he was gone. Sealed away like Doctor Anderson in one of those alien pods.

Caden could feel the presence dwelling inside his friend now, the weight of its awareness pressing against him. He wasn't sure how they had ever thought it was a curse. The truth seemed so obvious: when Vivienne had touched that underground column, she'd somehow absorbed an alien entity. One that was getting stronger, taking more control every day.

How much longer did Vivienne have before *she* became the shadow?

"*What* is starting?" he asked her.

Vivienne cocked her head to the side. It was an inhuman movement, and he resisted the urge to flinch back. "There was a plan in place long before the ship crashed here," she said. "I don't know what, exactly . . . I only get tiny whispers." She grimaced. "Anyhow. The crash changed everything, put it all on hold. But now everything is back in place. And so it's beginning." She took a deep, shaky breath. "The invasion."

Invasion.

The hairs on the back of Caden's neck stood on end. "And . . . what is the purpose of this invasion?"

Vivienne looked at him, her expression impossible to read in the darkness. "Isn't it obvious? They want to take over the planet, but they have to make room first. And that means they need to get rid of us."

It was as if Aiden was in his head whispering, *"No brick unturned, no tree unburned, no street unharmed."*

Caden swallowed. "So they want our extinction," he said.

"Exactly."

A low buzz filled the air, and outside their classroom, a light flickered on in the hallway. The school's backup generator must finally be kicking on, but only at half power. Was it conserving energy, or was something wrong with it?

The loudspeaker crackled and spat, and Caden jumped. Several other kids threw their hands over their ears.

"Is this thing on?" came a garbled voice. "Hello? Testing, testing . . . Eh, it's probably working."

"Who is that?" someone near Caden asked.

"This is your principal speaking," the voice said as if in answer.

"We have a principal?" someone else said.

"I thought there was just Ms. Lockett," another kid added.

The loudspeaker squawked again, and there came the sound of muffled cursing before the voice came back, a little clearer. "Ahem. So. I've just been given a message to read." The principal cleared his throat. "Attention all students and staff. We have a . . . oh. Oh my."

"'Oh my' what?" Caden craned forward.

"There's no mistake?" the principal asked. In the background came a muffled response. The principal sighed loudly. "No mistake. It appears we have a . . . a code black." He swallowed, the sound audible through the speaker. "I repeat, it's a code black. Please, everyone, make your way to the auditorium for further instructions. And may God have mercy on your souls." A pause. Then, "Wait, I wasn't supposed to say that last bit out loud. I'm dreadful at these kinds of things. Where's Ms. Lockett? Joan? Joan?" The loudspeaker cut out, and silence filled the room.

"What's a code black?" the boy behind Caden asked, but no one answered.

Caden certainly had no idea. Whatever it was, though, it must be pretty bad. Because he could feel Mr. Henry's fear crystalizing around him, radiating cold. *He* knew, and he was terrified.

"Everyone, leave your stuff at your desk and follow me," Mr. Henry said, his voice trembling. He moved stiffly to the door and fumbled with the handle, struggling to open it. The moment the door was open, Caden's classmates scurried out of their chairs to reach the light-filled hallway.

Caden and Vivienne waited, letting everyone else go before them.

"You're not planning on going to the auditorium, are you?" Caden whispered.

Vivienne shook her head. "Waste of time. They won't tell us anything in there. No, we need to meet up with Rae and the others."

By "others" Caden knew she meant the other kids from their short-lived internship. "Won't *they* be in the auditorium?"

"Nope. We came up with a contingency plan. Anything weird happens, and we meet up in the old lab. I'm pretty sure this," she pointed at the loudspeaker, "qualifies." She got up, slinging her backpack on and heading for the door, and Caden followed.

Out in the hall, Caden glanced back at their vanishing class before joining Vivienne, the two of them going against the stream like salmon. "What's a 'code black'?" he asked her as they avoided elbows and dodged around groups. Vivienne had spent a lot of time at the Locketts' house. Maybe she'd learned something there.

She hugged the lockers to let a large class go by them, her eyes wide with worry. "I don't know." She pushed away from the lockers and crossed the last several feet to the old science classroom, shoving the door open.

Inside, three other kids waited for them, and as Caden's eyes adjusted he recognized Nate, Becka, and Matt sitting in the gloom, the rest of the room reduced to shadows around them.

"You guys got here fast," Vivienne said.

"We had science class right next door," Nate said, pushing his glasses up on his nose. The fear rolled off him in sickening waves, but compared to Matt, he seemed downright stoic. Matt was shaking, his expression tight like he wanted to be anywhere but there. And his terror was so thick it was black, all of it vibrating around him like a string pulled way too tight.

Several minutes ticked past, and no one said anything else. They just waited. But eventually the hallway outside emptied.

"Where are Rae and Alyssa?" Nate asked the question they were all thinking.

"Maybe they forgot our plan?" Becka said.

"They wouldn't have forgotten," Vivienne said, annoyed.

Caden tried to ignore the feeling creeping into his stomach, a feeling like he'd just swallowed an ice cube whole, but it settled there, chilling all of him. Because he knew Vivienne was right; they wouldn't have forgotten. If they weren't here now, it meant they weren't coming.

He thought of his earlier sense of foreboding that morning. The feeling that he needed to warn Rae about Green On! as soon as possible. He hadn't seen her yet at school, and now it was too late.

No, he told himself firmly. There was no way Rae had gone to Green On!. She wouldn't have left without telling him first. He willed himself to believe that, even as the dread in his stomach thickened.

7.
RAE

The hallway was dark and empty. Rae kept a hand on the wall, half expecting Ms. Wallace to notice, to call her back. But she didn't. So Rae kept moving toward the front entrance of the school. She could hear her own breathing, a little too harsh, and the sound of her sneakers sliding on the hallway tiles. And . . . someone else.

Rae paused, and the footsteps behind her paused too, but a half-second too late. Rae's breath caught. In this dark hallway it was too easy to imagine all the horrors she'd seen inside the spaceship following her. She didn't want to turn around.

She could hear it breathing. Right. Behind. Her.

A sudden buzzing filled the air, and then the lights above her flickered on, dim and sputtering, but enough for her to see the rest of the hall stretching in front of her. Empty. And suddenly Rae knew she was being silly. She was in the school. A place filled with people, not monsters.

She turned.

Alyssa stood a few feet away, arms crossed, expression bored.

"Are you following me?" Rae demanded.

"Yeah."

"Why?"

"Because I don't want to be here either."

Rae opened her mouth, then shut it. Of course Alyssa didn't want to be stuck here in the school her mother loved so much. "Fine," Rae decided, just as the loudspeaker came to life.

Alyssa flinched, but it wasn't her mom's voice. It was a man's, nasally and flustered, the sound filtering through the closed door of the closest classroom. It was hard to understand until the words "code black," which rang loud and clear.

Alyssa gasped.

"What?" Rae said. "What does that mean?"

"It means the whole school is going into lockdown mode. No one in, and no one out."

"Why?"

Alyssa tossed her head impatiently. "As if I know that! It could be a million things in this town. Now, do you want to leave or not?"

The crackling of the loudspeaker ended, and the classroom doors on either side of them opened. "Let's go," Rae said as students began spilling out into the hallway. The last thing she wanted was to be stuck here. She started walking again, but Alyssa caught her arm.

"Not that way," Alyssa said. "It'll already be locked. All the entrances will."

"How do you know that?"

"My mom made sure I knew all the standard operating procedures for each code. Code black immediately triggers the school's automatic locking mechanisms."

"There are automatic locking mechanisms?"

"Of course."

Rae wasn't sure why that surprised her. In a town riddled with sinkholes and overrun with psychotic squirrels, it made a certain amount of sense to be able to swiftly and efficiently lock up the schools. "So we're already trapped." Rae swallowed down a rising sense of panic. Trapped. She hated feeling that way. It reminded her too much of the cabin in the woods, the sensation of burrowing between a rotting, bug-infested mattress and the splintery wood of the bed frame while Ivan stalked slowly closer, closer. *Ready or not, here I come . . .*

"I never said that." Alyssa smiled suddenly, her blue eyes crinkling, her whole face softening. Rae realized it was the first smile she'd seen on her face in weeks. "You're just lucky I decided to follow you; I'm probably the only one in this school who knows another way out." Her smile faltered a little. "Well, me and Vivi."

For a second Rae and Alyssa looked at each other, thoughts of Vivienne drifting between them like ghosts. It felt strange to be hanging out without her. Wrong, somehow. And Rae wondered if she should go find her and the others first. They'd probably be gathering in the science lab now.

But no. She didn't want to waste time arguing over what they should do next. She'd promised her sister they would tackle Green On! together, and code black or not, that was what she intended to do. "Lead on, fearless leader," she said.

Alyssa almost smiled again as she turned and headed back down the hall, weaving around people, ignoring anyone who called to her. Rae kept her gaze on the taller girl's long blond ponytail as she followed her over to the front office.

Alyssa paused at the door, glanced around, then pulled it open. "Quickly," she whispered. Rae hurried inside, the door closing behind her.

The office felt quiet, the air still, as if nothing living had been in here for years instead of days. "Who made the announcement?" Rae whispered.

"The principal."

"Is he here?"

Alyssa shook her head. "I don't know where he is, to be honest."

"He doesn't have his own office?"

"Oh, he does. But it's not in here. He moved it years back, said he didn't like being hassled by all the children. So he never told anyone where he moved it *to*." Alyssa shrugged, leading the way to her mom's office in the very back.

"But he's the principal! Doesn't he have to do . . . whatever it is principals do?" Rae wasn't really sure what that all entailed. Reviewing the other teachers? Giving detentions? It had to be important, though, right?

"My mom pretty much handles all of that." Alyssa grimaced. "Or she did."

"She will again," Rae promised immediately.

Alyssa nodded and took a deep breath, then opened the door to her mom's office, shutting it again behind Rae.

Rae had been in here twice before. Once when Patrick was offering her a place in his internship. And then more recently, when she'd been trying to get information from Ms. Lockett. This was her first time inside without an adult present, though, and she couldn't help feeling like she was trespassing. It just seemed unfriendly in here, like the spirit of Ms. Lockett was haunting it, ready to give out detentions.

Reluctantly, Rae followed Alyssa to the back of the small office. There wasn't much in here. A desk and chair in the far corner facing the door, two more chairs tucked neatly against the left wall, and a tall bookshelf across from them on the right. Nothing threatening. And no other exits.

"Why are we in here?" Rae asked.

"Did you ever wonder how my mom could get from one end of the school to the other without anyone seeing her?"

"No . . . could she?"

"It was, like, a superpower. Well, I *thought* it was a superpower. Only one time Vivienne and I were stuck here waiting for her to finish up her paperwork, and we discovered her secret." Alyssa went around to Ms. Lockett's desk. It was scarily organized, with baskets specifically labeled by pen color, paperclips all lined up in a row, and a stack of paper so neat it could have been in a binder. Crouching, Alyssa stuck her head under the desk.

Click.

The bookshelf swung outward, revealing a space behind it.

"A secret tunnel," Rae said flatly. "Of course there is." She resisted the urge to laugh, knowing if she started, she'd never stop. This place. This weird, weird place.

Reluctantly, she followed Alyssa through the secret door. She'd had enough of tunnels to last a lifetime.

8.
CADEN

To Caden's surprise, it was Matt who broke the silence first. "We should go to the auditorium and see if Alyssa and Rae are there."

"I already told you," Vivienne snapped, her nostrils flaring. "They wouldn't have forgotten."

"No, but maybe their teacher didn't let them slip away like ours did," Becka said. "Matt's right. It's worth checking."

"It's worth getting out of this creepy room," Nate said, wrapping his arms around himself and glancing into the corners.

Caden didn't blame him. Test tubes and microscopes and beakers had all been transformed by the darkness into ominous shapes. It almost felt as if there were something else in the room watching them.

The hairs on the back of Caden's neck stood on end, but when he reached out with his powers, he felt nothing. Only the fear of the others in the room with him. They were alone.

Still, by the time they finally reached the auditorium doors, he felt twitchy enough that, for once, he was eager to be in a room surrounded by other people.

They pulled open the doors and stepped inside. The room was dark—no generator-powered emergency lights in here—so someone had set up a line of candles on the stage. Caden was pretty sure Ms. Lockett would have had a fit to see them there, dripping wax and constituting a major fire hazard. In their flickering light he could see that the auditorium was packed, the entire school crowded inside, including all the teachers.

Despite the crowd, it was eerily quiet. Nothing but whispered conversations, as if everyone was afraid of attracting too much attention by talking loudly. He could feel that fear like a physical wall expanding outward, and he froze in place in the doorway.

"You okay?" Vivienne asked him.

He nodded, then noticed the way she had her arms crossed tightly, her hands gripping her elbows, shoulders hunched beneath her backpack. "Are you?"

She looked at him, dark eyes glittering with fear—fear . . . and hunger. "I'm as okay as you are," she whispered.

"That bad, huh?"

That made her smile, but only a little.

"Hey," a teacher said, the noise loud enough that a few people turned their heads. "Where were you?"

"Bathroom," Vivienne said immediately.

"All of you?"

"Safety in numbers," Becka said.

The teacher looked them over once. Mr. Pete from PE. Usually he was a rule stickler, but today he just nodded. "Have a seat over there." He gestured at a few empty seats near the back, and Caden and the others sat down.

"Have you seen them yet?" Nate asked. "Rae and Alyssa?"

"How could we?" Becka said. "It's so dark in here."

"How about I just give Rae a call?" Vivienne said, pulling out her phone.

Nate smacked himself in the head. "Should have thought of that."

"Probably," Vivienne said, flashing him a smile. It quickly turned into a frown, and she jabbed at her phone. "Huh."

Caden's stomach sank. He'd almost forgotten Aiden's warning about cell phones. "No reception, right?"

"Right," Vivienne said, peering at her screen.

"What?" Nate pulled his own phone out, glancing around once as if afraid the ghost of Ms. Lockett would swoop down and snatch it from his fingers. "No reception here either."

"Attention, students!" someone's voice boomed, so loud Caden actually jumped a little. He looked up at the stage where a short round man stood, his bald head gleaming despite the lack of overhead lights, his mustache bushy enough to hide his entire mouth.

"Is that the principal?" Becka asked.

"I think so," Nate whispered, eyes wide. "I can't believe he's actually come out of hiding. Things must be worse than I thought. And I already thought they were bad."

"I hate doing this sort of thing," the principal said. "Addressing students and whatnot. So I'm going to make this brief." He tucked his thumbs into his suspenders. "For those of you who don't know, code black means lockdown. Which means you all get to stay right here, in this school, for the foreseeable future."

"Foreseeable future?" someone called. "What's that supposed to mean?"

"It means I don't know when I can let you out. Obviously."

There was a collective gasp. "Why not?" someone else demanded.

The principal scowled, his mustache bristling like an angry cat. "Because normally the second stage of a code black is an evacuation. But unfortunately that is quite impossible now."

"Why?" another student said, the question echoing up and down the room.

The principal was silent for a moment, and then his shoulders sagged, all the energy seeming to leak out of him. "Because we *can't* evacuate. The entire town has been . . . well . . . ordered not to leave. Don't ask me why!" he said quickly, putting up his hands. "I have no idea. No one does. Or if they do, they're not talking."

"We're trapped?" someone in the auditorium said, and Caden could feel the spike of panic in the room.

"Why won't our phones work?"

"What's going on?"

"Are we in danger here?"

"What is Green On! doing? Can't they help us?"

The questions poured forth in a tide, the sound rising from whispers to yells, students standing, shouting, waving their useless cell phones in the air. And not just the students, but some of the teachers, too. They obviously knew as little as the rest of them.

"Please! Please!" the principal cried, holding his hands up high and taking a step back, then another, as if the noise were a physical force driving him away. He looked around, eyes rolling, clearly seeking some sort of exit. No wonder Ms. Lockett handled all of the school's interactions. She would have quieted this crowd and shut down all its questions with the sheer force of her authority. Caden had never liked the vice principal much, but in that moment, watching their principal sweating on the stage, he felt a grudging respect for her.

Would being trapped in an alien pod change her? He hadn't given that much thought before now. And what if they *couldn't* release her?

Rae was probably tackling those questions head on right now, diving into danger while he sat here uselessly in this auditorium. He gripped the arms of his chair and, reluctantly, peeled back his personal shields to check, extending his awareness out, searching for Rae's unique personal energy signature. Her own blend of determination and bravery layered over all her fear.

It was hard; the room was full of so much panic it made his own heart race, masking everything else.

"Please," the principal said again. "Stop shouting at me. This is exactly why I was told not to tell you all this."

"Who told you not to tell us?" another voice demanded. Caden thought it sounded a lot like Mrs. Murphy, his homeroom teacher. "Who's relaying all this information? We know it's not coming from *you* directly."

People quieted down at that, wanting to hear the answer.

The principal hesitated, sweat beading on the top of his head. "Er," he managed. "Well, that is . . . I mean, I'm not supposed to say—"

"His orders are coming from me," a woman's voice announced from somewhere to the left of the stage. Everyone craned in their seats, peering through the gloom as someone stepped out from behind the curtains and walked over to stand beside the principal. A woman, tall and slender with curly hair that gleamed red in the candlelight, her face round and rosy-cheeked. She wore a bright green pantsuit that should have been garish but somehow suited her.

"I'm sorry," the principal began. "I tried—"

"Not at all, Herbert." She put a hand on his shoulder and smiled at him. "I wanted to address everyone myself. You take it easy; you've done enough." Then she turned her smile out on the audience. "Hello, students and teachers. It's so nice to see all of you here. I'm Clara Thomas." She paused, and there were a couple of laughs in the audience. Because obviously everyone already knew who she was. Even Caden, who disliked anything that had to do with Green On!, recognized its CEO.

Clara was the friendly face of the company. The one who always showed up to sign the charity checks in person and take photos with the people of the town. With her wide blue eyes and curly hair, she exuded an air of innocence, a naivete that Caden knew had to be an act. But a convincing one.

At the sound of her voice, the crowd seemed to relax. As if just knowing Clara was there meant that everything was going to be all right. It was actually eerie how quickly that sense swept through the auditorium. Caden could see it as a wave of pearly-white calm crashing through the panic and washing it away.

"Now, I know this is scary," Clara continued, her voice deep and soothing. "But everything is going to be just fine. We just need you all to stay put for a little while."

"What's wrong?" a teacher asked. "Is there a problem at the lab?"

"I heard it was shut down?" someone else said.

"Is that why we're in code black?" another voice chimed in. Caden could feel the energy of the crowd shifting again, growing restless as fear rippled through them.

Clara's smile never wavered. "No, no. Nothing wrong at the lab. Just a routine training exercise that's gotten . . . well, a touch out of hand. But nothing to worry about!" she added hastily. "As I said, we just need everyone here to stay calm, and remain in the school, and we'll have it all sorted out before you know it."

Caden frowned, his brother's voice echoing in his mind. *Anyone who was still inside Green On! is already dead.* Something major had happened there. And while Caden knew Green On! had covered up things in the past, he doubted they'd be able to hide this. Only no one in the audience questioned it.

Caden glanced over at Vivienne. Her eyebrows were drawn together in concern, lips pressed tight. And for the first time he remembered that her mom worked at Green On!. Not only that, but she was often there late . . .

"I do require some assistance, however," Clara said, her tone changing, becoming sharper, more demanding. "I need to borrow one of your students."

"Who?" the principal asked.

And somehow Caden knew exactly who Clara was going to say. All thoughts of Mrs. Matsuoka vanished as Clara took a step forward, her eyes roving over the seats. "Rae Carter?" she called. "Can you come up here, please?

9.
RAE

The tunnels through the school were narrow and dark, but surprisingly clean in the light from Rae's cellphone. She had expected dust and spiders and cobwebs. Then she pictured Ms. Lockett, with her rigid appearance and perfectly organized desk, and couldn't imagine her tolerating anything dirty in the school. Even the secret passages.

Did she clean them herself, Rae wondered. Or did the school janitors know about these tunnels too? How secret were they?

Alyssa led the way, a silent shadow in the darkness lit by her own blue screen as she turned left, and right, and left. Occasionally Rae thought she heard footsteps nearby, and once someone's voice floated toward her as clearly as if they were standing by her side. But when she looked, there was no one there.

Probably these tunnels were haunted.

That made Rae think of how Ava had been possessed by some kind of demon. How it had taken over her sister's body and used her voice. Ava had been nothing more than a shell, the lines of her face molding to the thing beneath, turning into something ancient and angry until Caden drove it out.

He'd taught her sister how to protect herself afterward. Something about white light and holding protective images in your mind. Rae should have paid better attention, but at the time she'd been too angry with Caden for setting that whole thing in motion, and too scared. For a second there, she'd been sure all the things that made her sister *Ava* were gone forever. And she'd been powerless to stop it. All she could do was stand there and watch.

This was why she didn't like the supernatural stuff. Ghosts and demons and actual, literal, should-be-impossible magic. Give her a giant alien bug or other monster over that stuff any day. At least she could fight those.

"Where do you think you're going, little girl?"

Rae froze, the hairs on the back of her neck all standing on end. It felt suddenly colder in the tunnel, so cold her breath misted in the light of her cellphone.

Up ahead Alyssa kept walking, getting farther away. Rae forced her numbed feet to move, not wanting to get left behind. The tunnels had branched often enough that she wasn't sure she'd be able to find her way back on her own. She tried not imagining what it would be like to get lost in this labyrinth, winding her way in the dark as her cellphone battery died, listening to the echoes of those voices. The ones she definitely did *not* hear. Because they weren't real.

She sped up, but the whispers followed, phantom fingers sliding down her back.

"This is the way out," Alyssa said, stopping abruptly. She slid her hand along the wall, and with a soft *click*, a small rectangle popped open, revealing gray gloomy skies and the outlines of trees standing perfectly still.

Heart pounding way too fast, Rae followed Alyssa outside. She swore she heard something laughing as she shoved the door shut behind her. "There were ghosts in those tunnels," she said.

Alyssa sighed. "Yeah, I know."

Rae blinked. "You know?"

"I do. Mom's been trying to get rid of them for ages. I actually told her she should hire the Prices, but she—" Alyssa cut off abruptly.

"She what?" Rae pressed.

"She thinks they're, um, undignified. The whole ghost-hunting thing." Alyssa fiddled with a lock of her hair and looked away, her cheeks going pink. "My mom just pretends the things she doesn't like don't exist. Like the voices in the tunnels."

It was the opposite of what Rae's dad had taught her. He'd been big on truth, on facing things head on. In the end, that was probably what got him into trouble. But pretending things didn't exist hadn't worked out well for Ms. Lockett, either. Maybe if she'd been more willing to face the truth, she would have seen Patrick for what he was before she'd fallen into his trap.

Rae didn't like to think about that, though. Because *she'd* almost fallen into that trap too. Even after knowing Patrick was not to be trusted. She'd just wanted to believe so badly that he could help her that she'd been willing to ignore all her inner warning bells until it was almost too late.

"I, um, sort of did that to Caden, too," Alyssa whispered. "Before."

Rae nodded. "I heard."

Alyssa dropped her hands. "He probably hates me. I wouldn't blame him."

"I don't think Caden hates anyone. But he might like it if you apologized."

Alyssa's eyes widened. "I couldn't! What would I even say?"

"'Sorry for being mean'?" Rae suggested.

"As if that would help. I still said those things. It wouldn't unsay them."

Rae thought about Taylor, her former best friend. How would she feel if Taylor called her up and apologized? Would it help? She remembered how alone she'd been at her old school. No one would partner with her unless the teacher made them. Lunches were terrible—she spent most of them hiding in the bathroom. Way better than walking into a crowded cafeteria and knowing there would be nowhere for her to sit. Or, worse, that they'd leave one table open for her, in the middle, where they could all turn and stare at her as she ate.

Even now, humiliation boiled through her as she thought of those days. Humiliation and anger and hurt. No apology could take that away. Even though secretly, a part of her *was* waiting for an apology. But she realized now that it wouldn't matter.

She knew why Taylor had done what she'd done—Rae had been popular before. And by destroying her social standing, Taylor had managed to launch herself up. Apparently that had been more important than actual friendship. It would be nice to know Taylor was sorry for what she'd done; Rae would appreciate that. But it wouldn't change how she felt. And *she'd* only been an outcast for a year. Caden had been the school's outcast practically his whole life. Still . . .

"I don't think it would hurt," she said at last. Caden, after all, was a much more forgiving person than she'd ever be.

Alyssa nodded. "Maybe I will," she said. And she looked serious. "So, what's your plan now?"

Rae looked around. They were at the side of the school closest to the woods, the air heavy and humid against them. The storm seemed to have frozen, its pressure building without any release, the energy of all that pent-up rain and wind crackling through the air. It felt unsafe to stand here for too long. "My sister was going to pick me up after school ended."

Alyssa shook her head. "Her school will be on lockdown now too. Code black means everyone. She won't be able to leave."

Rae thought of Ava and her determination. "You don't know my sister. I think she'll still find a way out."

Alyssa looked at her hard, as if reading her face. "She's like you, isn't she?" she said at last. Then she nodded. "Okay, then, I guess we should wait for her? We'll want to keep close to the school and avoid the windows, though."

"We?"

Alyssa straightened. "Yes, *we*. I'm staying with you."

"But you don't even know where I'm going."

"To Green On!."

Rae stared at her.

"What? It's obvious. That's where all this," Alyssa gestured at the silent trees, the darkened school, the sky, "is coming from. Plus, you wanted to go there this morning. I doubt you've changed your mind. And I'm coming too."

Rae opened her mouth to argue, but just then she spotted a familiar car circling the school. Her heart leapt. Ava! Rae had known her sister would find a way out, but still. It was a relief to see her pull up to them.

Ava rolled down her window, grinning. "I was worried I'd have to break you out of there. Should have known."

Rae grinned back. "Yeah, you really should have."

"Who's this?" Ava jerked her chin at Alyssa.

Rae hesitated, then said, "My accomplice." She took a deep breath, imagining her and her sister alone for once on a mission, and then let it go. "She's coming too."

Alyssa awarded her with another one of her rare genuine smiles, and Rae knew she'd made the right decision. She just hoped Alyssa didn't get herself killed.

Or any of them, either.

10.
CADEN

Why does she want Rae?" Nate whispered.

"I don't know," Caden said, his heart thumping. "But I can't imagine it's for anything good."

"I guess I'm glad she's not here, then," Vivienne said.

Caden swallowed, glancing around the audience. Clara stood on the stage, still calling for Rae, and his anxiety rose. It didn't help that the other people in the auditorium were being strangely calm; despite learning that they would be trapped inside the school for who-knew-how-long, they just sat there, chatting quietly with one another, relaxed in their seats. And all because Clara had told them everything would be okay.

"Want to leave?" Vivienne whispered.

"Definitely," Becka said immediately. "The people here are seriously freaking me out."

"I'm with you," Nate said. "Let's get out of here before they start eating brains or something."

"Back to the lab?" Caden suggested.

They all nodded. All except Matt.

"Matt?" Becka said.

"I'm good here," Matt said, crossing his arms and settling deeper into his chair. They all stared at him, no one moving, and suddenly a torrent of words burst from him. "Look, every time I hang out with you people, I end up stomping through the creepy woods, or getting pulled into an evil dimensional hell world, or being chased by monsters, or . . . well. I never know what will happen next, but so far it's been pretty terrible. I mean, I like you. All of you. I do. And you're right; this is very strange." He nodded at the crowd. "But it also feels . . . I don't know. Safer here, surrounded by everyone else."

"It's not," Caden said flatly.

Matt shrugged. "I'll take my chances with the crowd."

"Matt . . ." Becka began slowly, eyes narrowing.

"No, Becka. Whatever you're going to say, save it. My dad only has me, okay? I have to think of him. I can't just go running off into danger again with the rest of you."

"*We* all have family too, you know," Vivienne snapped. "But we're not about to sit around like these sheep, pretending everything is okay when it's obviously not." Her nostrils flared, contempt rolling off her in plumes.

Caden frowned at her. It didn't feel like the Vivienne he knew. It *certainly* didn't sound like her. Whatever was happening right now in their town, it was affecting Vivienne, too. Speeding up her transformation.

"Hey, give him a break," Nate said. "If he's done, he's done."

"He's being a coward," Vivienne said. "But then, *you* would know all about that, wouldn't you?"

Nate's eyes widened behind his glasses, and Becka gasped.

Vivienne froze, and then she shook her head violently, as if trying to shake off a fly. "I'm so, so sorry. I didn't mean that."

Nate shrugged. "It's fine. I deserved it." His tone was casual, but Caden could feel the hurt pulsing around him.

"No, you didn't," Vivienne said. "You really, really didn't."

"Well, I did leave you and Rae to fight alien bugs underground without me."

"That wasn't your fault. I'm just . . . not myself right now. Can we please forget I said that?"

"Sure. Of course," Nate said quickly. "No problem."

Caden watched the whole exchange, his unease growing. Nate's emotions were a messy tangle around him, humiliation with a touch of guilt. It was exactly how Caden would expect him to feel. Just as he'd expect to feel remorse from Vivienne. Instead, he felt nothing from her. Nothing at all. As if any emotions she had were being blocked. Or erased . . .

"Matt, you know where to find us if you change your mind," Becka said. She frowned at Vivienne but didn't add anything. "Let's go." She slid out of her seat first, trailed by Nate. Vivienne paused just long enough to sling her backpack on before following after, leaving Caden to take up the rear. The moment they stepped out of the auditorium and into the hallway, he put a hand on Vivienne's arm, stopping her.

"Vivi," he began tentatively. "Are you—"

She turned and looked at him, and he froze like a mouse before a snake. He could see none of the things that made her *her* inside those pitiless eyes. And beneath his touch, a formless darkness vibrated just under Vivienne's skin, its presence cold, and hungry, and very alien. As it focused on him, Caden felt like he'd been caught out in the open in a hailstorm, the cold biting into him, so sharp he couldn't breathe, couldn't think.

No, Caden thought desperately, fighting against it. He pulled up his shields, imagining warm white light surrounding him. It worked, the cold lessening until he could breathe again. And then he focused that energy outward, imagining it flowing into Vivienne.

Nothing happened. Vivienne's lips curled in a small mocking smile. *You can't do anything to stop me, little human child. It's too late,* a voice spoke inside Caden's head, cold and clear.

"Hey, are you okay?" Nate said just up ahead. "You're bleeding."

Becka stopped and touched a hand to her nose. "Shoot," she said. "Yeah, I'm fine. It's just a nosebleed. All this weird atmospheric pressure. Anyone have a tissue?"

Vivienne lifted her head, nostrils flaring. And then she was gone, sprinting down the hall, a blur of movement headed straight for Becka.

Caden ran after her as fast as he'd ever run, already knowing he would be too late.

"Vivi, what—ah!" Becka screamed as Vivienne slammed into her, knocking her to the ground. Vivienne's lips pulled back in a snarl, and with a loud, guttural cry, she sank her teeth into Becka's throat.

11.
RAE

Rae frowned up at the sky. The clouds were so dark she kept expecting it to start raining, but so far nothing. Not a single drop. Not a breath of wind. It looked like the weather was being as weird as everything else in Whispering Pines.

Ava rattled the chain winding through the gate that blocked the road. It clinked but didn't budge, its lock firmly in place. "Hello?" she called. "Hellooooo!"

No answer.

On either side of the gate stretched a tall chain-link fence topped with barbed wire. The guardhouse just inside stood dark and empty. Beyond it, they could see the road stretching through the trees and leading toward the hulking cement block that was Green On!. So close, and yet so far.

Rae eyed the trees on either side of them. Just like the ones at the school, these stood silent. No animals. In the past, that had always been a bad sign. She shivered and inched closer to Ava's car, parked just in front of the gate.

"Well, that's super weird," Ava said, turning her back on the fence. "I can't believe it's not being guarded."

"Maybe all the guards are inside?" Rae suggested. "Code black could mean they had to lock down things here, too."

"Maybe." But Ava's eyebrows were drawn together, her face scrunched with worry. Rae didn't blame her; this whole thing felt wrong.

"Since we obviously can't drive there, what's the plan now?" Ava asked.

"It's not that far through the woods," Alyssa said. "We could try hiking there instead."

"Yeah, we could," Ava agreed. "If we could get past this." She patted the fence next to her. "I don't know about you, but I forgot my wire cutters back at the house."

"Ha ha. Very funny." Alyssa folded her arms. "The fence might not stretch all the way around. There could be another opening somewhere in there." She nodded at the woods. "I'm sure there's another gate at least."

"How do you know that?" Rae asked.

"Because there used to be another road that led to Green On!, until it got swallowed by the woods about three years ago."

"Swallowed by the woods?" Ava gave Alyssa a look of pure skepticism.

"Mm-hmm. It was all over the papers for a while."

Rae made a mental note to find those articles when this disaster was over. "I don't know," she said at last, staring into those woods. Silent and super creepy.

She knew part of the Watchful Woods had been turned into a sort of magical cage for the creatures of the Other Place. How far did that wall extend? She took a step closer to the trees, then another, reluctant to leave the road.

"Where are you going?" Ava asked. "You're not seriously planning on hiking there, are you? No offense to your friend here, but it's a terrible idea."

"Hey, at least I'm trying to come up with a plan," Alyssa snapped.

"I'm just checking something," Rae said, stepping onto the pine-needle-covered ground. No magical barrier stopped her. Maybe they *could* hike through the trees here.

"Check a little closer to the car, would you?" Ava said. "The trees are making me nervous."

Alyssa scoffed.

"What?" Ava said. "They're not acting normal. They're too . . . empty."

"Are they?" Rae asked, peering between trunks. With that charcoal-gray sky, all the shadows beneath blended together until it was impossible to see more than a few feet into the woods. Still, it almost looked like there'd been something else there. A darker shadow. Only now she couldn't see any sign of movement at all.

Rae took another step, then stopped. Her sister was right; it didn't feel safe so close to these trees. Still. "We *could* try to find the tunnel that leads to the spaceship—"

"You mean the one infested with big, murderous bugs?" Ava cut in. "No thank you."

"The bugs are gone now," Rae said. "Vivi and I made sure of that." She forced herself not to remember what it had felt like to be surrounded by all their corpses.

She still had nightmares about that moment. It was strange; the thing that continued to bother her the most, all these nights later, wasn't the terror she'd felt when coming face-to-face with those creatures. It was the guilt. The knowledge that she'd been responsible for so much death.

"Still, let's file that under Plan No Way in Hell," Ava said. She sighed. "I think we'll have to give up on Green On! for today."

"If you want to give up, fine," Alyssa said. "You can wait by the car or whatever. Just because *you're* too scared to go through the woods doesn't mean Rae and I can't do it. Rae, you're not scared, are you?"

"Rae," Ava said warningly.

"Rae?" Alyssa said.

"Shh," Rae hissed, trying to ignore them. She'd seen that shadow again, moving in the woods. She was sure of it. And she'd heard something. A rustling.

And then a cry sounded, long and eerie and oh-so-familiar.

Rae froze, her body rooted to the place with terror.

"Oh, no," Alyssa gasped, her face deathly pale. "I've heard that before."

"What is it?" Ava asked.

"Devourer," Rae whispered. The sound ended, but she knew

the creature was close. And they never traveled alone. Suddenly the fact that she could step into the woods seemed like a very bad sign indeed. If she could go in here, they could come *out*. "Let's get out of here. We can come up with a more solid plan at home."

"Good idea." Ava hurried over to the car, sliding into the driver's seat. This time Alyssa didn't argue; she got in the backseat quickly. Rae spared one last glance at the woods before rushing to the copilot side and getting in.

Ava turned the car on. "What's a Devourer?"

"You don't want to know," Rae said as Ava carefully turned the car around. They started back down the road just as a dark shape covered in blood and dirt plunged out of the tree line in front of them.

Ava screamed and slammed on the brakes.

12.
CADEN

"V ivienne, no!" Caden screamed, throwing his hands out toward her. He had no idea what he was doing, but he poured his will out like a net and imagined it wrapping around her, filling her with one simple command: *Stop*.

Vivienne froze, her teeth still buried in the flesh where Becka's neck met her shoulder. Becka was gasping, her eyes wide and afraid, her hands pushing ineffectually at Vivienne's head, feet kicking weakly.

Dimly Caden was aware of Nate flailing behind them, obviously not sure what to do. He ignored that, ignored everything—his own terror, his disbelief that this had worked—and focused on keeping his command clear and confident. *Let her go,* he ordered. *Now!*

Slowly, so slowly, Vivienne's mouth opened, blood streaming

down her chin, her eyes black and glassy as she looked at him. Becka started to crawl backward, and those eyes snapped back to her. Immediately she froze, a small whimper escaping her lips.

"Shh, shh, easy," Caden said, imagining a calm, soothing blue washing over all of them, as light and breezy as a summer day at the beach. "Easy," he repeated, and it seemed to help; Becka's shoulders relaxed, her eyes closing. Or maybe that was just blood loss . . .

A spike of fear jabbed through him, but he refused to let himself think about that. Becka would be okay. She *had* to be. Instead, he turned all his focus back on Vivienne, tightening his will around her. He felt the alien presence struggling against him, but despite its strength, it was still young and inexperienced.

Vivienne Matsuoka, come back.

At first there was nothing. Only a vast hunger, and the cold dark of a starless sky. But then slowly he sensed a small spark struggling beneath that. Vivienne. Only she wasn't strong enough to push off the alien presence that had wrested control.

Still staring into her eyes, he unclipped the pendant he always wore from around his neck. His mom had given it to him years ago as a way for him to remember who he was. Now it was Vivienne who needed that reminder. Tentatively he walked toward her, watching her nostrils flare, her body tense, every muscle straining.

"Easy, easy," he repeated.

"What's happening?" Nate squeaked. "What's she doing?"

"Shut up, Nate," Caden said, never taking his eyes from Vivienne. He felt his control over her straining, his own strength pulled taut. If this didn't work . . .

Moving carefully, as if he were approaching a skittish horse, he gently clasped his necklace around her neck and dropped the pendant so it landed under her shirt, nestled against her skin. The pendant he'd grabbed for comfort time and time again. The one that was such a part of him that it had absorbed his own energy signature.

Please work. Please. It wasn't a command this time, but a last desperate plea.

Vivienne blinked, one hand going to the lump under her shirt, and the spark inside her surged up and out. She blinked again, and she was herself once more.

Caden watched her dark eyes lighten, then fill with horror. "Oh, god," she breathed, wiping a hand across her mouth. She looked down into Becka's pale face, all the color draining from her own cheeks. "Becka." She reached for her, and Becka shrank back with a little cry. Vivienne flinched. "I'm so sorry. I'm so sorry." Tears streamed down her face, mixing with the blood still staining her chin, pinkish drops dotting her shirt.

"We'll fix this, okay?" Caden told her.

She shook her head. "We can't. We can't," she sobbed. "And it's just going to get worse." She scrambled away from him, away from Becka, moving until she hit the far wall. She curled herself into a tight ball, shaking violently, her face buried in her knees.

Caden let her go. He needed to check on Becka before figuring out what to do about Vivienne. Becka gazed up at him, her eyes half-lidded in shock, one hand clapped over her wound. Gently Caden pulled her hand to the side to study it. It looked terrible, the skin raw and torn, blood oozing from it in thick, dark streams, the floor beneath her sticky with it.

"Nate?" Caden looked up, but Nate was gone. Which meant it was all up to him.

Now the fear took over. He'd grown up dealing with magic and supernatural situations. But this? This was way beyond him. He had no idea what to do next, how to help her.

The bleeding. That was the first step. Stop the bleeding. He grabbed the bottom of his shirt and tried to rip a strip from it.

It didn't work.

"That's . . . embarrassing," Becka wheezed.

Caden glanced down at her. She was actually focusing on him now. That was encouraging, and his heart unclenched a little. "I know, right?" he said. "It always looks so easy in the movies."

He heard running footsteps and looked up to see Nate and Matt sprinting toward him.

"I got help," Nate explained, breathless, as he slid to a halt. "I wasn't sure if we should get a teacher yet . . . because . . ." He trailed off helplessly, but Caden understood.

Because Vivienne was the one who'd attacked Becka. Once they got an adult involved, there would be no hiding that. And then what would happen to Vivi?

Matt nudged Caden out of the way and crouched beside Becka, studying the wound. He hissed through his teeth, and she clapped her hand back over it. "It's going to be okay."

"Is it?" she gasped.

Matt nodded, his round face serious. "It is." He tore a strip from his own shirt as easily as if he were ripping a piece of paper, and Becka's eyes met Caden's.

"Don't say anything," he warned her.

She managed a small smile as Matt folded the cloth and gently pressed it to her neck, then ripped a second strip and used it to tie the first one in place.

"Do you have medical training?" Nate asked.

"Sort of. My dad's a personal trainer with the local women's soccer team. He brings me along sometimes to assist him."

"Lot of. Bite wounds. In that?" Becka asked, her words clipped and painful.

Matt flashed her a smile. "You'd be surprised. Those players are brutal. Now, can you sit up?"

In answer, Becka slowly pushed herself up to sitting, her movements stiff.

"Good, good. I'm going to carry you to the nurse's office where we can clean that wound and get real bandages. And some painkillers, too. Okay?"

"Sounds great," Becka wheezed. She draped an arm around his neck and allowed him to scoop his other arm under her legs and lift her as easily as if she weighed nothing. "I still . . . can't believe . . . she bit me." Her words were growing weaker, slurred around the edges.

"Yeah, what was *that*?" Nate said.

"It was . . ." Caden trailed off. How could he possibly explain it? He glanced over at the other end of the hall, expecting to see Vivienne there, wondering what she would say. Only, the hall was empty.

Vivienne was gone.

13.
RAE

The car screeched to a halt, Rae's seatbelt digging painfully into her chest.

"What are you doing?" Alyssa screamed. "Don't stop!"

"Wait!" Rae said. Because the dirty creature swaying in front of them wore Green On! scrubs that had turned a mottled brown with grime and crusted blood. *Not* a monster, but a person. And as her eyes traveled past the torn and stained uniform up to the face, she realized she *knew* him.

Rae was out of the car before anyone could stop her.

"Rae!" Ava shrieked.

Rae ignored her sister, running to his side. "Blake?"

His red hair was matted and covered in pine needles above a long nasty scratch visible on his forehead, and he had one arm wrapped protectively around his stomach.

He blinked at her, dazed. "Rae?"

"Yes, it's me. Come on, let's get you out of here." She took him by the arm, but he flinched away from her.

"How do I know it's really you?"

Rae frowned. "Who else would I be?" She heard a car door open, and then Alyssa was there with her.

"Blake! Oh my god, Blake," Alyssa said, staring at him.

Blake looked between the two of them, his eyes wide and frantic. "You don't understand! There are these spores all over the place, and they change you. They change you . . ." He swayed again, and this time he let Rae take his arm as Alyssa slid her own arm around his waist, the two of them half-carrying him to the car. "Zombies," he muttered.

"It's okay, shh shh," Alyssa cooed. "Just be calm. It's going to be okay."

Ava had gotten out now too, and stood watching grim-faced. Wordlessly she stood back as Alyssa and Rae awkwardly maneuvered Blake's tall frame into the backseat. "Hospital?" she said.

"I think so." Rae spared one last look at the woods. She felt sure her dad was somewhere in there. Whether inside Green On! or the spaceship, she had no idea. But the mystery of his location would have to wait a little longer. Blake needed medical help now. Sighing, she shut the back door and walked around the car to the front.

Another long, eerie howl tore through the otherwise silent woods. It sounded much closer. As if it were right there at the edge of the road.

Rae glanced beneath the nearby trees. Four glowing slitted

eyes looked back at her. "Oh," she whispered, frozen for one heartbeat, two.

And then Rae threw herself inside the car and slammed the door behind her. "Drive! Drive now!"

Ava didn't hesitate, and the car lurched forward just as a huge shape came hurtling toward them. It moved so fast, almost gliding, rapidly closing the distance between it and the car. Just up ahead the trees on either side dropped away and the road stretched clear and open. Rae clicked her seatbelt on as she focused on that space ahead, willing the car to go faster, faster.

Crunch!

Rae was thrown painfully forward once again, her seatbelt slicing into her as the car gave an anguished metallic scream, the front crumpling like an accordion.

They all sat there in stunned silence, the only sound a soft hiss from the front. Smoke rose from it in small, lazy rivulets, the same dark gray as the sky above them. Clearly they had hit *something*, but what? There was nothing visible in front of them to hit.

"What the . . . ?" Ava muttered. She shook herself and looked back. "Is everyone okay?"

"Yes, fine," Alyssa said, at the same time Rae said, "Peachy."

"Nope," Blake said firmly.

"I'm glad we have one honest person with us—ah!" Ava screamed as something huge and reptilian crashed into Rae's side of the car, so hard the whole vehicle lifted for a second before dropping back down on all four tires.

The thing backed off a few paces, eyeing them. Rae stared into those familiar slitted glowing eyes, like four crescent moons resting above a long snout stuffed with razor sharp teeth. It opened its mouth and shrieked.

"That, by the way," Rae said, her voice deceptively calm, "is a Devourer."

"I guessed," Ava whispered. She reached over and pressed the automatic lock for the doors.

The Devourer tilted its head at the sound.

"Not sure that's going to help," Rae muttered.

It slowly circled the car as the four of them shrank closer together in the middle.

"Do you think it can get in?" Alyssa asked, clutching at Blake's hands. "It can't, right? I mean, this is metal."

"Polar bears can rip a car door off," Blake said. "And that thing looks stronger than a bear." Fear seemed to have sharpened his focus, draining his earlier stupor.

"Shh," Ava hissed. The Devourer had almost completed its circle and now stood near the front of the car on Ava's side. It tried taking another step forward, then paused, its body flattening strangely against something.

An invisible wall.

Rae's stomach sank. This must be part of the Prices' magical barricade. The one keeping the Watchful Woods contained. Somehow it had expanded to block off this road now too.

Which meant they were trapped.

Even if *this* Devourer eventually left them alone, they wouldn't be able to leave the woods. They'd be stuck here, sitting ducks for the next hungry monster that came along.

The Devourer shrieked again, a sound of pure fury as it clawed at the impassable air. Then it twisted, leaping onto the roof of their car. Immediately the ceiling dented downward in the two places where its feet landed.

"Umm . . . are you sure about that polar bear stat?" Rae asked, hunching low in her seat.

"Yes," Blake whispered.

The car shook as the Devourer paced back and forth across it. Rae reached out to her sister, who took her hands, both of them squeezing tight. *Go away, just go away,* Rae thought at the monster. She waited, every muscle tense.

The Devourer stopped moving, but she could feel it crouching over them. Silent, and hungry, and calculating. What was it doing?

Screech!

A claw abruptly sliced through the top of the car.

Alyssa screamed. Rae would have, but the sound stuck in her throat. She couldn't move, couldn't breathe as that claw wriggled back and forth, hooking on a jagged piece of roof and then tearing it back with a sound like a can opening.

"Plan?" Blake gulped. "What's the plan?"

A long eel-like head thrust through the hole, teeth gnashing. Rae slid down until she was on the floor, still clutching her sister's hands. The thing's breath filled the car, hot and rancid, and her stomach churned. She couldn't stop looking at those teeth only inches above her. They were stained brown with old blood, the edges serrated like a shark's.

It shrieked, the sound echoing painfully inside the confines of the car as it thrust its way closer, the opening in the roof groaning and tearing, growing wider.

Those glowing eyes locked on Rae, and she knew she wasn't imagining the surge of triumph in their alien depths.

14.
CADEN

aden's heart stopped beating. He felt the emptiness between one heartbeat and the next, the feeling that he'd stepped outside of time, everything slowing down. The dimly lit hallway, Matt holding Becka, Nate hovering beside him. All of it seemed to freeze with him.

And then reality slammed into him.

Vivienne was missing. And in her current state, that was extremely dangerous. Both for her and for everyone around her.

He lurched to his feet.

"What is it?" Nate asked.

Caden scanned the hallway. The light overhead flickered, making it harder to see anything, the shadows growing and stretching, then receding in dizzying waves. No sign of her. Still, she couldn't have gotten far. Especially with the whole school on lockdown.

"Caden?"

"Vivienne's gone," Caden said. "We need to find her, fast."

"Do we, though?" Nate shifted uncomfortably. "Seems like maybe we should give her some space."

"Yeah, I'm with Nate on this one," Matt said, glancing down at Becka.

"You don't understand," Caden said.

"Understatement of the year," Nate said. "I mean, I knew Vivi could be a little quirky, and obviously she's under some stress, but—"

"It's not stress. She's—" Caden stopped. It wasn't his secret to tell, but at the moment, that no longer mattered. "There's an alien inside her, and it's taking her over, okay? So if we don't find her quickly, Becka might just be the appetizer."

Nate's face went pale.

"Is there anything you need from me?" Caden asked Matt.

Matt shook his head. "I can handle this."

"Becka?"

"I'm good," Becka croaked.

Caden highly doubted that, but it seemed like she was stable at least. "Then I'm going after Vivienne. Nate, you stay and help Matt."

Nate hesitated for one brief second, and then his shoulders slumped. "Ergo," he muttered sadly.

"What?"

"She's my friend. Ergo, I'm coming with you."

Caden thought about arguing, but in the end, he could probably use the help. "Let's go."

* * *

"You're sure she came in here?" Nate asked.

Caden frowned, his eyes closed, senses open. "Yes," he said at last. They'd been sprinting through the halls for the past twenty minutes, following Vivienne's energy signature. Luckily that had been easy for Caden; no one felt the way she did to his magical senses. But that search had ended here. Inside Ms. Lockett's office. Vivienne *should* still be here now; there was no way out.

Except . . .

His eyes opened, and he scanned the room.

"What?" Nate said.

"Rae and Alyssa must have left the school somehow. What if Vivienne got out the same way?"

"She's not in the school anymore?"

"I don't think so." Caden ran his hands over the bookshelf in the corner, then turned and started rummaging on the desk. He remembered how Rae had helped him search his mother's study for her Book of Shadows, and the way she'd found it hidden between drawers.

Ms. Lockett's drawers were all locked. But under her desk, he discovered a small metal switch. He flipped it, and Nate gasped.

"What?" Caden poked his head up. The bookshelf on the far wall had moved slightly, revealing an empty space behind it. "Ah. Secret exit."

"That actually explains a lot. Ms. Lockett was like some kind of ninja, getting from one side of the school to the other without being seen. This must be how she did it." Nate pulled on the book-shelf, widening the opening.

"Nice to know we've solved one mystery, at least." Caden brushed his hands off on his pants. "I'll take the lead."

Nate didn't argue, and Caden led the way past the bookshelf and into the corridor behind it, feeling suddenly very like Rae. He'd never considered himself to be particularly brave, but maybe some of her qualities had rubbed off on him. He sure hoped so.

Then he remembered that Rae had almost lost her eyes to an Unseeing, been swarmed underground by giant flesh-eating insects, and had narrowly avoided being trapped inside a pod on a space-ship. And as he followed the tunnels winding through the school, he couldn't shake the sense that he was walking into a trap as well.

15.
RAE

Rae stared into those glowing eyes, the color a swirling mix of yellow and green, like the fog that had once blanketed the Other Place. As the Devourer lunged closer, the car filling with the sounds of Alyssa and Blake screaming, Ava saying her name, the whining screech of metal tearing, those eyes were all she could see.

She was going to die. Here, in her sister's car. She would never see her dad again, even though he was so close.

No. Determination burned through Rae, and she surged upward and jabbed both her thumbs into the creature's top two eyes, driving forward with all the force she could.

It screamed in pain and tried to pull back, but the metal of the roof held it fast as Rae's thumbs sank in deep. She ignored the hot splash of gooey liquid trickling down her hands and arms and the terrible, mushy sensation under her thumbs and just kept pressing as if she might be able to force her hands through the monster's head and straight out the back.

And then an image flashed through her mind: the tunnel, the corpses of insects curled in piles around her, and the queen's upturned face as it died. So much death. Because of her.

Rae's stomach heaved, and she yanked her thumbs free with a terrible sucking sound. The Devourer thrashed its head around for a few more seconds before finally managing to rip itself back out of the car. Greenish blood dripped from the jagged slices of metal above them where it had cut itself in its desperation to escape.

"Rae?" Ava said.

Rae stared at her hands, the skin stained the same greenish color as the thing's blood. She thought she might be sick, but there was no time for that. She took a deep, steadying breath, then dropped her hands into her lap. "We need to get out of here." The Devourer was still shrieking out there; it was only a matter of time before the noise attracted more of them.

"The car—" Ava began.

"Is done, I know. And it wouldn't matter anyhow. The road is blocked." Rae kicked her door open and grabbed her inhaler from her backpack, stuffing it into her pocket.

"Blocked how?" Alyssa demanded, opening her own door.

"Magic," Rae said. She saw a flash of skepticism cross Alyssa's face before the taller girl glanced at the Devourer still writhing on the ground. She swallowed and didn't argue. Instead, she helped pull Blake from the car, supporting his weight.

"Where?" Ava said.

Rae jerked her chin at the woods. "We're too exposed on the road."

"But, you don't understand what it's like in there!" Blake's eyes were too wide, and for a second Rae thought he might try to bolt. Where, she had no idea.

Alyssa caught him by the arm. "We don't have a choice," she said grimly, tugging him toward the trees. Blake resisted for a second, and then he was sprinting, Rae and Ava right behind him.

Rae spared one last glance back at the wounded Devourer. It was on the ground, clawing at its ruined face, but it seemed to sense her gaze; it stopped moving, one perfect eye looking up and focusing on her. Where before there had been triumph, now she saw nothing but a cold, all-encompassing hatred.

She turned away, all the muscles in her back and neck tensed, ready to feel the monster slamming into her. It was a relief when the trees closed around her, turning the world to twilight and reducing everything to hazy shadows and blackened silhouettes. She kept running as fast as she could safely go in the gloom, stumbling over half-seen roots and thrashing through overgrown underbrush with the others.

"Plan?" Ava gasped beside her as they leapt over a fallen log, branches whipping their faces.

Rae was suddenly struck by the realization that this was her area of expertise. Ava might be older, but she'd never raced through the woods after a monster. Or away from one, either. She didn't have experience with this sort of thing.

"Shelter," Rae said. "Someplace we can hide."

"Green On!?" Alyssa suggested.

Blake stumbled, and only Alyssa's quick reflexes kept him from going down on his face in a patch of pine needles. Rae stopped running too. Even in the semi-darkness she could tell Blake was struggling; his face had gone even paler, his freckles practically glowing under all the dirt and blood, and he stood hunched over, both arms now pressed to his stomach. He wouldn't be able to run for much longer.

"We . . . can't," he gasped.

"Can't what?" Alyssa said.

"Go to . . . Green On!." He took a deep, ragged breath that ended in a wheeze. "It's bad there. I barely got out."

Rae and Ava exchanged glances, and Rae knew her sister was thinking about their dad. Was he safe, wherever he was?

"Bad how?" Ava asked.

Blake shook his head. "Monsters everywhere. And death. And blood."

"Yeah, that sounds pretty bad," Ava muttered, hugging herself.

"Okay," Rae said slowly, her mind racing. What if when Doctor Nguyen tried to free Alyssa's mom and everyone else trapped in those pods, she had released more than she bargained for? Rae could imagine all of the pods opening and a tide of aliens pouring out into the lab. An invasion, ready to exterminate any human they found.

Rae shook her head like that could clear it of those unhelpful thoughts. "But we can't stay here, in the middle of the woods. We need to go *somewhere*." Already her legs were itching with the need to keep moving. The woods were only going to get darker, and she had to assume the monsters from the Other Place could see better in the dark than she could.

And the woods, what she *could* see of them, had become strange. Even for this place. Several nearby plants definitely had tentacles trailing from them, and she spotted at least one tree that had been twisted into a bizarre shape. Even the ground under her feet felt spongier, the air heavy with moisture, as if the entire forest were slowly transforming into an alien planet.

"My uncle's yurt," Blake said at last. "We can go there."

"A yurt?" Alyssa frowned. "Aren't the walls made of canvas?"

"Yeah, and we all saw that thing slice through metal like it was a cake," Ava said.

The trees nearby rustled, and Rae heard a low, ominous growl that set her teeth on edge. "It's better than nothing," she said quickly. "Can you find it?"

Blake nodded.

"Then let's go." The only other place Rae knew of was the cabin where she'd almost lost her eyes to the Unseeing. With its wooden walls, it would probably provide more protection from the things that stalked through the forest than a glorified tent, but she couldn't bring herself to suggest it. Besides, she wasn't sure she'd be able to find it again on her own.

Ready or not, here I come . . .

Rae tried not to think about Ivan, or how it had felt to be stalked by him through that creepy cabin. But every time Blake stumbled or stopped to get his bearings, she could feel eyes on her back and knew they were running out of time.

The Watchful Woods had always felt creepy, but now they felt somehow *wrong*. Like a haunted funhouse mirror version, the trees all twisted, the animals strange. A squirrel zigzagged across a branch up ahead before a tentacle dropped on it, so fast it was gone before Rae could blink. She heard a small squeak, and then nothing, and quickened her pace. Yes, they definitely needed to find shelter.

"Oh, my . . ." Ava froze, staring into the shadows below a large fir tree.

Rae paused and looked. A deer lay on the ground, twitching, as its skin was rapidly peeled away by hundreds of little red worms. Rae's mouth fell open as she realized they were eating through the bones, too, just as fast.

"Are those the same bugs that were in our house?" Ava whispered in horror.

"No, those are something else."

Alyssa tugged on her sleeve. "Let's find that yurt. Blake says we're getting close."

Blake nodded, his face pale. Rae didn't know if that was from fear, or pain, or both. She took one last look at the deer as part of its skull collapsed, then shuddered and turned away. The shadows around them had lengthened, and she could imagine them hiding all sorts of monsters from the Other Place.

Rae picked up her pace, jumping at every little noise, until finally the trees opened up in a little clearing, and there was the yurt. Next to it stood an empty goat pen, all of it looking almost exactly the way Rae remembered from her last time here, when she and her friends had been searching for secret tunnels. They'd found one nearby that had led deep below Whispering Pines, and straight to the secret spaceship.

"Do you hear voices?" Alyssa whispered.

Rae pushed her memories away, concentrating. It did sound like there was a low murmur of voices coming from inside the yurt. Or maybe it was just the wind?

"Should we continue?" Ava stared at the yurt anxiously.

"We don't really have much of a choice," Rae said grimly. "At least whoever is in there is trapped just like us. Maybe they have a better idea of what's going on."

"Or maybe they're enemies," Blake whispered.

"Then let's go find out." She glanced around their small group. Alyssa looked determined, Ava resigned, and Blake pained. Not exactly the show of force she'd have hoped for, but it would have to do. "Time to meet the new neighbors."

Rae took the lead, wishing she had Caden or Vivienne with her. She loved her sister but really didn't know how she would react if things went wrong. Blake looked like he might collapse any second. And Alyssa? She'd been helpful so far, but Rae still didn't entirely trust her.

She strode up the three steps to the door, then waited a second, listening hard. There were definitely voices coming from inside. But the sky had already turned the dark purple of a deep bruise. Night was only moments away.

Squaring her shoulders, she grabbed the doorknob, and turned it.

16.
CADEN

The woods ahead felt different. It reminded Caden of a time when he'd been listening to music through headphones, and one side just stopped working. Everything seemed kind of muted. The trees stood there, strangely silent and unmoving, the sky above a dark smear. It almost made him feel as if he were looking at a photograph and not a living, breathing forest.

Nate eyed the trees nervously as well. "You're, um, sure Vivienne went in there?"

Fear surrounded him like a thick yellow cloud, but beneath it Caden could see his determination shining like a thin metal rod. Despite his terror, Nate had followed Caden outside the school and all the way to the closest edge of the Watchful Woods. Because Vivienne was his friend, and he wanted to help her.

And because he didn't want Caden to go it alone.

Caden let that thought warm him a little before nodding slowly. He took a step forward, then another, his hands up, his awareness open until he reached the barrier that enclosed the woods. The power of the spell trickled through him, most of it as familiar as his mom's favorite incense or his dad's jokes. But underneath their energy, he could feel that strange demonic taint. Almost like an aftertaste, something bitter that wasn't immediately apparent.

Nate started to walk past him, but Caden put out a hand, blocking him. "Don't get any closer."

"What? Why not?" Nate asked.

"Because if you step into the woods, you won't be able to get out again."

Nate blinked. "But . . . Vivienne—"

"Won't be able to get out on her own." Caden took a deep breath. "We'll need to go in and bring her out." *If we can,* he added silently.

Nate frowned. "I thought you said we couldn't step into the woods or we'd be stuck in there."

Caden turned his back on the trees, but he could still feel them. "That's why we need to find my brother first." He doubted his mom would be willing to let him go, but Aiden? He could be convinced. "And we'll have to do it quickly." If they didn't hurry, Vivienne would be in the middle of the forest before he and Nate managed to break the treeline.

The thought of going so far into the woods to find her made him feel queasy, and for a second he wondered if it would be better to just leave her be. There was no one for her to hurt inside that barrier.

Except herself.

That thought spurred him on. He knew the real Vivienne was still in there, fighting for control of her own body. He wouldn't abandon her now.

Nate was staring at him, a strange look plastered across his face. "What?" Caden said.

"I hate to break it to you, but you and me? We're not fast."

Caden sighed. "No, we're not. But what choice do we have?"

"I have an idea, but I'm not sure you'll like it." Nate shrugged awkwardly. "I'm not even sure *I* like it."

"At this point, I'll take anything; I'm fresh out of ideas."

Instead of telling him what it was, Nate turned and headed back toward the school. Caden followed, wondering what Nate had in mind and why it made him feel so uncomfortable. Whatever it was, it couldn't be worse than Rae's idea of breaking into someone's house . . .

Could it?

Less than thirty minutes later, they were biking down the road. Caden's bike was definitely too big for him, while Nate's had a lovely white wicker basket and pink flowers down its frame.

"If karma is a real thing, I'm screwed for the next ten years," Nate puffed, pedaling hard.

"Karma is real." Caden peddled along next to him.

"Great," Nate muttered. "Just great. I *never* steal! I don't even take extra plastic utensils from the food court, or school pens, or . . . or anything!"

"It's okay. We aren't technically stealing."

"No?" Nate glanced sideways at him, then quickly back to the road, his bike wobbling. "Pretty sure Brody and his sister would disagree."

Caden winced a little. Everyone knew the McAdams siblings never locked their bikes. They didn't have to; their dad was the chief of police. Who would steal from them? Under normal circumstances, no one. But today was definitely not a normal day. So when Nate had suggested it, Caden had agreed immediately. "Well, we're not keeping them," Caden said at last. "We're merely borrowing them for the greater good."

"Hopefully karma realizes that," Nate said.

At least while there was a lockdown, Brody and Beatrice would have no idea their bikes were gone. If all went as planned, Caden and Nate would return them before anyone was the wiser. And if things *didn't* go the way they hoped, well, a couple of stolen bikes wouldn't matter.

Caden tried not to think about that, but he could feel the pressure of the Watchful Woods building as if it were a boiling pot, and his family's spell was the lid. The things in there were getting restless, ready to escape. The moment they spilled out, they'd pour over the whole town.

And they wouldn't stop with Whispering Pines.

Caden stood so he could pedal faster, wishing he'd be able to outrun that thought. It was bad enough having the responsibility of a whole town on his shoulders. Now, he could feel the weight of the world, and it made him realize how small he was. How small they *all* were—his family, his friends. If they were all that stood between the world and an alien invasion, things were pretty grim indeed.

The next few minutes passed in silence, aside from the steady howling of the wind all around them. The kind that meant it would begin raining soon. Caden wanted to say something to Nate, but part of him was worried the noise would attract unwanted attention. Plus, peddling was getting harder. He never realized how many little hills there were around here until he was peddling up yet another one of them.

Nate was the first to speak. "It's getting dark," he huffed. "Too dark."

"We're almost there," Caden told him, but he knew what Nate meant. It felt like night was crashing down on them, although they should have had a few hours of daylight left. Worse, none of the Green On! streetlights had turned on. It looked like the whole of Whispering Pines was without power.

In the gloom, the town almost felt eerier than the woods. No cars passed them, honking for them to get out of the way. No one stood in front of their houses, watering their lawns, or collecting the mail, or anything. And even though the creatures of the Other Place should be trapped behind his family's magical barrier, Caden wasn't convinced that all of them had been caught.

He pictured Carly's mangled body, torn and bloody, abandoned on the edge of his yard by the Devourers. It was too easy to imagine more of them stalking the streets now, sliding through the shadows . . .

They turned down his road and biked past Rae's house and his, both dark. He had almost been hoping he would see Rae there, home safe. But knowing Rae, she was probably deep in the woods by now.

"Where are we biking?" Nate gasped. "I know you said something about finding your brother, but I'm pretty sure we just passed your house back there. Also, my legs and butt are killing me."

"It's not too much farther." Caden didn't feel like telling him the details of where they were going yet. If Nate was struggling with the ethics of stealing a couple of bikes, how would he feel about Caden's family confiscating an entire house? Even Caden didn't know how he felt about that.

Several long, surprisingly hilly streets later, Caden turned into the driveway of Doctor Anderson's house. He could feel eyes on him as he and Nate hopped off their bikes. They propped them against the nicely painted picket fence, then opened the gate to the yard.

Caden glanced up at the porch. A shadowy figure stood there, watching them. For a second Caden's heart lurched, before the figure took a step forward, the shadows lifting to reveal Aiden.

"Nice bike," Aiden told Nate.

Nate shrugged, obviously not caring what Aiden thought. Caden envied him that; despite everything, he still struggled with the part of himself that craved his brother's approval.

Aiden turned his gaze to him. "I was wondering when you'd show up."

Caden couldn't hide his surprise. "You knew I'd come here?"

Aiden smirked. "I knew you'd want to go inside the forest."

"How?" Caden hadn't even known that until recently.

"Because, dear brother, your friends are in there, and you've always fancied yourself a bit of a hero. Better watch that instinct; it'll get you killed."

17.
RAE

The doorknob didn't turn. Rae rattled it. "Locked," she whispered to the others.

"Then knock," Alyssa said. "Quickly!" She glanced over her shoulder, and Rae followed her gaze to the trees looming all around them.

Before, the air had felt like a solid thing, unmoving and heavy, the trees standing unnaturally still. Now, a breeze whispered through those branches, setting them to creak and moan, the air crackling with energy. Maybe the storm that had been building all day was finally about to open up on their heads.

She knocked, softly at first, then harder. "Hello? Anyone?" She listened. The voices she'd heard before had gone quiet. "Hello—*ahh!*"

The door had flown open so violently Rae stumbled back,

almost falling off the top step. A tall man in a bright green hazmat suit loomed in the doorway, one hand gripping a large metal canister that had to be a weapon of some kind.

"We come in peace!" Rae held up both her hands, heart racing.

The man scowled at her, his dark eyes glancing past her at Ava, Alyssa, and Blake just behind her. "Where did *you* all come from?" He squinted suspiciously. "You're too young to be part of Green On!."

"We're interns," Rae said, not wanting to get into their whole life story. She felt way too exposed, standing there in that clearing, and she kept picturing the hatred in the wounded Devourer's eyes. "Can we talk about this inside, maybe?"

"Let them in, Roland," a woman said from somewhere in the yurt. "It's not safe to keep the door open so long."

Roland gave Rae one last good look, then stepped to the side. Tentatively Rae and the others filed past him. "I'm going to check on our perimeter," he muttered. "Make sure nothing else is creeping around our borders."

"Wait!" a man called after him. "Your helmet!"

"And end up like Takeshi? I don't think so." Roland gave Rae and the others one last mistrustful glare before leaving, closing the door firmly behind him.

"Pleasant man, that one," Ava said.

Rae managed a small smile, suddenly glad her older sister was with her. Her smile wilted as she took in the rest of the yurt. Four people stared up at her from their place huddled together in the middle of the single room, wedged between a narrow bed and an overcrowded bookshelf. Two of them wore hazmat suits like the man who had just left, and the other two were in Green On! lab coats. All of them clutched weapons, their expressions wary, their bloodstained clothing smeared with dirt.

Rae swallowed. "Hey," she said. "I'm Rae."

"Hi, Rae," the woman in the lab coat said, smiling tiredly. "I'm Amelia." She wiped the back of one hand across her forehead, smearing the dirt caked there. "Sorry about Roland. It's been kind of a rough day."

"What happened to Takeshi?" Rae had to ask.

"Oh, he was ripped in half about a quarter mile that way," the other woman, a short blond in a hazmat suit, said, gesturing vaguely to the left. She tapped her own helmet, which sat on the floor beside her. "Something in the atmosphere out there really messes up the visibility of these things. Poor guy didn't see it coming." She shrugged. "At least it was quick."

Rae felt suddenly queasy. Maybe it was the words, or the casual way the woman said them, but she couldn't help picturing the scene. "Oh" was all she managed.

"This is Nicole, by the way," Amelia said, shooting the blond woman a dark look. "That's Doug," she indicated the man in the lab coat, who lifted his hand in a half-hearted wave. "And Bernard." She pointed at the man in the hazmat suit. He was older than the rest of them, with extremely bushy eyebrows and a completely bald head. He scowled, his arms crossed tightly.

"I'm Ava, this is Alyssa, and this is Blake," Ava said.

"Isn't this cute? It's like a regular little picnic in here," Nicole said, her voice sharp and mocking. "Your friend is bleeding all over the floor, by the way."

Rae glanced at Blake. Alyssa had her arm around him; it looked to be the only thing holding him up. He swayed in place, his face almost gray.

"Let's lay him down so he can rest," Alyssa suggested.

The other adults shuffled a little, and Alyssa managed to get Blake over to the bed. He lay back with a groan, then immediately turned onto his side, his arms clamped over his stomach as if trying to hold his guts in.

"Blake?" Rae stepped closer. "Are you okay?"

"No," he said, eyes closing. His red hair was dark with sweat, and the front of his scrubs stuck to him, the material soaked through with blood. "I think my stitches have opened."

"Does anyone here have medical supplies?" Ava demanded.

"I have a first aid kit," Doug said. "There's not much left in it, though."

"Better than nothing." Ava held out a hand for it.

He unzipped the backpack sitting at his feet and pulled out a small kit, then stood. As he moved, Rae noticed a gleam of metal at his hip. A machete, strapped to his thigh. It reminded her of the one she'd been given from Green On! back when Patrick had sent her and Vivienne into the tunnels to take on an entire swarm of giant, flesh-eating centipedes. She wished she had a weapon like that on her now too.

"I'll do it," Doug said. "I'm trained as a medic."

"Oh, good," Ava said. "My mom's a nurse, but that's about it for my qualifications. I can help, though."

"Thanks." He smiled at her, then moved beside the bed and began gently peeling back Blake's shirt.

Rae caught a glimpse of torn skin and blood and quickly turned away. She felt slightly guilty about leaving her sister to help alone, but that didn't stop her from moving to sit next to Amelia, who sat slumped beside Nicole. Bernard leaned against the bookshelf across from them, still scowling.

"So, um, how long have you been here?" Rae asked.

"In the yurt?" Amelia said.

"Yes."

"Since early this morning. We were supposed to meet up with the rest of our team, but . . ."

"No one else showed," Nicole said harshly. "They're probably all dead."

"Don't say that," Amelia snapped.

"Why not? It's true. Not like it matters; we'll be joining them soon enough."

As if to punctuate her words, something outside gave a long, mournful howl. Rae shivered and hugged her knees to her chest as Alyssa sank to the floor beside her.

"Who is the rest of your team?" Alyssa asked. "For that matter, who are *you*?"

"That's classified info," Bernard spoke up suddenly.

Nicole snorted. "Oh, let it rest, Bernard. No one here is going to be talking to anyone."

Rae and Alyssa exchanged a glance. "I'm not planning on dying here today," Rae said firmly.

"Me, neither," Alyssa said.

Nicole shrugged. "Youthful optimism. I like it. Hold on to it while you still can. By my calculations, that'll be, oh, say, another few hours? Less if the monsters can smell that one's blood." She pointed over at Blake, who was panting now and making small, terrible gasps as the medic worked on him. She shook her head. "Told you we should have left them outside," she muttered.

"We're part of the E and R department at Green On!," Amelia said quickly, shooting her companion a dark glance.

"E and R?" Rae frowned.

"Experimental and research."

And suddenly Rae knew *exactly* where she'd heard it before. It was the department in charge of finding "alternative" renewable energy sources. The one Patrick had taken over when he joined the company. They were behind her friends' recent mission to the Other Place, and the ones working on the spaceship now hidden below their town.

Rae's mom had recently admitted that her dad was somewhere in Whispering Pines, working with a secret organization at the heart of Green On!. One that dealt with the safety and protection of Earth.

Why hasn't Dad been in contact? Rae had asked.

Because he's not allowed to, her mom had said. *The organization he works for, they were furious that he released the extraterrestrial— apparently they had been keeping it for interrogation—and so he has been on probation for the past year. Which meant no contact with the outside.*

Rae could feel a hard knot of anger building up inside herself, but she smothered it. Anger would not get her the answers she needed. She took a deep breath, trying to be calm. Collected. Like Caden would have been in this situation. "Do you know Chris Carter?" she asked.

The air in the yurt seemed to grow chillier. The three adults sitting in the middle all stopped moving and exchanged worried glances. Behind her, Rae could feel her sister's attention sharpening and knew she was listening too.

"You *do* know him." Rae curled her hands in her lap, trying to hide her excitement. "Where is he? What's he doing? Is he okay?"

"That information," Bernard said sharply, "is classified."

"Stuff it, Bernard. Seriously," Nicole said.

"Why do you want to know about Chris?" Amelia asked.

"He's our dad," Ava spoke up.

"And he's been missing for a year," Rae said. "So if you know anything, please—" her voice broke, and she had to stop, afraid she might start crying. "Please tell us," she managed in a ragged whisper.

Bernard scowled and crossed his arms over his chest, but Amelia nodded thoughtfully. "Rae and Ava Carter. I remember him talking about you . . ."

Hope flared in Rae's chest. "He did?"

"All the time. It was what kept him going when . . ." She looked down at her hands.

"When what?" Ava demanded.

"When things got rough for him," Amelia finished. "Some of

the higher-ups thought he was a spy at first. They thought he'd been working for the aliens. They . . . well. They weren't kind to him."

"What does *that* mean?" Rae said, her hope turning to terror. It almost sounded like they'd tortured him. But that couldn't be right.

"Where's Roland?" Bernard asked suddenly. "He's been gone a long time."

"After they determined he wasn't a spy, they had a problem: he knew too much," Amelia continued, clearly refusing to let anyone distract her from what she wanted to say. "They couldn't just let him go. And his knowledge of the energy systems on extraterrestrial crafts is second to none. They needed him. *We* needed him. But he, um, wasn't feeling the most cooperative. So Hahn Nguyen convinced your mom to move here, where Chris could receive regular updates on your lives. It helped motivate him."

Nicole laughed again. "Oh, come on, are we really going to sugarcoat this?" She looked Rae right in the eyes, her own a clear pale blue, sharp and unapologetic. "Honey, you were brought to Whispering Pines for one reason and one reason only: you're a hostage. As long as Chris is a good little boy, nothing happens to his family. But the moment he isn't . . ." She smiled grimly.

A cold lump settled in Rae's stomach. Did Doctor Nguyen *know* that was the real reason Green On! wanted Rae and her family in Whispering Pines? "What kind of organization *are* you?" Rae whispered. "I thought you were supposed to be the good guys." Although lately she had begun questioning who the good guys really were.

"We are," Bernard burst out, his face reddening, the color spreading to his ears and across the top of his head. "We are trying to save the world! Something your father couldn't seem to under-stand. No, he flatly refused to help. Refused! Even though we *knew* an alien attack would be imminent, especially after he released one of those creatures. An attack that could lead to the extinction of the human race! He left us no choice."

Rae stared at his red face, knowing her own was just as red. White-hot rage burned in her chest, and she had to keep her hands clenched in her lap to stop herself from flying at him. How *dare* he talk about her father like that? Her dad who always searched for the truth, no matter where that path led him!

Behind them, the medic had finished patching Blake up. "That's as good as I can do for you," he said. "Really, you need to get to a hospital, but as long as you don't do anything too wild, those ban-dages should hold for a day or two."

"Thanks," Blake said weakly.

"I'm sure my dad had good reasons to not want to help you," Rae managed, her voice shaking.

"Well, we did keep him locked inside a cell for six months and then refused to let him speak to his family," Nicole said. "I can see how he might not feel cooperative after that."

"The ends justify the means." Bernard sniffed. "You know that."

The door of the yurt burst open, and everyone froze, but it was just Roland finally returning.

"Took you long enough," Bernard snapped.

Roland didn't say anything. He just stood by the door, his face gray, sweat beading on his forehead.

Rae stuffed all her anger deep inside. For now. There was only one question that really mattered in this moment. "Where is my dad now?"

Amelia rubbed one of her temples, looking suddenly exhausted. "He's—"

Roland took a strange, jerky step forward, his hands in fists at his sides.

"Roland?" Bernard frowned at him. "Are you okay?"

Rivulets of sweat ran down Roland's face. His lips pulled back in a terrible grin, his eyes bloodshot as they focused on Bernard's face. And then he moved, so fast it was a blur, grabbing Bernard by the front of his hazmat suit and hauling him to his feet as easily as if he weighed nothing.

Amelia gasped, and Alyssa grabbed Rae's shoulder as Roland pulled Bernard's face close to his and spat in it.

"Roland!" Nicole was on her feet and running toward him, fists flying, Amelia right behind her. "What are you *doing*?"

"No!" Blake shrieked. "Don't get near him! Can't you see? He's infected!"

But it was too late. Roland dropped Bernard, one hand snaking out to grab Amelia by the throat, the other gripping Nicole by the top of her short hair, pulling them both toward him. He opened his mouth wide, thick ropy strips of saliva dripping from his teeth.

Rae was on her feet, torn between the instinct to run and the desire to help.

Roland spat a gob of something greenish-yellow into Amelia's eye, then hacked all over Nicole before letting them both go. Bernard, meanwhile, had staggered to his feet, his eyes wild, unfocused.

But Rae could see them turning pink as sweat pooled across his face, and she knew whatever had happened to Roland was happening to him now too.

His eyes locked on hers, and his lips pulled back in a horrible mockery of a grin.

18.
CADEN

Caden stared at his brother, hope rising in his chest. "You know where Vivienne is? And Rae? Is she in there too?"

"Rae's in there," Aiden said.

"Of course she is," Nate muttered, shaking his head.

"That's all I know," Aiden continued. "I felt them pass the wall, but once they're in there," he pointed at the Watchful Woods, "they're lost to me."

Caden's heart sank. "Is there any way to track them?"

Aiden shrugged. "You might be able to. But I doubt it."

Caden turned to stare at the trees. They were clumped together so thickly they were like a wall, naked branches intertwined in eerie patterns. He squinted and realized it wasn't like a wall at all but a cage. Even if it weren't full of murderous alien creatures, it would be impossible to search. He was going to have to get more help.

"Maybe Mom would know—" Caden started.

"No," Aiden cut him off. "She can't help you."

"Why not?" Caden glanced at his brother and caught a hint of some kind of emotion from him, something furtive and dark that wound around him like an eel before vanishing as he regained his usual control. "Is something wrong?" Caden asked.

Aiden hesitated. And in that pause, Caden could feel his heart turning to ice in his chest. "The spell . . . almost collapsed," Aiden said at last. "Mom managed to save it somehow. To be honest, I'm not sure *what* she did, and I can't ask her, because she lost consciousness immediately afterward. Dad, too."

Caden took a step back, the weight of his brother's words hitting him. "They're *both* unconscious?"

Aiden nodded. "Them, and most of the coven. They are using everything they have to keep the spell in place, but it's not going to last much longer." His mouth twisted. "You remember what I told you before? About what will happen if the spell collapses?"

Caden remembered all too well. "That all the monsters in the woods will pour out into the town."

Nate made a small noise, his arms wrapped around himself. He'd seen the things that currently dwelled inside the woods. He knew what they would do to the people of the town.

"And that's the best-case scenario," Aiden said quietly.

The worst case meant that everyone currently tied to the spell—Caden's parents, Aiden, the rest of the coven—would die in the backlash.

And Caden would be the only one left to clean up the mess.

"Can't we do anything?" Caden asked.

"*I'm* doing everything I can right now," Aiden said grimly. He ran one finger against the large silver ring encircling his thumb. The one he'd mysteriously acquired while inside the Other Place. Caden frowned at it. Yesterday it had burned a deep, dark crimson, but now that color had faded. Only, when he squinted, he thought maybe he could still detect a reddish glow . . .

Caden blinked and looked away. "What does that mean?" he asked.

"It means, dear brother, that I'm keeping the spell stable using whatever means necessary. But it's only a temporary solution." Aiden turned back to the woods, his eyes dark. "I'm not strong enough to hold it for much longer." He grit his teeth, the admission obviously painful for him. Caden really looked at his brother, finally noticing the deep circles under his brown eyes and the way his cheeks had sunken in, making him appear gaunt and much older than his sixteen years.

"How long?" Caden asked.

Aiden ran a hand through his short spiky hair. "Six hours," he said at last. "And then the spell will come down."

"Six hours?" Nate burst out. "That's it? That's all you can do?"

Aiden shot him a cold look, and Nate immediately shut his mouth.

Caden took a deep breath. "I know I can't be a part of the spell." His brother had made the reasons for that very clear. "But is there some other way I can help?"

"Are you sure you want the answer to that question?" Aiden lifted one eyebrow, waiting.

Caden swallowed. He'd felt this way before, like he was standing on the edge of a cliff, about to jump into unknown waters. In the past, he would have tried backing slowly away. But ever since he'd met Rae, he felt compelled to leap, because he knew, given the same choices, Rae would always take the plunge.

"Tell me," Caden said.

And Aiden did.

19.
RAE

Rae stared at Bernard in horror. He swayed on his feet, his strange smile stretching wider, the tendons in his neck standing out as if all his muscles were straining against some invisible force.

"What's happening to them?" Ava demanded.

"I told you!" Blake was almost sobbing in terror. "There's some kind of spore in the woods. It changes you. It makes you into . . . into *that*!"

That. Some kind of disease-spreading zombie.

Rae stared into Bernard's bloodshot eyes. Was he aware in there, like a passenger strapped to a runaway car? Or had all the things that made him who he was been erased by whatever alien substance was now taking him over? Terror filled her heart and weighed down her limbs. She'd faced death before, but not something like this.

Behind Bernard, Amelia climbed stiffly to her feet, her movements jerky, like a puppet just getting used to its strings. Her eyes had gone the same pinkish color as Bernard's and Roland's, her lips pulling tight to expose all her teeth. "Run," she panted, staring wildly around the room. "Run."

Rae backed away a step, bumping into Ava behind her. Run where? The zombies were between them and the only door out. And then she realized: this was a yurt. The very thing that made it less secure from the monsters outside might save them now.

Canvas walls.

"Your knife," she said, turning to Doug, the one non-zombified adult in the room. His own eyes were almost as wide and wild as Amelia's.

"I . . . I can't!" He clapped his hands protectively against his chest. "They're my colleagues! I'm a medic, not a murderer!"

"For the walls!" Rae snapped as Bernard took a shaky step closer, saliva dripping from his teeth, the other three closing in behind him. "Not the people!"

"The . . . oh." Doug fumbled the giant blade free as Roland suddenly jerked to a stop behind the others, then collapsed to the ground. His body shook like a leaf in a windstorm before going abruptly still. A second later and a sprout burst from his right eye, shooting up several inches, the eyeball bursting into goo around it.

Vomit rose in the back of Rae's throat, and she clapped a hand over her mouth. She, Blake, Alyssa, and Ava all moved as a group toward the wall, the medic stumbling ahead of them, the blade trembling in his hand.

Amelia darted forward, impossibly fast, and Rae instinctively grabbed the bed Blake had been lying on and knocked it over onto its side, fear giving her strength. Alyssa and Ava were both at her side in an instant, shoving the heavy wooden frame. It slid forward, crashing into Amelia, who stumbled back into Bernard, both of them going down in a tangle of limbs.

Nicole sidestepped, barely seeming to notice her fallen comrades as she continued to advance.

"Hurry up!" Ava yelled.

"The walls," Doug panted, "are tougher . . . than you think."

Rae risked a glance back at him. He'd managed to work his machete through a clear space of wall beneath one of the yurt's small windows. Rae would have considered using one of them as an exit, but they were so narrow she didn't think they'd all be able to fit. Grunting, Doug wiggled the blade, slowly slicing downward.

Rae looked back, then gasped. Nicole was right there, reaching for her, so close Rae could see her own face reflected in the bloody eyes.

Crash!

A small metal cooking pot slammed into the woman's chest, knocking her back a few steps. Another pot missed her by inches, but the third clipped Nicole in the side of the face, spinning her around.

"I'm out of cookware," Ava said.

"Almost . . . there . . ." Doug grunted.

Rip!

"Aha!" he yelled in triumph. "Go, go, go!" Pulling one of the sides back, he moved so Blake could exit first, followed by Alyssa.

"Rae," Ava began, hesitating when it was her turn at the make-shift exit.

"Go, I'm right behind you!"

Ava ducked through. Rae started after her just as Bernard flung himself toward her, one big hand grasping her wrist, his fingers so tight she felt her bones creaking.

Rae cried out and tried to pull away, but Bernard was so strong. He opened his mouth wide, a terrible gurgling sound coming from the back of his throat as he tugged her face nearer.

Thwack!

Blood spattered in a messy arc.

Rae stared at the hand still gripping her wrist. A hand, with no arm attached. Only blood, and the white glint of bone.

"Oh, god, I didn't mean to. I didn't *want* to," Doug babbled, his machete tumbling to the ground, his face green. He stumbled back.

Right into Amelia.

"Look out!" Rae darted forward, scooping the machete up. Time seemed to slow down as she pulled her arm back, the machete raised.

Amelia had both arms wrapped around the medic in an embrace that would have seemed affectionate if not for the expression on her face—mouth gaping, saliva dripping, eyes rolling. She barely looked human.

But she was. Rae knew that, and so she hesitated, unable to swing the knife.

Amelia hocked a disgusting glob straight into the medic's open, gaping mouth, then released him. He dropped to his knees, choking and spitting. Behind him, Rae caught a glimpse of Bernard falling to his back like Roland had, his whole body twitching as a strange alien plant burst from his left eye, the stalk shooting up several inches before widening into some kind of glowing, pulsing spore.

The medic wiped his mouth and turned to Rae. She gasped. His jaw twitched, and his eyes were already growing pink.

"I'm sorry," she whispered, guilt stabbing through her. He'd saved her, and now she was going to leave him behind.

"Rae!" Ava yelled.

"Go," he whispered, sweat beading along his forehead. "Be fast."

Rae tightened her grip on the machete and ducked outside.

20.
CADEN

D o you know why Green On! chose to put their lab here, of all places?" Aiden asked.

"Someone discovered geothermal vents in the woods," Caden said, remembering the articles he'd read online back when he was investigating Patrick Smith. "So a bunch of scientists thought this would be a good spot to work on developing alternative energy sources."

"Oh, good. I see you've mastered the art of Wikipedia."

Caden sighed. "Am I wrong?"

"No. Not wrong. That *is* the 'official' reason."

"And the *real* reason?" Caden asked.

"This place is also a spiritual vortex."

"I know. Mom told me." She'd said that the line between dimensions was thinner in Whispering Pines, which meant it attracted more of the supernatural elements. It was one of the reasons why her ancestor had been able to create the Other Place here.

"It's not a coincidence," Aiden said.

"What are you talking about?" Caden frowned, confused. He could feel Nate watching the two of them, his mouth still clamped shut, his uneasiness wrapping around him like a cloud.

"Haven't you ever wondered why there are so many oddities in this town?" Aiden asked. "Why it's riddled with sinkholes and tunnels? Why strange things happen here all the time, and no one seems to notice?"

"Of course I've wondered that," Caden said. Especially after he met Rae, who made him see how strange Whispering Pines really was.

"It's *because* of those geothermal vents. They're not just releasing hot air, but a kind of cosmic energy that warps the reality around it."

Caden stared at his brother. "They're doing what now?"

Aiden sighed and scrubbed a hand back through his short dark hair. "I'm not explaining this well."

Nate made a small noise in agreement.

Aiden glanced at him. "Something you want to add?"

Nate shook his head hurriedly.

"I didn't think so. Why don't you go scamper off over there and let the adults talk, eh?" Aiden made a shooing motion with his hands.

"Hey," Caden said. "Nate's trying to help."

"And isn't that sweet of him?" Aiden smiled, wide and fake. "Thank you, Nate. Now go away."

Caden started to argue, but Nate shook his head. "It's fine. I'll just . . . scamper, I guess." Nate shot Aiden one last dirty look, then walked a few feet away, his arms crossed.

"You didn't have to be so rude," Caden said.

"Focus, Caden. This is important. We don't have time to get into all the details now, but you do need to know that at its heart, Whispering Pines is a sort of . . . portal. That's really what a 'spiritual vortex' is, a place where the energy of other dimensions is able to flow through into our own."

"How do you know this?" Caden asked. "Mom never said anything about it."

Aiden laughed. "Oh, Mom. I'm not even sure *she* knows the whole truth of it. Let's just say I have a different source for my information these days." He stroked his index finger over the ring on his thumb, and Caden caught a glint of crimson glowing within the twisting silver bands, like a banked coal deep in the heart of an otherwise cold fire.

"And what do you have to give in exchange for this information?" Caden asked, staring at that ring.

"Is this really the time to discuss those details? The clock is ticking, little brother."

The clock *was* ticking. Caden could feel time slipping away. The longer they stood here talking, the farther Vivienne and Rae would both be from them. And the weaker his parents would become, the barrier spell draining them. "Fine. What is it you need me to do?"

"It's simple, really." Aiden smiled, cold and sharp. "You just need to find those vents and destroy them."

"I need to . . . what?"

"Destroy the vents, and you destroy the mouth of the vortex. Get rid of that, and it should trigger a backlash of energy that will wipe out the Watchful Woods . . . and everything in them."

Caden gaped at his brother. "*What?* I can't do that! What about the people in there?"

"Sometimes you have to sacrifice the few for the good of the many." Aiden's mouth twisted. "Green On! itself taught me that." He gave a short, bitter laugh. "Kind of ironic that their lab will be part of the sacrifice."

"I'm not going to sacrifice my friends." The whole reason Caden had come to his brother in the first place was to get help finding and retrieving Vivienne.

Aiden sighed. "Fine. Take this." He reached into his jacket pocket and pulled out a small pouch, dangling it in front of Caden's face.

"What is it?"

"So young, and so suspicious." Aiden opened the pouch enough for Caden to see inside. A handful of deep blue stones speckled with hints of amber and gray sat nestled inside.

"Lapis lazuli?"

Aiden nodded, closing the pouch up again. "Each of them has been spelled with a purpose: to return to me. If you see your friends, or anyone else in the woods—unlikely as that is—you can give them one of these. It should lead them here."

"I didn't realize that was possible."

The corner of Aiden's mouth drew up in amusement. "There is so much more to this life than you could possibly imagine, little brother. So much you don't know. This?" He shook the pouch. "This is nothing. The things I could teach you, if you'd only let me . . ."

Caden bit his lip. There was a time when he'd wanted nothing more than to be just like his brother. Then, more recently, when he'd wanted the exact opposite. Now, though? He wasn't sure what he wanted. "Maybe when this is over," he said at last. "If we survive this." He eyed the pouch. "In the meantime, you'll open the barrier for anyone I find?"

"I will."

"You promise?" Caden asked.

"I swear it." Aiden's eyebrows were drawn together, his expression serious. A solemn oath. Even Aiden wouldn't break one of those lightly.

Still, Caden had a hard time trusting his brother, but he took the pouch anyhow. What else could he do?

"You'll have to be quick, though," Aiden said. "Remember what I said: six hours, and then the barrier goes down. Once that happens, the aliens will pour into our town. It will be a slaughter; you and I both know it. And if you destroy the mouth of the vortex without the barrier in place, the blast won't be contained to these woods. You understand?"

Caden nodded. He understood exactly what Aiden was saying: It didn't matter whether or not he'd found Rae and Vivienne. He needed to destroy the vortex before time was up regardless. Could he do it?

He pictured the things from the Other Place pouring through Whispering Pines, killing everyone he'd ever known, and then spreading from there. Unseeing infiltrating all the major cities, leaving a plague of zombified children in their wake. Devourers roaming the streets. And who knew what else.

"How do I destroy it?" he whispered.

"With this." In one quick motion, Aiden tugged his ring free and tossed it at Caden.

Caden caught it automatically, then wished he hadn't. It felt icy cold, as if the warmth of Aiden's skin had been unable to touch it.

"Put it on," Aiden ordered.

Reluctantly, Caden slid the ring over his left thumb. He thought it would be too big—Aiden's fingers were thicker than his—but it fit as if made for him. Because of course it did. "Why do I need this?"

"When you get to the vents, drop that inside. It'll absorb the vortex's energy."

"How?" Caden asked. That seemed too easy.

Aiden hesitated, his eyes going dark and flat. "*She* will eat the energy," he said at last.

She.

Caden looked down at the ring on his thumb and wanted to chuck it far, far away. "The demon," he whispered.

Aiden gave one short nod, his expression unreadable. And while Caden could usually read the emotions of others, his brother was like a brick wall, impossible to discern. "She'll protect you from the blast," Aiden said. "It's part of the deal. Since you're a Price, you'll be safe."

"And Nate?" Caden glanced over at his friend, who was obviously listening but pretending not to.

Aiden's jaw twitched, like there was more he wanted to say, but he was stopping himself.

"Should he stay here?" Caden thought of going into the Watchful Woods alone. Just him, and the darkness, and the creatures that dwelled inside it.

"No," Aiden said. "It'll be safer in the forest if there are two of you."

"Really?" Caden doubted it would make a difference to the monsters of the Other Place if he was alone or with one other person. He still wouldn't appear threatening.

"Well, safer in the same way that surfing in the ocean is safer if you bring along a friend." Aiden flashed a quick smile, and in that moment he looked so like the old Aiden, the person he'd been before his time in the Other Place, that Caden's breath caught. He hadn't realized how much his brother had changed. And even though he hadn't really liked that old version of Aiden, he felt a sharp pang now for his loss.

His brother had been cruel and selfish, but there had been a sort of innocence about him too. A carefree confidence that had radiated through his entire being. He'd believed that, no matter what, things would always work out in his favor. But after nine months of torture inside the Other Place, followed by a brief captivity within the bowels of Green On!, and then whatever deal he'd made recently with a demon, that innocence had been drained away, leaving behind this new version. Someone harder and more cynical, his soul forever scarred by the darkness.

"What about the blast from the vortex?" Caden asked, shaking off his weird sense of nostalgia. "Nate isn't a Price. Won't it kill him, too?"

Aiden's expression changed, his smile growing hard and brittle, a fragile thing. "No, he'll be fine. You just need to be touching him, and he'll be protected too."

Caden frowned. He didn't think protective magic worked that way. But maybe demon magic was different. "Are you sure?"

"Of course I'm sure. Stop worrying about other people so much and focus on your own safety. That's what matters. Now, are you ready to go?"

"Not really."

"That's the spirit." Aiden turned to Nate. "You can stop hovering and join us now."

"I wasn't hovering," Nate muttered, walking toward them.

Aiden smirked. And then he closed his eyes, his hands moving as he muttered something soundlessly to himself.

The trees just beyond the old stone wall shivered as if caught in a sudden windstorm, and then shifted away from one another, leaving a gap about a foot wide.

Nate gasped.

"The trail won't remain for long," Aiden said, his eyes opening. "But while you wear my ring, you should be able to feel the pull of the vents. That will guide you." He gazed into the forest, his eyes narrowing. "Better go quickly."

Caden glanced at Nate. "You can stay—"

"Nope," Nate said. "I told you I'd help you find Vivienne, so I'm coming. Otherwise I'll never be able to face her." His cheeks went pink, and Caden knew they were both thinking of how she'd called him a coward.

"No one would blame you if you changed your mind," Caden said quietly, laying a hand on Nate's arm. "Really."

Nate wasn't like Rae; bravery didn't come naturally to him.

Caden could feel Nate's fear battling with his sense of loyalty, but Nate shook his head, his eyes fixed on that narrow dark ribbon ahead of them, his jaw set and determined.

"What part of *quickly* do you fools not understand?" Aiden snapped.

Caden dropped his hand from Nate's arm and reluctantly walked forward. He half-expected to feel some sort of resistance as he climbed over the stone wall and past the spell's barrier, but there was nothing, just a sudden shift in the wind, a stillness, as if it had been cut off from him. Seconds later he stood beneath the trees, Nate breathing heavily behind him.

"Remember," Aiden called after them. "Six hours, tops."

Caden pulled his phone out and looked at the time. Quarter past five. He shoved his phone back into his pocket, pulled his hoodie closer around himself, and walked deeper into the Watchful Woods.

Something cried out in the distance. A long, anguished scream, as if the one making it were in unspeakable pain. The sound abruptly ended, leaving behind a silence that was so much worse.

"Well, that's ominous," Nate muttered.

Caden managed a weak smile. "At least it wasn't coming from one of us."

"Not yet." Nate hunched his shoulders and glanced uneasily up at the woods around them. The sky overhead was the color of wet concrete. It should have been very dark inside the forest, but instead the trees seemed to be emitting a gentle greenish glow.

Not the trees, Caden realized. There was something *on* the trees that gave off that light. A strange sort of ropy vine. Or maybe it was a fungus? Caden peered at one. It spiraled up the length of the tree trunk, the whole thing about an inch thick with a spattering of larger knobs, each the size of his fist, jutting from it.

"What's that?" Nate leaned in beside him.

The knob closest to them began to swell, glowing brighter as it expanded. Nate gasped and yanked Caden back, the two of them falling to the ground just as the thing exploded outward in a puff of green seeds.

Nate whipped the collar of his shirt up and over his nose and mouth and scrambled away from the seeds gently drifting down. Caden had no idea what any of this meant, but he imitated his friend, holding his jacket collar up and scooting backward until he was far enough away that none of the seeds could reach him.

"What is it?" he asked.

Nate's eyes were wide behind his glasses. "I'm not sure, but I can't imagine it's a good thing."

"It's just a plant."

Nate gave him a look like he couldn't believe the idiocy that had tumbled out of his mouth, and Caden thought of the tentacled "plant" that had almost killed him inside the Other Place. "Yeah," he said slowly. "Okay, you've got a point."

"Even under normal circumstances, plants can be very danger-ous. These ones?" Nate shuddered dramatically. "I just don't think we should get too close. We *definitely* shouldn't let them touch us."

Caden nodded and pushed himself to his feet, brushing dirt and bits of leaves off his clothes. His left hand felt heavy, and he couldn't help glancing at the ring now encircling his thumb. Aiden's ring. A reminder of what he had to do.

"Um, Caden?" Nate said.

Caden blinked and shoved his hand into his hoodie pocket. "Sorry. Lost in thought."

Nate nodded. "I understand. What your brother said is a lot to digest. Frankly, a week ago I wouldn't have believed most of it—vortexes and magic GPS rocks?—but right now anything seems possible. The thing that seems *most* possible, though, is that standing around here is going to get us eaten."

The trees nearby rustled, and Nate flinched.

"Right," Caden said. "Of course."

He closed his eyes, orienting himself. He could feel the forest pulsing with life, most of it alien. Briefly he attempted to find Vivienne, but it was impossible. She'd changed so much and so rapidly that he wasn't even sure he'd recognize her personal signature anymore. Rae was still the same Rae—she was that rare soul who was so wholly and completely herself, and he doubted she'd ever change—but even she was impossible to sense in the midst of all that wild.

Would he be able to destroy the woods, knowing that they might still be in them?

He pushed that thought away for now.

"This way," he said, opening his eyes and pointing toward the vents. Aiden was right; he could feel the tug of their energy and knew it would lead him where he needed to go. He just had to hope that somewhere along the way, he'd find his friends too.

21.
RAE

It should have been dark outside the yurt—there was no moon, no stars, the evening sky was wrapped in a thick blanket of roiling gray clouds—but a glow seeped up from the ground, painting everything with a soft greenish tint.

Rae froze. That glow reminded her of the yellow-green fog of the Other Place. It didn't roll across the landscape like the heavy fog of that alternate dimension, but there was no mistaking the similarities. The Watchful Woods was changing, the atmosphere adjusting to its new inhabitants, becoming an alien world.

She didn't belong here.

"Rae!" Ava yelled from just beneath the trees. "Run!"

Rae caught a ripple of movement from the corner of her eye and turned as a huge shape hurtled toward her, sliding across the grass like water flowing downhill, impossibly fast—the Devourer, its good eyes locked on her face, the injured ones still weeping thick greenish gunk. There were other shadows moving through the grass behind it. Rae didn't know if they were Devourers too, and she didn't stick around to find out.

She ran for the trees as fast as she could, the machete held out at her side so she wouldn't accidentally cut herself. Ava watched her, eyes wide, arm around Blake's waist to help support him. There was no sign of Alyssa, and Rae just had to hope she was okay.

"Go!" Rae yelled at her sister.

Ava took off, practically dragging Blake, his steps slow and clumsy. He would be easy prey, but Rae knew her sister would never leave him, even to save herself.

Rae reached the trees, darting underneath creaking branches and over wiry underbrush. A tentacle whipped past her face, and just ahead she caught a glimpse of a strange fungus protruding in thick, ropy vines along the trunk of a tree. It pulsed like a heartbeat, and she instinctively veered away from it.

Up ahead she could just make out her sister running with Blake, could hear the snapping of branches. If Rae kept running in this direction, she'd lead the monsters right to them. So she made a quick decision: she turned away from Ava, heading in the opposite direction.

She just hoped she'd be able to find her sister again in the forest. If they both survived long enough. She could feel her lungs tightening, her breath escaping in a terrible, high-pitched wheeze, and knew she wouldn't be able to keep this pace up much longer. The machete's weight threw off her stride, making her slower, but she couldn't bring herself to drop it.

The Devourer was going to catch her. It was just a matter of time. Minutes, if not seconds. And when it did . . .

She tightened her grip on her weapon.

And then hands grabbed her free arm and yanked her sideways, and suddenly she was falling.

She hit the ground with a soft *oof* that crushed the remaining air from her lungs and lay there, stunned, as someone shoved a pile of dead leaves over her. "Alyssa?" Rae wheezed.

"Shh," Alyssa hissed.

Rae went as still as she could, trying to silently suck air back in. She could hear the crunching of taloned feet through leaves, a creature snarling, and then the long, eerie cry of the Devourer's hunting call. It knew she'd hidden herself, and it was searching for her.

Rae trembled, her thin leaf covering rattling slightly with the movement, but she couldn't help it. Her fingers tightened on the machete at her side, her heart pounding so loudly it was all she could hear. Could the Devourer hear it too? Could it smell her?

Alyssa lay pressed in on her other side, both of them frozen. Listening.

It sounded like the Devourer was moving away from them, the snapping of undergrowth growing fainter from above. Rae started to relax.

And then the crunching of leaves grew louder again as the Devourer circled back. The branches overhead creaked, and Rae tensed. Next to her, Alyssa's breath came in tiny, terrified gasps.

Click-click-grrr.

Rae squeezed her eyes shut. It was right above them. She could feel it standing there, searching for them among the leaves, could smell its foul breath.

Ready or not . . .

For a second Rae was back in that cabin, wedged between a rotting headboard and a bug-infested mattress as the Unseeing searched for her. She remembered the certainty that any second she would be discovered, and terror filled her now, turning her mind into a blank sheet of panic, her whole body numb. She was going to die here, in this place. A horrible, bloody death.

Alyssa's fingers met her own, their hands clasping tightly, and some of Rae's terror ebbed. No matter what happened, at least she wasn't alone this time. She let that thought give her comfort, and then she let go of Alyssa's hand, gathering all her strength, all her courage. If this didn't work, she'd be dead.

She flung herself up, leaves flying in all directions, her machete raised high.

She caught a glimpse of the eel-like face, the glowing eyes, and swung.

The Devourer was too fast; it dodged, her blade missing its neck, embedding itself in the creature's shoulder instead. Shrieking, it lunged at her, knocking her back down again.

Rae smacked into the dirt, spots dancing across her vision. She blinked them away as the Devourer loomed over her, ooze dripping from its two ruined eyes, green blood congealing around the blade in its shoulder, its teeth stained blackish. So many teeth. Rae couldn't look away from them as that mouth opened wide, the long, snakelike tongue extending—

Thwack!

The Devourer staggered back as Alyssa slammed a tree branch into its head.

"Take that!" Alyssa swung the branch again, catching the monster in its injured shoulder. It screamed, then twisted around, teeth snapping, and the branch broke apart.

Alyssa backed up, her hands held out.

Rae lurched to her feet, launching herself forward and grabbing the hilt of her machete. It was slippery with blood, but she managed to yank it free with a sound like wet cloth tearing.

Snarling, the Devourer turned on her, slashing out with its talons.

Rae stumbled back, holding her blade with both hands, blocking one swipe, then a second, before the third caught her weapon, knocking it out of her grasp. The Devourer's mouth curled in a murderous smile, and it advanced. Rae backed up, hitting the tree behind her. Trapped. She braced herself.

"No!" Alyssa threw a rock. It bounced harmlessly off the monster's back. It never took its remaining eyes off Rae. She read her death in their glowing depths—

A mass of tentacles dropped down from the tree above, enveloping the Devourer like a cocoon and whisking it up so fast it didn't even have time to struggle.

Rae and Alyssa stared up in horror. The branches above them shook, showering them with dead leaves and bits of twigs as the forest filled with the sounds of bones crunching, followed by a horrible sucking noise. Then silence.

A few shards of bone dropped to the ground around them.

"Let's not stay under this tree," Alyssa said.

Rae nodded, unable to think of any words to say as she followed Alyssa away. While she was grateful to . . . whatever it was in the tree, that was still one of the most horrifying things she had ever witnessed. And she'd seen a lot of horror.

"That was awful," Alyssa said flatly.

"Understatement of the day." Rae shook her head. She still couldn't believe that had happened. She should be dead. They *both* should be.

She looked at Alyssa, remembering how the other girl had squeezed her hand, their fear a shared thing, and it felt almost like she were seeing her for the first time. Alyssa's hair was snarled with leaves and twigs, dirt was smeared across her forehead, her blue eyes were glittering. She looked fierce and brave and determined, and Rae felt a rush of gratitude that she was here with her now.

"Thank you for saving my life back there."

Alyssa nodded. "Of course." Her lips curved in a wide smile. "And it felt good to smack that thing in the head. Like really, really good."

Rae laughed. "I can imagine."

Alyssa's smile froze, her eyes widening. "Wait. Do you hear something?"

Rae listened. Something was moving fast through the forest, branches cracking around it. "Devourers hunt in packs," she whispered, remembering the way they'd moved through the Other Place. She and Alyssa exchanged a look. "Hide," Rae said.

They dove behind a large Douglas fir. Rae just hoped it didn't contain any carnivorous tentacled creatures. She adjusted her grip on her blade and waited as the sounds of movement drew closer.

22.
CADEN

Down!" Caden hissed.

Nate ducked immediately, crouching beside Caden behind a tangle of underbrush as something large and sinewy crashed through the trees nearby. Caden could feel it searching for them, and he closed his eyes and mentally gave it a push.

We're not here. Keep moving along.

He met with resistance, as if his magic were hitting an invisible wall. He could feel the creature still searching for them, its hunger palpable. It knew prey was nearby. Caden's magical suggestions weren't working.

Nate squeezed his eyes shut, his shoulders hunching as the creature scuttled closer to their hiding spot. Caden could hear it breathing, a wet, rasping sound. He caught a glimpse of six long, spidery limbs covered in short black hair supporting a round torso. It had no head that Caden could see.

It paused, its body quivering, and now Caden noticed the mouth in the middle of the torso like a giant sucking hole, big enough to swallow a person's head. He tried not to imagine what that would feel like as the creature turned, searching.

Caden tried again, digging deeper inside himself, picturing an invisible web that he tossed at the creature. *Go away. There is nothing for you here.* This time he felt the web catch, his own essence spinning out to power the spell. The creature gave a low, frustrated moan and then skittered away, vanishing into the woods.

Caden sagged back, wiping a hand over his forehead, exhausted. That was the fourth close call in the last ten minutes. The forest was teeming with things that wanted to eat them, and they all seemed much more resistant to his magic than the creatures in the Other Place had been. Unbidden, his mother's words whispered through his mind.

I felt something early this morning. A pressure coming from Green On!, as if a tide of creatures had flooded through the labs and were pushing at our boundary . . .

"What *was* that?" Nate asked.

"I have no clue," Caden said, pushing himself to his feet.

"I saw some scary things in the Other Place, but nothing like that. It was like an ogre and a spider had a baby. Horrible." Nate stood more slowly, brushing twigs off his shoulders. He looked almost as tired as Caden felt. People thought constant fear was all adrenaline and nerves, but that could only sustain someone for so long, and it took a lot of energy. Nate had burned through his reserves early on and now was just hanging on by a thread.

Caden didn't want to add to his friend's fear, but they were in this together. Nate deserved to know what he now suspected. "I think the pods on the spaceship must have opened."

Nate stopped patting at his clothes. "What?"

"Rae said Doctor Nguyen was going to try to open the ones that held Ms. Lockett and the other humans. Maybe something went wrong and she opened all of them . . ."

Nate's eyes widened. "So the woods aren't just full of creatures from the Other Place but also literal, from-outer-space aliens?"

"I think so."

"Great. Just great."

"If it makes you feel better, I think both sets of creatures are equally willing to eat you."

"Strangely that does *not* make me feel better." Nate went quiet, but Caden could see his emotions swirling around him like a gathering storm, his thoughts arriving at some dark conclusion. "If that's true," Nate said finally, "and all the pods opened, what would that mean for Doctor Nguyen?"

Caden shook his head.

"Yeah, that's what I thought." Nate pressed his lips together in a thin line that almost hid their trembling. Grief surrounded him in clouds of deep, dark purple, and Caden remembered that Nate had once looked up to the scientist. "What about everyone else at Green On!?" Nate asked, his voice choked.

Caden hesitated, but he'd chosen honesty with Nate, and he

would stick to that path. "Aiden believes that anyone who was in the lab early this morning is dead."

Nate nodded. He visibly composed himself, the grief fading until only a pale echo of purple remained, coloring him like an old bruise. "Well, there's a good chance we'll be joining them on the other side."

Caden shifted, uncomfortable with how true that was. He was so very tired that even his bones ached, and he didn't know how many more aliens he'd be able to turn away before his energy ran out. And since the vents were somewhere near the lab, he and Nate would be heading straight into the thick of it.

"How close are we to Green On! now?" Nate asked.

Caden closed his eyes, trying to figure out where in the forest they were. To his surprise, they'd gotten farther than he'd thought. "You know, we're actually almost there."

"I don't know if I should be excited or horrified," Nate said, and Caden understood: who knew what condition the lab would be in when they got there? "But it's got to be better in there than out here."

Caden felt a prickling sense of foreboding and knew, instinctively, that Nate was wrong. It was going to be worse. So much worse. But this time he kept that truth to himself, and the two of them resumed their slow, painful trek through a forest that had seemingly changed overnight.

Trees had been twisted into strange shapes, tentacles drifting from them to brush lazily against the ground. Things with too many eyes peered out at them from behind trunks. Mist rose around their feet, thick and cloying. And always there was that ever-present glow. But the worst part was the noise.

Caden heard none of the usual sounds of the Watchful Woods. No birdcalls, no rustling deer. Instead, the night was alive with high-pitched shrieks and guttural moans. The victorious cries of creatures on the hunt and the agonized wails of the things they were eating. It was a constant backdrop to the sounds of his own breathing, the pounding of his heart, and his too-loud footsteps.

On top of all of that, Caden felt like he were getting scraped raw, his personal shields down, his awareness spread thinly around them. He was like a sweater being unraveled in a million directions as he searched the forest constantly, alert to their next threat.

He mentally brushed against something just ahead and froze.

"What?" Nate whispered. "Another monster?"

"No," Caden whispered back. "It's something else." Was he wrong, though? He reached out again, feeling for the life nearby.

He *wasn't* wrong!

He launched himself forward, fighting past gnarled brush and several aggressive tentacled plants.

"What is it?" Nate gasped, struggling after him.

But Caden didn't have to say anything because she was in front of them now, her brown eyes wide in surprise.

Ava Carter, looking so like Rae it made Caden's heart ache, with her arm around Blake's waist, half-supporting him.

"Caden?" she said. "How are you here?"

"Is this real?" Blake asked, squinting at Caden.

"It's real," Caden said. "And long story," he added to Ava.

"Is Rae with you?" Nate asked her eagerly.

And even though Caden knew she wasn't—he'd have sensed her—he couldn't help his brief surge of hope.

Ava shook her head, her face crumpling. "We got separated back near the yurt."

Caden's heart sank. "How long ago was that?"

"It was—" Ava stopped as something loud crashed through the trees above them. Everyone went still, listening. A moment passed, then another. "False alarm?" Ava said.

And then a dark humanoid shape dropped down. Right onto their heads.

23.
RAE

As the footfalls drew near, Rae leapt out from behind the tree, her machete raised. And froze, her arm still in mid-swing. "Vivi?" she gasped, staring into a pair of dark eyes that were shockingly familiar.

"More or less," Vivienne said, her arms crossed, posture relaxed. As if she didn't notice the giant knife hovering inches from her head.

Rae quickly lowered her arm, holding the machete at her side. Her heart was still racing, her breathing too fast, too constricted. Nothing made sense. How was Vivienne here? Was she dreaming? It *felt* like a dream, with the trees hovering silently over her, the air heavy with moisture, everything glowing gently.

"Vivienne!" Alyssa screeched, leaping up to join them.

"Shh!" Rae and Vivienne both hissed.

Alyssa flinched. "Sorry," she whispered. "Got carried away."

All three of them glanced around, but the forest seemed quiet, no monsters rushing toward them. Yet. Rae knew it was just a matter of time, though.

Alyssa leaned in and gave Vivienne a quick embrace. Vivienne just stood there, arms held awkwardly at her sides, as if she'd forgotten what a hug was. "I thought I might never see you again!" Alyssa let her go, beaming. "Does this mean we're not trapped by that weird invisible wall, then?"

"No, we're still trapped," Vivienne said. "It's a one-way entrance only. I could get in, but I can't get out, and neither can you."

"Oh." Alyssa's smile vanished, and Rae felt her own shoulders lowering in disappointment.

"Why did you come here?" Rae asked.

"I had to get away from the school. I couldn't be there any longer."

"But why *here*?" Alyssa asked. "Why the forest? Seems like the last place I'd want to go if I weren't already stuck here." She glanced at Rae. "No offense. I know coming out here was sort of my idea and all."

"I came because Patrick is here," Vivienne said.

Rae felt like the air in her lungs had turned to stone. "Patrick? *Here?* Like in these woods here?"

"Not the woods," Vivienne said, her face grim. "The ship."

"You mean in the pod?"

Vivienne shook her head. "He's free."

Rae swallowed down a rising tide of horror. She had pushed

Patrick into a pod herself. If he were truly free, she could only imagine how angry he'd be with her. She'd rather face a dozen Devourers than him again. At least they would just kill her. She had no idea what Patrick would do.

"How do you know this?" Alyssa asked. "Did my mom get released too?" Her face filled with hope.

Vivienne stared back, her eyes seeming to soak in the greenish glow of the forest, turning them strange and alien. "We can't tell her that," she muttered.

"What?" Alyssa said.

Vivienne blinked, and she was herself again. "I don't know," she said. "Maybe everyone is free now."

Rae thought of all the other pods she'd run past on that spaceship. Patrick and Ms. Lockett and Doctor Anderson . . . and hundreds, maybe thousands of aliens. She ran a hand through her sweaty bangs, then glanced around. They were standing next to a shallow, leaf-strewn pit. Just beyond it, the ground opened up in a yawning hole. Rae stared into that darkness, so black even the green glow couldn't do anything to soften it. She suddenly knew exactly where they were.

"You're going through the tunnels."

"Yep," Vivienne said.

"Do the tunnels lead to the spaceship?" Alyssa asked.

"They do," Vivienne said.

"Then I'm coming with you."

Vivienne shrugged. "If you want. Rae, you in too?"

Rae had the sudden urge to turn and run, and keep running

forever. She did *not* want to go back into those tunnels. They were so dark, and the walls were so close, and this time she wouldn't have Caden around to help her along. Besides, Ava was out there in the forest somewhere. She couldn't just leave her.

"Did you see Ava on your way over here?" she asked.

Vivienne shook her head.

Rae turned the machete in her hands, thinking. There was no way to find her sister. She would just have to hope that, wherever they were, Ava and Blake were safe. But Vivienne needed her now. And maybe her dad did too.

Her shoulders slumped. "I'm in," she said miserably.

Rae wasn't sure what she was expecting—a smile, maybe? Some words of encouragement? But Vivienne just nodded, her face expressionless. "Let's go then," she said, leading the way to the mouth of the tunnel.

Rae followed, trying not to worry about the monsters potentially waiting for them in the darkness below as Vivienne opened her ever-present backpack and pulled out a rope, skillfully tying it off and dropping the end into the hole of the tunnel.

Vivienne looked up, meeting Rae's gaze, her own eyes flat. And Rae was suddenly reminded of that moment in the cavern below when Vivienne had faced down one of the queen bugs. She'd killed it, and then she'd turned and focused on Rae. Only it hadn't been *her* in there. Something else had stared out from within the confines of her friend's familiar face. Something cruel and inhuman.

It had reminded Rae of a hooded cobra, all cold-blooded and hypnotic, and she hadn't been able to look away.

Vivienne's eyes had that same alien cast to them now. She flashed Rae a smile—a quick baring of teeth—and raised one eyebrow in a silent challenge. And then she grabbed the rope and swung down, disappearing from view.

Rae stood there, heart racing.

"You want me to go first?" Alyssa asked her.

Rae shook her head, her hands trembling as she carefully tucked her machete into the belt loop of her jeans, hoping it didn't slice her butt on the way down. She grabbed the rope, the rough fibers digging into her palms. And as she climbed down, she couldn't help thinking that Vivienne just might be the most dangerous thing lurking in those tunnels.

24.
CADEN

Caden saw the dark humanoid shape dropping like a spider from the trees above, and for a second he felt like he was back inside that rickety cabin in the woods, watching Rae struggle beneath the Unseeing as it pinned her down and attempted to steal her eyes. He'd felt so helpless, unable to go to her, Aiden's ghostly voice urging him to reopen the rift to the Other Place instead. Whispering that it was the only way to save her.

Blake screamed, and Caden blinked away the cobwebs of memory. A lot had happened in the weeks since Rae was attacked. He wasn't the same boy he'd been. He certainly wasn't helpless anymore.

Caden narrowed his eyes, taking in the reality of the scene in front of him. Blake lay on his back in the dirt, his hands up, pushing against the chest of the Unseeing straddling him. It appeared almost human, except the arms and legs were too long, and the face was all mouth with only a slit of a nose. Where eyes should have been there was nothing but smooth skin.

Ava ran at it, trying to shove it off Blake. It casually backhanded her, sending her tumbling, its focus never wavering from Blake. As if Ava were nothing but a fly to it, a small irritation.

Dimly Caden was aware of Nate hurrying to her side, but he kept his attention on the Unseeing. It loomed over Blake, its hands rising up over his face while it used its knees to keep him pinned to the ground. *Let him go*, he told it, his words a silver chain that looped around the creature's throat, pulling tight.

The Unseeing snarled, its palms lowering.

Caden pulled harder, sweat beading on his forehead. This *had* to work. He'd been able to bend these creatures to his will in the past. But never, he realized, when they were about to feed. That urge might be too strong for his magic to overcome.

Let him go! Caden put everything he had behind that command.

"Never," the Unseeing growled.

Blake screamed again, a terrible sound, as the Unseeing's palms dropped, the long spiderlike fingers splayed on either side of Blake's face.

Whack!

The Unseeing toppled sideways. It lurched back to its feet, impossibly fast, but Ava was faster. She swung a large branch like a club at its head again, catching it just under the chin with another satisfying *whack!* that sent it staggering back into the trunk of a tree. Its feet slid in the dirt, arms stretched out. One of its grasping hands caught a length of ropy fungus, which it used to keep its balance.

Ava swung again, but this time it was ready for her; it caught the branch mid-swing and yanked it from Ava's grip, then snapped it in half over one spindly leg. Blood ran down its forehead and stained its pointed teeth as it turned to her. "You shouldn't have done that," it hissed.

Ava took a step back, her hands up—

The fungus the Unseeing had been holding exploded outward, enveloping its head in a puff of bright green. It made a strange, strangled cry and toppled to its knees, hands scrabbling at its face, nails tearing long, bloody rivulets into the skin.

Caden moved closer to Ava, wanting to protect her, even though he wasn't sure what he could possibly do. His last plan hadn't been very effective. Certainly less effective than her methods.

"What is happening?" Nate whispered, pressing in beside them. Blake leaned heavily on his other side, his breathing labored.

"I have no idea," Caden whispered back. "But I think we're about to see what that fungus of yours does."

The trees near them rustled, and Caden glanced over his shoulder.

Another creature dropped onto all fours in the dirt behind them, its spindly body long and so skinny that all its ribs showed, its limbs grotesquely stretched. Its cheeks were hollower, the jaw elongated, but the eyes—or rather, the spaces where eyes should have been—were familiar. Another Unseeing.

Caden felt his heart stop as the thing scuttled toward them.

"Look at all these eyes," it crooned. "So . . . pretty . . ."

Caden, Nate, Blake, and Ava all drew so close together their shoulders touched.

The Unseeing lurched upright, vibrating with eagerness as it sniffed the air. "I smell fear, and blood." It turned, somehow inspecting each of them despite its lack of perceivable vision. "Brown eyes today." It turned its focus on Caden. "Yours, I think. So deep. So lovely."

Caden wondered what would happen to the rest of Whispering Pines if he died here now. His finger brushed against the ring on his thumb.

"I can help you," came a soft whisper scratching at the back of his mind.

Caden hesitated. He could feel the power inside the ring, enough to save them all, if only he dared tap into it. Maybe—

The first Unseeing staggered to its feet. "Mine," it gasped.

The newcomer paused, tilting its head to the side, considering. "There's enough here to share, brother. Don't you think?"

The first Unseeing took a step toward them, its whole body twitching. All the muscles in its neck stood out in sharp relief as its lips pulled back, back, back, revealing every single tooth in a horrible grin that looked too large for its face.

"Brother?" the other Unseeing asked, and there was a hint of emotion in its voice. In a human, Caden would have marked it for fear. "What are you—" It didn't get a chance to finish before its "brother" suddenly rushed forward, movements jerky, and tackled it to the ground.

Caden bit back a gasp as the two creatures thrashed in the dirt, long limbs flailing, teeth gnashing. It was impossible to tell which was which.

"I vote we run," Nate whispered. "All in favor?"

"Absolutely," Ava said. Caden took one of Blake's arms, Nate the other, and together the four of them hurried away from the Unseeings. They didn't say a word until the sounds of the fight died away behind them.

"What the heck was that?" Ava finally burst out, her steps slowing. "Why did it attack the other one like that?"

"Infection," Blake wheezed, stumbling to a stop so abruptly that Caden almost dropped him.

"Are you okay?" Caden asked him. Blake's red hair was matted with dirt and sweat and something that looked suspiciously like dried blood, and his face was so pale his freckles stood out like ink spots.

"Well . . . they say what doesn't kill you makes you stronger. But so far, I feel like what hasn't killed me is just softening me up for the next thing to try to kill me. And the next." Blake grimaced. "I've had a rough day. A rough *few* days, really." He clutched his stomach. "I'm so done with all of this."

"You've survived this long," Ava said. "What's one more monster attack, right?"

"Let's not say that too loudly," Nate said uneasily.

Caden nodded. It was never a good idea to challenge the universe. "So, infection?" he prompted.

"Those plants," Blake said. "They release some kind of spore

— 163 —

that turns you into a zombie, makes you attack other people and infect them, too."

"Like in the yurt," Ava said, her eyes widening in sudden understanding.

"Yes. Apparently it works the same way on the monsters, too."

"You know, I've read about a fungus like that," Nate said, perking up. "It's called ophiocordyceps unilateralis, and it grows in some tropical rain forests. It infects the ants that live in the trees, hijacking their bodies and making them transport it to its ideal location before killing them off and—"

"And you sound way too excited about this," Ava said. She shook her head and muttered, "Weirdo."

Nate looked offended. "It's called science. And it's important. We know why the fungus in *our* world attacks the ants—it can't move on its own, so it's basically using them as transportation devices in order to spawn more of itself. But why is *this* fungus infecting things here this way? Maybe," Nate mused, his eyes glinting, "it's helping to change the atmosphere. It feels different in here. More humid. Almost like . . ."

"Like the Other Place," Caden finished for him. "I know." It felt as if this part of their town already belonged to the aliens. And if Caden failed in his mission, soon the rest of Whispering Pines would follow suit.

And then the world.

The clock is ticking, little brother.

Caden pulled the pouch Aiden had given him from his pocket and opened it, plucking one stone from inside. It was a little larger than a marble, and polished smooth. "Here." He held it out to Ava.

"What's this?" she asked, taking it.

"It's . . ." Caden trailed off, not sure how to explain it.

"A magical GPS device," Nate supplied.

"*That* hardly sounds scientific." Ava frowned down at the stone in her palm, then curled her fingers around it. "How does it work— ah!" She dropped it abruptly.

"Don't lose it!" Caden scooped it back up.

"It *moved*!"

"I know," Caden said. "It's trying to lead you back to the wall. If you go in the direction it tells you to, you'll be able to get out of the woods." He held it back out to her.

Ava stared at it, looking skeptical. "Where did you get it?"

Caden swallowed. This would be the tricky part. "From my brother," he admitted.

Ava crossed her arms, scowling. "No, thank you."

"Can you find your way out without it?"

She sniffed and didn't say anything.

"Ava, please. I know you don't trust Aiden—"

"Ha! Biggest understatement of the year, that."

"—but he's the only one who can get you out of here safely," Caden finished.

"He kidnapped me and tried to rip my soul from my body. I'd rather stay in here than go anywhere near him again."

"I'll take it," Blake said, holding out his hand.

Ava gave him a wounded look.

"Sorry. It's just . . . I need to get out of here before the next thing tries to eat me, infect me, or burst from my chest."

Caden handed over the stone. Blake closed his fingers around it protectively. "You have to go with him," Caden told Ava. "The woods aren't safe, and they're about to get even less safe soon."

"I can't leave until I find Rae."

"I'm looking for her, too," Caden said.

"Then I'll stay with you and help."

Caden shook his head. "Someone needs to get Blake out of here."

"Nate can do it."

"I'd feel safer with you," Blake said. "No offense, Nate."

"None taken. I saw Ava handle that Unseeing."

Ava managed a small smile at that, but it vanished quickly. "I can't abandon her, Caden. You understand that, right?"

Caden looked into Ava's wide brown eyes—so like Rae's—and did understand. But at the same time, the woods were dangerous. It was bad enough dragging Nate through them; he didn't want to be responsible for Ava, too. Especially since Rae would never forgive him if something happened to her sister.

"You're not abandoning her," he said, gently weaving his emotions around her. Reassurance, a desire to go home, a sense of duty toward Blake. "I'll find her. I have . . . well. Ways to look that you don't." He felt that strange resistance again, as if his magic were trapped inside a bubble within him and he was trying to force it through a tiny crack.

"I still think I should help you." Ava thrust her jaw forward, looking exactly like an older version of her sister. Determined, stubborn, impossible to move.

Caden nodded slowly, trying to figure out a way to reach her and change her mind. What emotion was the strongest motivator? And then it came to him: guilt.

Your mom needs you, he whispered in her mind. *If something were to happen to* both *you and Rae, she'd be alone . . .* He layered emotions over that thought. Worry over what her mother would do, all alone. An uncertainty about how she would cope. A reminder of how much she struggled when her husband vanished.

"I understand why you think that," Caden said out loud. "But Nate and I can travel faster if it's just the two of us."

Ava stared hard at him as if trying to read his thoughts. And then she sighed. "Fine. But I'm trusting you. Don't let me down."

"I won't," Caden promised. But he could feel the ring on his thumb tightening, its coldness seeping into his skin, and knew it wasn't necessarily a promise he'd be able to keep.

If he didn't find Rae by the time he reached the vents, he'd have no choice but to destroy the woods with her in them. Her, and Vivienne.

"I guess we'd better go, then," Ava said, still looking uncertain.

Blake nodded enthusiastically. "Yes, please."

"Good luck," Ava whispered before setting off through the woods with Blake. Caden watched them go and hoped that they, at least, would be safe. When he turned away, Nate was staring at him.

"What?" Caden asked.

"Nothing," Nate said. But his expression was wary, and Caden could feel tiny pricklings of suspicion floating around him.

"Are you sure? Because it seems like there's something."

"It's just . . . she changed her mind so quickly. I didn't think she would."

Caden shrugged, hoping he didn't look guilty. Not that he had anything to feel guilty about, since he hadn't done anything wrong. He wasn't really trying to control Ava; he was just giving her a little nudge, and for her own good too. But the way Nate was still looking at him made him feel uncomfortable.

So what? If Nate suspected anything, Caden could always change *his* mind too.

Caden realized he was rubbing his index finger over the ring on his thumb and immediately stopped. And as he and Nate resumed their trek through the forest, he had to wonder if that last thought had come from him, or from the demon.

He wasn't sure which would be worse.

25.
RAE

Rae's sneakers sank into the soil of the tunnel, and the darkness seemed to swallow her whole. The tunnel was definitely as scary as she remembered, and for the hundredth time in the last minute, she wished she had stayed on the surface looking for her sister. If all the aliens from the pods really were loose, would they be up in the forest or down here?

She just hoped Ava and Blake were okay.

"Wow, it is super dark and creepy down here." Even though Alyssa spoke quietly, her voice seemed to fill the air, like a beacon to the creatures that might be waiting for them. "Do we have a flashlight or anything?"

"I think Vivienne usually has one." Rae looked at Vivienne. Her friend stood with her back to them, staring down the tunnel. "Vivi?"

Vivienne glanced over. It was impossible to see her face clearly in the darkness at the mouth of the tunnel, but she didn't seem quite . . . right. "What?" she asked.

"Do you, um, have a flashlight?"

Vivienne nodded, then slid her ever-present backpack off her shoulder and rummaged inside, pulling out a single headlamp. She tossed it to Rae, who barely managed to catch it.

"Thanks," Rae said.

Vivienne didn't respond, just turned and started down the tunnel into the dark.

Alyssa nudged Rae and gave her the 'what's up with her' look.

Rae hesitated, but in the end she just shrugged. How do you tell someone that their best friend was turning into an alien? Rae had no idea how to even begin that talk, and now didn't seem like the time to try. Not with the darkness pressing in on all sides, trying to smother them.

She pulled the headlamp on, adjusted her ponytail, and turned on the beam. The light seemed faded and weak, and she just hoped Vivienne had remembered to change out the batteries from the last time. "I guess we'd better follow," she whispered.

"I guess so," Alyssa said. They shared an uneasy glance, and Rae felt another rush of gratitude that Alyssa was there with her. Alyssa wasn't always the nicest person, and sometimes she could be hard to be around. But standing here with her in that dark tunnel, Rae knew that, no matter what happened, she trusted Alyssa to have her back.

When Rae had first arrived in Whispering Pines, she'd thought

Alyssa was another version of Taylor, her former best friend and the reason her last year in California had been so terrible. Taylor had been happy to be Rae's friend when Rae was at her best—happy, popular, confident. But the moment Rae had started to struggle, Taylor had dropped her like a bad habit. She'd wanted nothing to do with Rae's troubles and had made sure no one else wanted anything to do with her, either.

Despite Vivienne's increasing strangeness, Alyssa had never turned away from her. She hadn't given up on trying to find a way to help Jeremy, either. And now, when Rae needed a friend the most, she was there, literally ready to battle monsters with her. Rae's dad had always told her that through adversity, you learned who a person really was. And Alyssa, it turned out, was nothing at all like Taylor.

"Thank you," Rae whispered.

"For what?" Alyssa asked.

Rae hesitated, not sure how to put it all into words. Taylor's betrayal had left a wound inside Rae that had never quite healed. But in some ways, her friendship with Alyssa felt like a second chance. Like she was erasing that hurt and replacing it with something better. "For being my friend," Rae said at last.

"Wow, that's cheesy." Alyssa shook her head. "But you're welcome. And . . . I'm glad we're friends."

Rae grinned. "Me, too."

Rae carefully slid the machete out from her belt loop, hefting its weight in her hand. It felt reassuringly solid, the length of the blade gleaming in the light from her headlamp.

"I wish I had one of those too," Alyssa whispered as the two of them set off after Vivienne. "I don't even have a pocket knife."

Rae thought of the giant centipedes she'd seen the last time she was down here and knew it wouldn't matter. She doubted her machete would even slow them down.

As they walked deeper into the tunnel, every sound seemed amplified. The scraping of Rae's shoes, the harsh rasp of her breathing, the rapid pounding of her heart. She'd almost forgotten how much she hated being down here, feeling the weight of all that dirt above her. Knowing if she stretched her arms out, they'd bump into the tunnel walls on either side.

A wave of claustrophobia rose up in her, and she swallowed it down, trying to keep her focus on the thin strip of ground illuminated in front of her. Alyssa stuck close behind her, her footsteps too loud, her breathing fast and shallow, and Rae found herself missing Caden and his soothing presence. Still, having Alyssa around did make her feel better; at least she wasn't the only one terrified of the dark enclosed space.

And despite their fear, both she and Alyssa were willing to go down below Whispering Pines in the hopes that they could rescue people they cared about. The thought that she might really see her dad again helped ground Rae as the tunnel narrowed around them, the ceiling lowering until they were forced to crawl.

Rae remembered this part from before. She concentrated on the feeling of rough dirt under her left hand as she crawled, awkwardly keeping the long blade of the machete pointed straight ahead. She tried to ignore how the ceiling brushed against her back, the sides of the tunnel squeezing in, but she couldn't stop the fear that it would continue shrinking until she was wedged inside it, trapped for all eternity.

Rae forced herself to keep crawling. Left hand, right leg. Right hand, left leg. She knew the tunnel would widen again. She just had to keep moving forward.

The air felt too thick. So thick it was suffocating, almost like she were inhaling soup. And it was hot, too. She didn't remember *that* from before.

She tried to keep her breathing even, but she could hear herself wheezing now, her lungs rattling with the effort. By the time the tunnel widened enough for her to stand again, spots were dancing in front of her eyes, and she had to put a hand on the wall to steady herself.

It felt spongy beneath her fingers, the dirt moist.

She blinked away the spots, but they expanded, filling her vision with a soft greenish glow. She blinked again, then rubbed her eyes with the back of her free hand. The glow remained. Frowning, she turned off her headlamp.

The tunnel remained bright enough to see, its contours gently illuminated. Vivienne stood motionless a few feet away, her hands balled into fists at her sides.

"That's creepy," Alyssa whispered. "It looks just like the mist—"

"From the Other Place," Rae said. "I know."

"Shh!" Vivienne whipped around to face them, her eyes picking up the glow, gleaming like a cat's. "The tunnels ahead are not empty."

"N-not empty?" Alyssa swallowed audibly. "Um, what exactly does that mean?"

"It means you'll want to be quiet." Vivienne paused. "Unless you'd like to be bug food, that is." Her lips curved up in a small, mocking smile that looked completely wrong on her face. It reminded Rae of how Ava had looked when she'd been possessed by Prudence, like someone else was wearing her skin like a mask.

Vivienne turned away from them, darting forward, her footsteps silent. Rae waited until she'd disappeared around a bend in the tunnel, and then she waited some more, her heart hammering against her rib cage.

"There's something really wrong with her," Alyssa said quietly. "Isn't there?"

This time Rae didn't try to deny it. "Yes."

Alyssa nodded but didn't ask any questions. Maybe she didn't want to know more. And even though Rae normally would have scoffed at that—her dad had never turned away from the truth, so neither should anyone else—recently she'd started to understand how comforting not knowing could be. If you remained ignorant of the details, you could pretend things weren't so bad.

Unfortunately for Rae, she knew the truth: things were very, very bad indeed.

"We'd better follow her," Alyssa whispered. "I don't think she'll wait for us otherwise."

"Just a second," Rae wheezed. "Can you hold this?" She passed Alyssa the machete.

"Wow, that's lighter than I'd have thought. I wonder what kind of metal this is?" Alyssa swung the blade around, and Rae took a hasty step back. Safely out of range, she pulled her inhaler out of her pocket and took two quick puffs before tucking it away again, her hands shaking as the medicine shot through her like a burst of adrenaline.

"I'm ready," she whispered, and Alyssa reluctantly passed her back the large knife. Clutching it tightly, Rae turned the corner, all her senses alert, visions of swarming bugs scuttling through her brain.

The tunnel stretched ahead of her, illuminated by the now-familiar soft green glow. A few trailing roots had made their way down through the ceiling, and several rocks jutted out of the sides, sharp and jagged, but otherwise it was empty. Nothing moved in that light.

Rae let out a breath.

Something brushed against her arm. She almost screamed but managed to choke the sound back just in time. It was only Vivienne, standing half-hidden in a small alcove next to her.

"You waited for us," Rae said.

"I didn't think you'd notice this opening otherwise," Vivienne whispered, her voice so soft it was like the tunnel itself sighing.

She was right; it wasn't an alcove behind her, but a crevice.

"If we're very careful, and very quiet, we might be able to slip past them without fighting," Vivienne continued.

"Them?" Rae swallowed.

Vivienne glanced at her, amusement shadowing her face. "You go first."

"Me? Why me?"

"Because you're the leader." The way Vivienne said it, half-serious and half-mocking, made it impossible for Rae to know if Vivienne actually believed that or not. For that matter, Rae wasn't sure what she believed herself. Was she the leader? Did she want to be? She looked down at the weapon in her hand and knew the answer.

"Okay," she whispered.

"Alyssa, you follow Rae," Vivienne said.

Alyssa whimpered, her eyes huge.

"I'll go last and guard your backs." Vivienne flashed them both a feral smile, and suddenly Rae wasn't so sure she *wanted* her at her back. "No, wait," Vivienne said abruptly, her face going suddenly unsure. She paused, her head tilting, as if she were listening to something. "Actually, you're right. I probably *can* protect best from behind."

"Who's right?" Alyssa asked. "Who are you talking to?"

Vivienne blinked. "No one. Nothing. Just thinking out loud." Her gaze sharpened on Rae. "Well?"

Rae took a deep breath, adjusted her grip on her machete, and slipped past Vivienne. For a second the stone walls of the crevice squeezed in on her, scraping against her shoulders, and she had to fight down a brief surge of panic. She would *not* be trapped here. Then she was through and stepping into the mouth of a large cavern.

And into one of her worst nightmares.

The entire ceiling was draped in giant, milky-white egg sacs, some of them still moving, all of them way too visible in that eerie greenish glow. Rae tried hard not to look at them, knowing they would be full of bodies. Hopefully just animals, like the one about six feet away that clearly held a deer—she could see one hoof sticking out, and a pair of antlers—but she couldn't be sure. And it wouldn't matter anyhow; even if there *were* people trapped in there, she couldn't help them.

And it wasn't just egg sacs in that room; the walls shivered and trembled, the ceiling undulated, and the entire floor seemed to be moving as centipedes of all sizes skittered around, busy setting up this . . . this mess hall.

Alyssa nudged her from behind, and Rae forced her numb feet to move. She kept her back to the wall, trying to watch the whole cavern at once as Alyssa squeezed out of the crevice.

Alyssa stifled a gasp. "Bugs," she whispered. "Hate bugs."

Rae put a finger to her lips as the nearest centipede—a monster the length of her leg—turned in their direction. It tilted its head, considering, antennae moving back and forth.

Alyssa clapped a hand over her mouth, eyes wide with terror, as behind her, Vivienne went completely still.

Something began shrieking inside one of the larger egg sacs hung near the center of the room, and all the centipedes turned toward it. Attentive. Eager. The egg sac convulsed as the thing inside thrashed, tearing at the sticky mess encasing it. Rae caught a glimpse of one long-fingered hand, an all-too-human foot, and then the head burst through.

An eyeless horror, huge mouth stretched wide to show off jagged teeth. An Unseeing, not a human.

Rae barely had time to register that before the Unseeing made one last pitiful sound, and something exploded from it in a burst of gore. Two somethings. Centipedes, each the size of a puppy, and covered in blood and goo.

The other centipedes in the room surged forward, swarming up the sac and feeding noisily on the Unseeing as it feebly kicked its legs for the last time.

Rae felt sick. She took a deep, steadying breath, and immediately regretted it. The entire room stank of blood and decay and something worse, some dry musky insect smell. Gagging, she swallowed it down, motioned for Alyssa and Vivienne to follow her, and forced herself to move. Now was their chance, while the centipedes were distracted.

One step, two steps . . .

Click, click, click. A large shape scurried along the ceiling just above their heads, thousands of legs moving rapidly. Rae froze. Alyssa was staying so close behind her that she crashed into her back. Rae stumbled forward a few steps before staggering to a stop, her heart pounding, but the bug kept going, ignoring them.

Rae let out a breath, then turned to shoot a look at Alyssa.

Sorry, Alyssa mouthed. Behind her, Vivienne didn't even glance over, her gaze remaining locked on the ceiling, tracking the movement of another bug.

Rae resumed inching her way along the edge of the cavern. This time Alyssa gave her a little space before following. Rae couldn't hear Vivienne at all, but assumed she was still trailing behind them. An opening on the other side of the cavern led out into another tunnel. Rae had to hope that if they made it that far without attracting attention, they were safe.

Almost there. Twenty feet. Then fifteen. Then ten. The tunnel beyond looked empty, and Rae started to believe they were really going to make it.

Click! Click!

Rae glanced up.

The biggest alien centipede she had ever seen hung above her. Even bigger than the queen she'd faced last time.

Rae's mind went blank with panic as it dropped, landing in front of her, its front half rearing back to reveal the round face, the eyes—black and pitiless—the mandibles opening and closing. *Click. Click. Click.*

Rae was so close to it she could see her own reflection frozen in the thing's cruel gaze. Time seemed to slow, then stop completely, the details of the moment etching themselves into Rae's brain. Her hands sweaty on the machete handle, the room swimming around her, the saliva dripping slowly from the centipede's mandibles. If it attacked, she'd fight it.

But she would lose.

Another shriek, long and agonized, and the centipede swiveled away from Rae and toward the source of the noise, its legs a blur as it scurried up the wall and across the ceiling.

Rae didn't waste any more time. She practically threw herself forward, diving through the opening and into the tunnel on the other side of the cavern. The lovely, narrow, empty tunnel. Her feet carried her several feet down it before she was able to skid to a stop and turn.

Alyssa and Vivienne were both sprinting toward her.

Rae grinned at them. "We made it," she said. "We actually—"

Something slammed into her from behind.

26.
CADEN

The tall, imposing chain-link fence that surrounded Green On! loomed above Caden in the eerie green twilight of the forest, the barbed wire at the top reminding him of monster teeth.

"We made it," Nate huffed, putting his hands on his knees. He sucked in a long, tortured breath, then straightened, adjusting his chipped glasses. "I can't believe we really made it."

"Believe it," Caden said, staring through the fence and into the compound beyond. The main building was still pretty far away; this must be the back of Green On!. A smaller building squatted near the fence like a giant concrete toad, ugly and unassuming. But something about it drew his eye . . .

He had the sudden strange sense that this place, right here, was the correct spot. The vents, and therefore the mouth of the vortex, had to be close by.

"I thought for sure we'd be eaten," Nate continued, relief making him babble. "Or at least, gnawed on a little." He paused. "Actually, to be more accurate, I thought for sure *I'd* be eaten."

"While I what? Skipped on ahead?"

Nate shifted, looking uncomfortable. "I mean, I didn't think you'd be skipping, exactly. Just running very fast."

"We've already established that's not a skill I have." Caden glanced at Nate. Not even a hint of a smile. "You know I wouldn't leave you behind, right?"

"Wouldn't you, though?"

Caden frowned, not sure where this was coming from. He'd never been anything but nice to Nate. He'd thought they were friends, even. And then he realized. "This is about Rae, isn't it?"

Nate shrugged and looked away.

"I don't want to leave her behind either. Or Vivienne."

"But you will."

Caden opened his mouth to argue, then shut it again. Since leaving Ava and Blake, they hadn't seen any other sign of human life in the woods. And Caden had looked; he'd kept his senses as wide open as possible, searching for any possible trace of his friends' energy signatures. And nothing.

That *nothing* scared him more than he wanted to say. It might mean they were just out of his range. For all he knew, they'd made it back to the barrier and found Aiden on their own and were safely outside the forest.

Or they were dead.

He shoved those thoughts away. He had a job to do here. All

of Whispering Pines—and the entire *world* beyond—was in danger. No matter how much he cared about his friends, he had to do whatever it took to stop this alien invasion here and now, or it could mean the extinction of all of humanity. Nate knew that.

Caden was suddenly furious. He curled his hands into fists at his sides, wanting to lash out. Nate with his suspicious looks and little judgmental comments. Didn't he understand what was at stake here? Didn't he know what Caden was dealing with?

"Let's go," Caden said, his voice harsh. He strode along the side of the fence, not looking to see if Nate followed. It wasn't *his* fault that Vivienne had gone sprinting into the woods. And it wasn't his fault Rae was in here too. They'd made their choices, and now he would have to make his.

His fury grew as he stomped alongside the fence. He'd told Rae again and again not to just throw herself into danger. To think first and make a careful plan. But no. She always had to rush in, trying to save everyone, and look where it got her. Into a whole bunch of trouble.

Like now, trapped in a forest full of monsters. A forest that, if all went well, he would be destroying soon.

He paused, one foot lifted, as the reality of that thought hit him: He'd made it to the lab without finding his friends, which meant when he destroyed the aliens in the Watchful Woods, he'd be killing them, too.

His anger was nothing more than a shield. Something that stood between him and a whole complicated well of other emotions. Guilt, terror, grief . . . He let the anger go and allowed everything else he felt to wash over him, leaving him empty and defeated.

He'd never had a friend before Rae, but now that she was here, he couldn't imagine his life without her in it.

"Um, Caden?"

"What?" Caden looked back.

Nate stood a few paces behind, his hand over his mouth, eyes wide behind his glasses. "I, uh, think I found us a way in." He pointed, and now Caden saw it, too. Beneath the fence was a large hole where something had dug through the dirt, clearly intent on getting inside.

Or desperate to get out.

Caden moved closer, noticing the way the fence was bent outward at the bottom here, the chain links at the end jagged as if pieces had been torn free from the metal, their edges stained with blood.

He exchanged a look with Nate, and all their earlier resentments vanished. It was just the two of them here now. And Caden had to admit he was very grateful not to be alone in this instant.

"Should we go through it?" Nate asked, voice small.

Caden looked past the fence. The smaller building was only about twenty yards away now. Close enough that he could see a metal door set into the side. "Yes," he said, trying to sound confident.

Nate shuffled from foot to foot, the green glow of the forest painting his face a sickly color as he stared at that hole and the blood above it.

"You were the one who said it had to be better inside the lab," Caden pointed out.

"Yeah, well, I've reconsidered." Nate sighed. "But I've made it this far. I guess there's no going back."

Caden ran his finger over the ring on his thumb. "No," he said quietly. "No, there's not." He dropped to his hands and knees, careful to avoid the jagged fence edge as he slid forward onto his stomach, slithering through the dirt under the fence and then pulling himself back up on the other side. He stood and brushed at his jacket as Nate slowly army-crawled his own way through.

It looked even creepier standing on the inside and looking out at the forest surrounding them. Trees moved strangely, despite the lack of a breeze, their branches rippling like the arms of an octopus.

Caden turned his back on the forest, surveying the area around him. Now that there wasn't a fence blocking his view, he could see the bodies. Some were alien—a Devourer lay nearby with a giant burned hole in its chest, its mouth wide open. But most were human, dressed in Green On! lab coats or, in a few cases, hazmat suits, the helmets torn off and discarded.

"Do you think . . ." Nate swallowed audibly. "Is there anyone still alive in here?"

Caden hadn't felt the presence of any life. But then, he wasn't entirely sure how far his awareness stretched. "I don't know," he said at last. He didn't know how many employees had been in the building when the invasion started. Hopefully not too many. Still, over half the town was employed by Green On!. This place would be haunted for years if any of it survived.

Thwack, thwack, thwack.

Caden frowned, searching for the noise. It sounded like flesh hitting metal . . . His eyes fell on the body of a woman nearby. She'd fallen beside the fence, only a few feet from the hole, her hands outstretched, her pale hair braided tightly back from her face. She was moving, her arms and legs smacking into the chain links.

Caden couldn't look away, frozen in horrified fascination as the woman's whole body shuddered, her face twitching. Abruptly, an alien plant burst from her left eye, shooting upward until it hovered about a foot above her face. It was thick and ropy, glistening in the light, and covered in small pulsing sacs.

Caden gasped and took a step back. Nate clutched at his arm, pulling his shirt up over his mouth with his free hand, and the two of them moved quickly away.

Only now the other bodies nearby began shuddering, too. As if the presence of fresh blood in the area had triggered some kind of response. Another alien plant burst from the ear of the man lying closest to them, and then from the mouth of the body just behind, and Caden didn't think twice; he ran toward the small outbuilding, Nate racing beside him.

They reached the metal door. There was a keypad to the side of it, and Caden's mind went blank with panic. He didn't have the code! He could hear sounds now from behind him. Terrible moaning sounds, and he risked a glance back. One of the bodies lying nearby stretched its mouth into the rictus of a smile, eyes wide and unseeing, a plant growing from out of the top of its head. The spores hanging from the plant whooshed open, and tiny particles started to float through the air—

Nate whimpered and lunged for the door, grabbing for the handle. It opened.

"Not locked?" Caden gasped. "Why?"

"I don't even care right now," Nate said, darting inside.

With one last glance at the figures moaning and twitching around them, Caden followed him into the dark, pulling the door firmly shut behind him.

27.
RAE

Rae hit the ground hard. The machete flew out of her hand, all the air wheezing from her lungs. She blinked back the spots dancing in her vision as she struggled to turn and face her attacker.

A giant shape loomed over her in the dimly lit tunnel. One with a long, narrow face and six arms, each limb segmented like the legs of a spider and covered in jagged spikes.

Rae gasped for breath, scrabbling backward on her hands, her mind numb with terror. There was nowhere to go, no place to hide. The monster seemed to fill the whole tunnel as it skittered toward her, its hot, rancid breath bathing her face. Its lips drew back, the mouth opening impossibly wide, saliva dripping from its teeth and splattering against her skin.

Her fingers brushed against smooth metal behind her. The machete. She reached for it—

The creature lunged forward, teeth snapping.

Instinctively Rae squeezed her eyes shut, bracing herself.

Nothing happened.

She opened her eyes.

Vivienne was straddling the thing's neck, her hands gripping its jaws, forcing them shut. Her own mouth was open in a silent snarl, her eyes filled with the same greenish glow as the alien's beneath her.

Rae froze, entranced. Her friend was completely transformed. Gone was the easygoing girl who'd instantly accepted her on her first day at Dana S. Middle School. In her place was . . . Rae didn't even know. But this new version of Vivienne—so fierce, so strong, so *alien*—managed to wrestle the monster to the ground despite being less than half its size.

She pinned its head down as it thrashed and squirmed.

"The key," Vivienne said, her voice scarily calm, "is the head. Control the head, and it doesn't matter what the rest of the body wants to do."

Rae shivered, wondering if Vivienne was only talking about the alien she was fighting. Rae risked a glance at Alyssa, who stood with her back pressed against the tunnel wall, her hands clenched over her mouth, eyes wide.

Alyssa and Vivienne had been best friends since they were old enough to walk. What must it cost Alyssa to see her friend like this now? She didn't know Vivienne's secret. All she knew was that her friend was suddenly this killing machine.

The creature gave a strangled cry and, in a burst of speed, managed to get its legs under it and fling Vivienne off. She twisted in midair, hitting the low tunnel ceiling with her feet and rebounding back.

The next few seconds were a blur of motion—Vivienne snarling and tearing at the monster with her teeth, her nails, as it screeched and tried to claw her back, its own teeth snapping.

Rae had thought this alien was fast, but it was nothing compared to Vivienne's speed. She danced around its attacks easily, raking deep, bloody gouges in its side and along its chest, before tearing one of its arms from its body with a loud, sickening *rip*.

It keened in pain, one of its other arms clutching at the wound as it stumbled back. Vivienne laughed, advancing on it. And Rae wondered if the *real* Vivienne was still there, looking out through her eyes, trapped in her body as it killed this creature so brutally.

No *if*, Rae thought, determined to believe it. Vivienne *was* in there. And Rae wouldn't leave her to commit this violence alone.

She grabbed the machete and pushed herself to her feet, running at the alien. "Vivienne, drop!"

Vivienne instantly flattened herself to the ground, and Rae leapt over her, swinging the machete with both hands, putting all her strength into it.

The blade sank into the creature's neck, just below its elongated head. The impact shuddered all the way up Rae's arms, and she felt the skin and muscle give way as her knife cut deep before catching on the bones of the neck inside.

It was the most horrible sensation Rae had ever felt. Worse

than when she'd sliced into the Devourer's shoulder in the woods.

She let go of the machete and stumbled back as the alien toppled over, blood pouring from its neck. It scrabbled at the wound with its remaining five arms and then went still, the glow fading from its eyes.

Rae rubbed her hands against her pants and took slow, careful breaths. She felt too hot in this tunnel. Too closed in.

She'd killed it.

It had tried to kill her first. It was evil, a hungry thing made for rending flesh. It needed to die. But still . . .

"Um, guys?" Alyssa's voice was a tiny squeak.

Rae turned slowly, feeling like all of this was unreal. The tunnel, the blood, the corpse in front of her. But the sight of the terror on Alyssa's face snapped her back into the present.

"The bugs," Alyssa gasped, pointing. "I think . . . I think they can smell the blood."

Rae twisted to look back at the opening to the cavern behind them. Hundreds of long, squirmy bodies poured from it, coating the walls, ceiling, and floor of the tunnel until it looked like the earth itself was moving.

"Run!" Vivienne yelled. "Now!" She grabbed Alyssa and shoved her past the dead alien, pushing until the other girl began to sprint. Rae followed, pausing only to grab her machete and yank it from the corpse, its handle slippery with blood and gore and—

And she wasn't going to think about it. *Just run*, she told herself.

She ran, the *click-click-click* of thousands of legs echoing behind her. And then an even more awful noise—the unmistakable sound of eating as the things fell upon the alien's body. She just hoped it would distract them long enough for her and her friends to get away.

Just ahead, Vivienne and Alyssa had inexplicably stopped running and were standing, staring at the wall.

Rae skidded to a halt. "What are you—" she began. And then she saw it. A large metal door with a button engraved in the wall next to it.

The elevator.

She remembered how they'd stumbled on this before, back when it was her, Vivi, Nate, and Caden. It had led them directly to the spaceship. She hadn't realized they were so close to it now, but the tunnels seemed different in this strange glow, as if they had shifted directions. For all she knew, maybe they really had.

Click. Click.

Rae glanced back over her shoulder. The giant queen stood less than thirty feet away, her top half lifted, her upper legs waving gently as if caught in a breeze. Her black eyes focused on them. Considering.

The hairs on the back of Rae's neck stood on end. She jabbed the elevator button.

"I already did that," Vivienne said.

Rae jabbed it again anyhow.

"That won't speed it up." Vivienne sounded way too calm.

"Maybe not, but it feels like it helps," Rae snapped.

The centipede shifted, its body rippling, and Rae knew it was about to charge. She already knew how fast it would be. The tunnel from here stretched straight and long—they'd never be able to out-run it. The elevator was their only hope.

"Come on, come on," Rae whispered, willing those doors to open.

The centipede dropped to the ground, its segmented torso bunching.

The elevator doors started to open—

The bug sprang forward, legs skittering madly against the rock, mandibles open wide. Rae shifted her grip on her machete, trying to be ready as it launched itself at them.

"Now!" Vivienne darted through the doors, yanking Rae and Alyssa in after her into the tiny box of an elevator. She immediately pressed the button to send them down.

The doors snapped shut just as the centipede crashed into them, screaming. Rae stumbled back against the far wall of the elevator, heart racing. She barely had time to brace herself before they were falling, shooting downward so fast it felt like she'd left her stomach behind.

Alyssa gave a little cry and fell on her butt. Only Vivienne stood there in the center of the elevator, her balance perfect, motionless except for the movement of her dark hair. And her eyes, which roved all around the tiny space, then flicked to Rae's.

Rae wanted to look away, but she couldn't. Vivienne's face was smeared with blood. Her hands, too, were red to the elbows, the sleeves of her jacket soaked.

Ding!

The elevator stopped with a lurch, and this time Vivienne actually did stumble. Rae put out a hand, and Vivienne caught it. And her eyes, for just a second, were the eyes of a frightened thirteen-year-old. Wide and terrified. "Rae?" she whispered, sounding lost, her fingers tightening on Rae's.

Rae's heart squeezed. Vivienne. She *was* in there. Rae swallowed. "Yes, Vivienne. I'm with you."

Vivienne opened her mouth like she wanted to say something more, but then the moment was gone, her eyes going flat and hard. "Vivienne isn't here anymore," the thing inside her friend said. She bared her teeth, white against the crimson staining her face.

The doors opened, and she dropped Rae's hand and stepped out.

28.
CADEN

Caden and Nate stood at the top of a metal stairwell lit by a dim red light. Neither of them wanted to go down it.

"After you." Caden extended a hand in front of him.

"Oh, no, after you," Nate said. "I insist."

"I'm pretty sure in horror movies, it's the person in back who gets eaten first."

"Then at least it would be done with quickly. It's the suspense I don't like." Nate managed a small smile. "Nice try, though."

Caden couldn't help smiling back.

Thump!

Something threw itself at the door behind them, and they both jumped.

"I guess that's our cue," Nate said nervously.

Caden nodded, and reluctantly started down the stairs.

They led down to a cramped metal platform barely big enough for the two of them to stand on, which led to yet another set of stairs, and another platform, the pattern seeming to continue forever. As they descended, it grew hotter, the air thick with humidity. Nate had to keep pausing on each platform to wipe the steam from his glasses.

At the third pause, Caden felt it: a tug, as if something had hooked him through the belly button. He frowned, peering down at the next set of stairs. It must be the vortex. Now that he knew it was there, he could feel it, the pull so strong it cut through everything else. Even the thick cloud of Nate's terror was no match for it.

Caden glanced at his companion. Nate rubbed his lenses with the bottom of his shirt, his mouth pressed into a small, thin line. His face seemed rounder without the defining features of his glasses. Softer, and more childish. "Caden?" he said.

"Hmm?"

"Do you remember the first time you saw a ghost?"

Caden paused. If the question had come from just about anyone else at their school, he would have thought they were looking for a way to make fun of him. But Nate wasn't like that. Either he was legitimately curious, or he was hoping to take his mind off the creepiness of their current surroundings by focusing on past creepiness.

"Yes, I remember." Caden reached for his pendant, his fingers closing on thin air before he remembered he'd given it to Vivienne. He dropped his hand. "I don't think anyone ever forgets the first time they see a ghost. They might convince themselves that what they saw wasn't real, that it couldn't be possible. But they never really forget."

"I know," Nate whispered. "I saw one after my grandfather's

funeral. We were at the cemetery where he was being buried, and there was a lady by a gravestone. She was crying so hard her whole body shook, but it made no sound. And she wore this dress . . . I just knew it was old. High collar, long skirt, like something out of a history book."

"You're sure she was a ghost?" Caden asked.

"Oh, yes. There was just something . . . off . . . about her."

It was how most people described their first ghost sightings: "something off."

"Also," Nate said slowly, "she scared the heck out of me."

"Why? What happened?" Caden asked.

Nate put his glasses back on. "She seemed so sad, I wanted to ask her what was wrong. But the moment I took a step toward her, she stopped crying and whipped around. Her eyes met mine. And she gave me this *look*." He shivered. "Even now, I can still see it. Like she blamed me for all her misfortunes."

"I'm sure she didn't blame *you*, exactly."

"It seemed pretty personal."

Caden shook his head. "She blamed the living. You were just the proxy for the rest of us."

"Well, whatever I was, it was terrifying. I couldn't move, couldn't blink, and she just started drifting toward me. And I knew if she touched me, I would die." He rubbed his chest. "Luckily my mom noticed I wasn't paying attention to my grandfather's burial sermon. She grabbed me by the arm and yanked me around to face his graveside. When I looked back, the woman was gone."

Caden nodded, thoughtful.

"Would I have died?" Nate asked.

"You mean, if she touched you?"

"Yes."

"No. Ghosts can make you feel . . . certain ways if you don't know how to shield yourself from them. That was just her manipulating your emotions." *Probably,* he amended silently. Some ghosts really could kill with a touch, but they were rare. And right now, Nate didn't need to know about them.

"Well, that's good to know," Nate said. He was quiet for a minute, and Caden glanced at the next set of stairs, knowing they should keep moving but not wanting to.

"When I was little," Nate said abruptly, "my mom was always telling me I had an overactive imagination. There were no such things as monsters under the bed or in the closet. She wanted me to grow up and stop believing in fairy tales. But after that day at the funeral, when I saw *her* and realized what she must be, I knew I was right to be afraid. There really *were* things—impossible, terrifying things—that existed. Even if no one else saw them." He shrugged. "I guess I've been sort of a scaredy-cat ever since."

"And yet here you are." Caden extended his arms to take in the stairwell, the lab, the forest around them.

"Here I am," Nate agreed, giving a small, rueful smile. "Trust me, I'm more surprised than anyone." He cleared his throat. "So. What about your first time?"

Caden hesitated. In some ways, his experience was similar to Nate's. "Oh, you know," he said at last. "My mom is in the ghost-hunting business, and sometimes she'd take me with her to work. I was with her on a job the first time I saw a ghost." He kept his voice casual, like it had been no big deal.

"Oh? What happened?"

"Nothing much. My mom was there to lay her spirit to rest. So she did." He turned away from Nate and started down the next stairwell, hoping to avoid any more questions. Because it had not been nearly so simple.

He could still picture the ghost, how her long hair swirled around her gaunt face in a breeze only she felt. And the way her eyes, when they fixed on him, were huge and dark and glistening with unshed tears. She hadn't been ready to go yet. *Please help me,* she'd whispered. *Help me.* And Caden, soft-hearted and foolish, had tried.

He remembered how he'd scattered his mom's protective salt ring in the middle of the ritual. *"Wait, Mom. She just needs you to listen to her,"* he'd said. Right before the candle snuffed out. And suddenly the sad ghost he'd seen transformed into something horrible, her eyes burning a deep, dark crimson as she'd reached for him with hands like claws.

He'd been too young, then, to really know how to properly shield himself, and her psychic energy had nearly torn him apart. It had felt like getting blasted by sand, but on the inside of his body.

He couldn't really remember what happened next—most of it was a blur—but his mom had rushed him from that house so fast, she hadn't finished the cleansing and had to go back and complete it later, even though that meant refunding the client. Mostly, Caden remembered his dad, and how furious he'd been about the whole thing. Soon after that, his mom began sending him to daycare when she worked instead of carting him with her.

Aiden had been super annoyed about that, he remembered now. He'd missed out on the whole thing because he'd already been in elementary school at the time. But after that, their dad didn't want either of them going on any more jobs.

Caden had overheard their mom arguing with their dad about it. She'd said Caden was too sensitive, but Aiden wouldn't make that kind of mistake. Even now, years later, Caden could feel the familiar burning sense of shame when he thought of that conversation.

"Caden is too much like you," his mom had told his dad. *"Soft-hearted."*

"You mean kind? Compassionate? Those aren't bad things," his dad had said.

"In this line of work, they can be a liability. He's too easy to manipulate. He needs to learn—"

"He's still young," his dad had snapped. *"Let him learn when he's older."*

"Aiden already knows better—"

"Aiden is young too. Let him be a kid for once. No more house visits with them. I'm serious."

"Fine. I'll give it a few more years."

Caden blinked away the memory. It was the first time he'd realized how much better his brother was at all the paranormal stuff. The first time he'd longed to be more like Aiden. Aiden, who already knew better. Who wasn't too sensitive. Who could handle anything.

Only now as Caden walked through the darkness with Nate, he wondered: was it really so bad to be sensitive? Better that than to be whatever Aiden was. At least *he* cared about other people. Aiden cared only for himself and, possibly, for his family. Everyone else could vanish off the face of the Earth and he wouldn't care.

Caden frowned as he reached the bottom of the stairs, something about that thought bothering him. He glanced at Nate. Nate, who Aiden had claimed would be safe with him as long as they were touching when the blast went off.

"Why is it safer to surf with a friend?" Caden asked abruptly.

"Hmm?" Nate seemed to pull himself from his own thoughts.

"It was something Aiden said before we stepped into the woods. Is it because then you'd have someone looking out for you?" That was how he'd taken it at the time.

Nate laughed, a small, joyless sound. "I'm sure that's not how your brother meant it." He adjusted his glasses. "Surfing with a friend reduces your chances of a shark attack by fifty percent. You know, because the shark might eat your friend instead of you."

"Oh," Caden said. That sounded a lot more like the Aiden he knew. The one who viewed other people as spare parts to be used or sacrificed as needed.

Stop worrying about other people so much and focus on your own safety. That's what matters.

And Caden was hit with the sudden horrible certainty that the magic that would protect him from the blast wouldn't really extend to anyone he was touching.

No, Caden told himself. Even Aiden wouldn't lie to him about something as important as that. Would he?

"Is that an elevator?" Nate asked.

Caden blinked, staring through the gloom. At the other end of the platform, instead of more stairs, gleamed a pair of metal doors. "Maybe it goes back up?" he said. They walked closer, and Nate tapped the button next to the doors. A down arrow was clearly etched into the wall.

"Or not," Caden said.

"We probably need some sort of clearance to access it," Nate said, studying the panel below the buttons.

Caden reached out and pushed the down arrow. It lit up, and a moment later, the doors swung open with a quiet *ding*.

Caden met Nate's gaze. "Okay, something's definitely wrong," Nate said. "A code black in town? This place should be completely locked down. Instead, it's all wide open."

"A computer glitch?" Caden suggested.

Nate frowned and adjusted his dirty glasses. "Maybe," he said doubtfully. "Or maybe someone has hacked into the system and removed all the clearances."

"Why?"

Nate shrugged. "To make it easier to come and go?"

"Who would be able to do that?" Even as Caden asked the question, he knew. If the pods on the spaceship really were open— and they'd seen enough strange aliens in the woods to convince him of that—then that meant Patrick was free too.

The elevator made an angry buzzing noise.

"Maybe this leads to the spaceship, like the last elevator we found," Nate said, dropping his voice.

Caden looked at the small metal box. "Only one way to find out." And he stepped inside.

29.
RAE

Rae started to follow Vivienne from the elevator, but Alyssa caught her by the wrist, holding her back. "So, are you going to tell me what's wrong with her?" Alyssa asked quietly. "Or am I supposed to just pretend this is all normal?"

Rae hesitated. It wasn't her secret to share. But when she looked back at Alyssa, she knew she couldn't keep it to herself anymore. Vivienne . . . the *real* Vivienne . . . would understand.

Vivienne isn't here anymore.

"Do you remember last summer when she went spelunking with her mom?" Rae said, pushing the memory of Vivienne's last words from her mind. Rae didn't want to think about them or the flat way Vivienne had said them. No emotion, no humanity.

Alyssa nodded.

"Apparently she found something. A sort of column. And

when she touched it . . . she began changing. She thought it was a curse at first, so Caden's mom gave her a large protective amulet that she carried around in her backpack for a while." Rae wasn't sure what had happened to it after Vivienne had used it to help Aiden stop a demon. Maybe it had been destroyed in that battle.

"So *that's* why she started lugging that thing everywhere," Alyssa said, eyes widening. Then they narrowed. "That was also when she started acting . . . different. My mom said it was just her teenage hormones kicking in." Alyssa snorted. "Some hormones. But then, I don't think my mom actually believes there's much difference between a teenager and a monster . . ." Alyssa's expression shifted, turning wistful. Sad.

"We'll find your mom," Rae said, guessing at the sudden change.

Alyssa nodded. "She's . . . well. A little harsh, I know. But it's out of a sense of duty. She just wants to protect everyone."

"I know."

"And Vivienne . . ."

"She's not a monster," Rae said.

"It looked bad, Rae. The way she attacked that thing back there." Alyssa shuddered. "I never thought I'd be scared of my own friend."

"She's scared of herself, too."

Alyssa bit her lip. "Poor Vivi," she whispered. "So, since you said it's not a curse, what is it?"

"An alien embryo."

Alyssa stared at her. "What?"

"It's been growing inside her. And now . . ." Rae swallowed. "Now, I think it's taken over."

Alyssa went pale. "Can't we do anything about it?"

"I hope so," Rae said. The elevator doors started to close, and she stopped them with a hand. "For now, though, the best we can do is stay near and try to help her."

Alyssa nodded, looking suddenly unsure. But this time when Rae stepped from the elevator, she let her go, falling in behind her.

The tunnel continued straight for about twenty feet before it veered sharply to the left, exactly the way Rae remembered. As they reached the corner, her steps slowed, and she took a deep, careful breath, then poked her head around.

The tunnel widened here into a giant cavern, far larger than the bug-infested one they'd left behind. The two times Rae had been here before, the entire space had been lit by floodlights. Now, only that eerie green mist illuminated the space. And the thing in it.

The spaceship.

It loomed in the center of the cavern, massive and glimmering, the green lighting turning it from silver-blue to a vibrant teal. The way its surface rippled reminded Rae of the ocean, and she couldn't look away. She'd never seen anything so beautiful.

Alyssa gasped, and reluctantly Rae forced herself to focus on the rest of the scene. If the pods on board really *had* opened, then this place should be crawling with things. Only, as she did a quick scan of the area, she saw nothing. Just Vivienne's silhouette, standing motionless beside the plastic barrier that had been set around the spaceship. There were no guards, no scientists, and no alien creatures.

Rae frowned, feeling uneasy. It didn't seem right for it to be so empty down here. If the aliens had escaped, was Doctor Nguyen onboard the spaceship when it happened? She didn't always like or trust the woman, but Rae didn't want anything bad to happen to her. Tentatively Rae stepped around the corner, walking slowly until she stood next to Vivienne.

Vivienne stared up at the ship, her head tilted way back at an angle that looked painful. Unnatural. Alien.

Vivienne isn't here anymore.

No, Rae told herself. That was a lie. She'd seen her in there. And she'd get her back.

"Do you smell it?" Vivienne asked quietly.

"Smell what?" Rae asked.

"All the blood."

Rae shifted uneasily. Now that Vivienne mentioned it, there was a hot metallic scent to the air. Suddenly the lack of people around took on a much darker meaning.

Rae made herself look—*really* look—at the cavern around her. At first glance it appeared empty, but now that she wasn't distracted by the spaceship, she noticed several long streaks staining the floor. They looked black . . . the color blood would be if it had soaked into the dirt. Staggering back, she turned in a circle, noticing the other splotches—large ovals of black, tiny spatters of it, more smears everywhere she looked. Her mind reeled, spinning out images of people dying, bleeding, their bodies dragged away and devoured . . .

She shut those images down. There was no way to know what had happened out here, and for once, Rae was grateful to remain ignorant.

Vivienne gave herself a little shake, as if coming out of a trance. "Let's go board the ship."

"Now?" Rae said, exchanging an uneasy look with Alyssa. That *was* why they'd come out here, but it felt wrong somehow. As if the ship—and whatever still dwelled inside it—were waiting for them. A spider lurking in the center of a web. Rae thought of Caden, and how often he'd told her not to rush into things. How listening to that advice had saved her the last time she was about to run after Patrick. "Maybe we should come up with a plan first, or—"

"I'm going now," Vivienne snapped. "If you're too scared to come with me, then stay here. You'd just be in my way anyhow." In one smooth motion, she leapt over the plastic barrier, landing lightly on her feet on the other side.

"Vivi, wait!" Rae hurried toward the opening in the barrier, rushing after her. But Vivienne didn't look back, and she didn't slow her stride. She was all the way around to the other side of the spaceship before Rae and Alyssa caught up with her. "How will we—" Rae began.

The doorway leading inside the spaceship silently opened, the ramp extending out to meet them.

"Get in," she finished in a whisper. Now she *knew* something was wrong.

Vivienne stepped onto the ramp.

"Wait!" Rae said. "We can't just waltz in there. We need . . . we need a plan or something." *Caden would be proud of me*, she thought.

"We don't have time for a plan," Vivienne said. "I'm going in now." She half-turned back. "The only question is, are *you* coming with me?"

Rae knew she should say no. This was obviously some kind of trap. But there was that look in Vivienne's eyes again. A lost, haunted look. A glimpse of the real Vivienne trapped inside.

And despite all her misgivings, Rae knew she could never abandon her friend. "Yes." She tightened her grip on her machete.

"Of course," Alyssa said.

Vivienne flashed them a quick smile. "Thank you," she whispered, her hand clasped around something near her throat. As Rae walked up the ramp to join her, she realized it was a very familiar pendant. *Caden's* pendant.

"Why do you have that?" Rae asked, feeling a strange twinge inside. Fear, maybe? Was she worried Vivienne had done something to Caden? But no. She couldn't believe her friend would be capable of hurting him. She just couldn't.

Vivienne noticed her looking and dropped her hand. "He thought it would help me." She shrugged. "Maybe it has. Hard to say."

"Huh." Rae shoved her strange surge of emotions down. She didn't have time for any complicated feelings right now. The spaceship waited. "Ready?"

Vivienne nodded.

"I guess so," Alyssa said, joining them on the ramp. The three of them shifted until they were standing shoulder-to-shoulder, like they had been the day Rae had made the track team, days or weeks or possibly lifetimes ago. And then they walked together through the doorway and onto the ship.

30.
CADEN

Caden clutched at the wall as the elevator plunged downward. He counted the seconds until, finally, the elevator slowed and then stuttered to a stop. The doors popped open, bathing the inside in a soft green glow.

"If I never go in one of these secret elevators again, it will still be too soon," Nate muttered as he staggered out the door. "That was terrible."

"Can't say it was my favorite thing either." Caden followed him, listening to the *swoosh* of the doors closing behind him. A second later and the elevator rose up again, as if it were in a hurry to meet more people above. Caden glanced back uneasily. It was silly to feel abandoned by an elevator, but something about its rapid retreat made him uncomfortable, like it was another sign that they were well and truly on their own.

"I guess we answered *that* question." Nate pointed. "Look."

The hallway leading from the elevator opened up into a large underground cavern. And looming in the center of it was the spaceship.

Caden stared at it, his mouth dropping open. It was larger than he remembered, its smooth metal surface seeming to soak in the greenish light that filled the cavernous space, the color undulating across in ripples and waves. The whole thing was rounded like the underside of a spoon, and yet it wasn't a perfect disk. It was hard to tell exactly *what* its shape was; much like with a ghost sighting, something about it just seemed off, as if it didn't quite belong in their physical realm, and any attempts to pinpoint exact details were impossible.

"I almost forgot how unreal it looked," Nate whispered. "Like something out of a movie set."

Caden only nodded, his eyes glued to that rippling surface. It was almost hypnotic, the way colors seemed to race across it only to vanish again. It pulled him toward it, and he let his feet move, carrying him closer. He could feel the tug of energy, the way it reached for him, welcoming him like an old friend.

And abruptly he stopped, realizing it wasn't the ship he was feeling at all. It was the energy pulsing beneath it.

The mouth of the vortex must be right here.

31.
RAE

The last time Rae was inside the ship, it had been lit by a faint red light. But now the floor hummed beneath her feet and the walls all glowed a gentle yellow. It did not seem like the ship was quite full-powered, but it was definitely easier to see than it had been before.

Not that they really needed it. This area was as empty as Rae remembered. Nothing but curving walls of metal bending in all directions. She took the lead, her steps echoing too loudly, the air seeming to magnify the sounds as she followed the natural curve of the wall.

The doorway leading to the next section of the ship stood open as well. Rae stepped through it cautiously, remembering how startled she'd been before to come face-to-face with a giant centipede trapped in a pod. Only this time, no bug greeted her. The pod was still there, but its door hung open, the glass inside empty.

Rae's heart squeezed in her chest, her whole body going cold. As she turned and looked down the rows and rows, all she saw were more empty glass cases. "No," she whispered, her steps quickening until she was running, checking pod after pod.

Every single one had been abandoned.

She pictured the things she'd seen—monsters with too many tentacles, too many mouths, things that looked like they'd slither or squelch. Creatures that didn't belong in her world. All of them, unleashed.

"Rae!" Alyssa gasped from somewhere behind her. "Rae, stop!"

But Rae *couldn't* stop, her feet carrying her through the next doorway and into another room full of empty pods. She felt like if she stopped, all the missing creatures would come pouring after her. It wasn't logical; if they were still on the ship, she'd have seen them. But still, her feet kept moving, panic building in her chest. Flashes of the last time she'd been here filled her mind. The monsters in the pods, Patrick stalking her through the rooms, how trapped she'd felt.

And then she caught a glimpse of movement up ahead in one of the pods.

Not *all* of them were empty after all.

Her feet slowed, the panic receding, leaving her mind clear. What was she *doing*, sprinting through the spaceship, not waiting for her friends? If Caden were there, he'd be the first to tell her exactly how foolish that was.

Blinking, she turned to find Alyssa sprinting behind her, face flushed and blond ponytail swinging. She stopped next to Rae, breathing hard. "You," Alyssa began.

"I'm sorry, Alyssa."

"You just took off! We shouldn't split up!"

"I know, and I'm sorry about that, too."

"Too?" Alyssa said. "What *else* are you sorry about, then?"

Rae moved to the side so Alyssa could see the pod.

Alyssa's eyes widened, her face going white. "Oh," she whispered. Inside floated Ms. Lockett, her eyes open and unseeing, her mouth wide in a silent scream, one hand pressed to the inside of the pod that imprisoned her. "Mom!" Alyssa rushed over, checking the door. "Why didn't she get released with everything else?"

"I don't know," Rae said. "But it looks like none of the humans did." Doctor Anderson was still imprisoned in his own tube, and now she noticed a few other people—adults she didn't recognize, some in Green On! lab coats—floating in their own silent pods as well. She looked carefully at all their faces, but didn't see Doctor Nguyen amongst them. Or her father, either.

Rae rubbed a hand over her face, not sure if she was relieved or disappointed not to see him here.

Alyssa pressed her own hand against the outside of her mom's pod so that only glass stood between their two palms.

"Where's Vivienne?" Rae asked, glancing around.

Alyssa looked back, her expression lost. "I . . . I don't know. She *was* right behind me."

Fear clutched Rae's heart. Had something happened to Vivi? Rae knew it would be all her fault. If she hadn't run on ahead, then—

Footsteps stopped her thoughts, and she relaxed a little. But the figure who stepped into view was definitely *not* her friend.

Patrick paused beside an empty pod a few feet away. He looked almost the same as he always had: nondescript black suit, perfectly styled dark hair, and a smile so wide Rae could see every single gleaming tooth. Only his eyes betrayed him. Where they used to be the warm blue of a summer sky, now they were black.

Completely black. No color, no white, as if the darkness of his pupils had leaked outward, expanding to take up all the space.

"Hello, Ms. Carter." His smile dropped away, leaving his face blank and terrifying, those alien eyes focusing on her face with an intensity she could feel in her gut. "I wondered when you'd show up."

32.
CADEN

Caden approached the ship slowly, his steps cautious. It was surrounded by a thick plastic barrier that had been swarming with guards and scientists last time. This time, the area around the ship was completely empty. It made the hairs on the back of his neck stand on end.

Maybe they'd all been evacuated.

But the moment he got close to that barrier, he was hit with a wave of negative energies, and he knew something terrible had happened here. He closed his eyes as the echoes of it washed over him, his mind filling with screams, images playing behind his eyelids: people in lab coats running, shrieking, trying to hide as a swarm of monsters crashed into them. Caden had an impression of tentacles, and teeth, and hunger. Of blood and death and terror.

And then the quiet that came after. Complete and utter silence.

He opened his eyes, trying to banish the images from his mind, but they kept replaying over and over like a bad television show.

"Have you seen this?" Nate said, his voice trembling.

Caden didn't want to look, didn't want to see. But he made himself walk toward his friend, already suspecting what he'd find.

Nate pointed at the ground. A stain stood out against the dirt, long and dark, as if something had been leaking as it was dragged across the cavern floor.

Not some*thing*. Someone.

Caden took a deep breath. It was a mistake; the whole cavern smelled like death. His head swam, and he let his breath out slowly, trying to regain his equilibrium.

"It's blood, isn't it?" Nate said quietly.

Caden nodded.

"There's more." Nate pointed at several other stains nearby. "But . . . no bodies."

"I think . . ." Caden swallowed hard, the images from before flashing through his mind. He banished them. "They were all dragged into the tunnels. And then eaten."

Nate's skin turned a ghastly greenish color. "Oh," he managed. "That's, um, rather efficient."

Caden shoved his trembling hands deep into his jacket pockets and looked at the spaceship again, this time focusing on the inside, trying to somehow see past the outer surface. According to Rae there had been hundreds, maybe thousands of pods in there, all containing different alien species.

They must have caught the people out here completely unawares.

Focus, Caden, he told himself. If he didn't find those geothermal vents and destroy the mouth of the vortex, then the deaths here would be nothing more than a warm-up act.

He ran his finger over the ring on his thumb. It felt like it was pulsing with its own inner heartbeat, the metal throbbing against his skin, his own heartbeat slowing to match until the two beat in sync. It should have been horrifying, but he was distracted by the feeling of a deeper vibration coming from outside himself. One that seemed to shiver through his bones.

He drifted closer to the plastic barrier until he stood pressed against it. Dimly he was aware of Nate circling around behind him, muttering something under his breath as he studied the abandoned computer monitors. But most of Caden's attention was on the thin strip of plastic that separated him from the ship.

Part of the plastic barrier had been torn away. If he let himself look, he'd see the claw marks along the edges. So he didn't look. Not closely. Instead, he stepped through the space, walking forward until he was close enough to reach out and touch the side of the ship.

It still drew his eye, making it hard to look anywhere else, but he forced himself to drop his gaze down. There was something directly below the spaceship.

Steam.

Caden crouched, studying the wafting tendrils of air. From this close, he could feel the heat radiating from them, could smell the telltale rotten egg scent of sulfur.

The ship must have crashed right on top of the vents. Maybe

the vortex itself had pulled the craft toward it, like some kind of supernatural magnet. Caden had no idea; he wasn't really clear on how a vortex worked. If he survived this, he'd have to ask Aiden more questions. Right now, though, there was only one that needed an answer.

Aiden had told him that all he needed to do was drop the ring into the vents. If he did that, it would cause a magical blast that would kill everything in the Watchful Woods . . . including Rae and Vivienne. And possibly Nate as well. But it would also save Whispering Pines, and maybe even the world itself.

Caden had thought if it came down to it that he would be able to sacrifice his friends for the good of the world. But now he was here, facing that very real possibility. And . . . he wasn't sure he could do it.

He rubbed again at the ring on his finger. It wasn't just pulsing now, but throbbing, the metal warm and silky. It *wanted* to be dropped inside those vents. He could feel its eagerness mixed with the frustration of being so close to its goal.

Aiden would do it, the ring hissed in his mind. *He would be strong enough.*

Caden felt the weight of those words, the truth of them. His brother wouldn't think twice about sacrificing others if he felt it was necessary. Aiden had always been good at doing whatever needed to be done in order to achieve his goals. And maybe that *was* a kind of strength. Caden was the one who worried about collateral damage, who concerned himself with the feelings of others, who was too sensitive, too softhearted.

But that could be a strength too.

Caden had already decided he didn't want to be like Aiden; maybe it was time he stopped comparing himself to his brother. Aiden had his own way of doing things. Caden would find a different way.

"Caden?" Nate crouched beside him, pale face scrunched with worry. "Are you okay?"

Caden nodded. "I'm fine. But I'm not ready to destroy the vortex. Not yet."

Nate stared at him, and Caden waited for him to say something encouraging, to remind him that the fate of the rest of their town rested on this moment. The fate of the world, even. If he didn't stop this invasion now, it could mean the extinction of the human race. Against that, what were a few small lives?

Instead, Nate put a hand on his shoulder and gave it a small squeeze. "I'm glad" was all he said.

Caden smiled. Of course Nate wouldn't believe in sacrificing their friends either.

And Caden knew it might still come to that. Like Aiden had said, they didn't have a lot of time left. He glanced at his phone. Already almost two and a half hours had passed. But that still gave them a few hours to find their friends first.

Caden stood, backing away from the hot vents and wiping his sweaty hands on his pants. And then he felt a presence rushing toward them. He froze, his mind going blank in panic.

"What?" Nate said, that single word cutting through Caden's paralysis. He couldn't just stand here.

Caden grabbed Nate by the arm and tugged him down, close to the vents, ignoring the way the heat immediately bathed him in sticky, stinky humidity. That didn't matter. All that mattered was that the steam was thick enough to hide them. "Something's coming," he whispered.

"Aliens?" Nate gasped.

Caden shook his head. "People."

"Then why are we hiding?"

Caden couldn't explain why they didn't want these people to discover them. He just knew it would be very bad. "Because," he whispered. "Trust me?" He'd meant it as a statement, but it came out a question, all his vulnerability on full display.

"I do," Nate answered immediately.

And despite their creepy surroundings and his own terror, Caden felt strangely comforted.

33.
RAE

Alyssa's face went red. *"You,"* she said, spitting the word with such vehemence it sounded like a curse.

"Me?" Patrick raised an eyebrow. "What about me, Ms. Lockett?"

"You kidnapped my mom!"

"Did I? As I recall, your mom came to *me* and insisted on staying near Green On! until all her students were returned to her. I merely found her a convenient place to wait."

"A convenient place?" Rae gaped at him. "You stuck her in a pod!"

"And thus saved her from some of the . . . unpleasantness of the past twenty-four hours."

"Why is she still in a pod?" Alyssa demanded. "If the aliens were freed, why weren't the humans?"

"How simplified that statement is. Dividing the world into *humans* and *aliens*, as if we are so very different."

"Answer her question," Rae said, refusing to be distracted.

"These pods, as you call them, each have a different locking mechanism. For instance, you'll notice none of the embryos on board were released either. I simply used a similar lock for the humans. Including our dear Ms. Lockett."

"You monster," Alyssa choked out.

"Monster?" Patrick's eerie black eyes widened. "Thanks to me, your mother, at least, has been quite safe. Others haven't been as lucky." He made a show of looking over his shoulder.

Rae looked past him, noticing for the first time the blood sprayed across the floor nearby, streaks of it smeared against the walls and splattered on some of the empty pods. A *lot* of blood. A shiver ran down her spine, and she looked quickly away again, then gasped.

Patrick was suddenly standing much closer. So close he could almost have reached out and touched her.

She hadn't even seen him move.

She raised her machete, hands trembling. "S-stay where you are." She could feel Alyssa moving beside her, silently offering her support. It should have been reassuring, but she doubted the two of them could take him on. He was no Devourer, but something much more intelligent and dangerous. They needed Vivienne. Where could she have gone?

Unless . . . unless Patrick had caught up to her already. What if he'd done something to her?

Fear clutched at her heart with icy fingers, and she tried not to imagine Vivienne frozen inside her own pod, mouth open and screaming soundlessly.

Patrick feinted to the left, and Rae adjusted her grip, moving the machete so the blade stayed between her and him.

"Come now, Ms. Carter. Are you really prepared to swing that at me?"

Rae wasn't sure. She remembered the sickening feeling of slicing into that alien creature's neck back in the tunnels . . . The thought of doing that to Patrick—to someone she'd had actual conversations with, someone who *seemed* human, at least most of the time—made her stomach roil. "If I have to," she managed, her voice only trembling a little.

He nodded once, his expression thoughtful. "I suppose you might. I made the mistake of underestimating you last time; I won't do that again."

Last time Rae had been armed with a giant EpiPen specially designed to work against Patrick's extraterrestrial nature. It had rendered him unconscious long enough for her to shove him into a pod. She wished she had something like that again. She could stab him with a needle no problem. It was the idea of slicing that bothered her. Of killing.

Of murder.

"What do you want from us?" Alyssa demanded.

"From *you*?" He cocked his head to the side. "Absolutely nothing. You, Ms. Lockett, are merely a loose end waiting to be tied. Now, I believe—"

It all happened so fast; Rae blinked, and Patrick was on them. He grabbed Alyssa by the throat and tossed her into the wall. Rae swung her machete at him, all moral questions washed away by the desire to protect her friend.

Patrick caught the blade in his bare hand. It should have sliced right through. There should have been blood and missing fingers. Instead, a shock ran through Rae's arm, and she felt like she'd just driven her blade into stone.

Patrick grinned at her, a twisted leering expression very different from his usual practiced smile, his black eyes gleaming like an insect's. He gave a sharp twist of his hand and yanked the machete from Rae's grip, so hard her fingers went numb, then brought it down on his knee.

It shattered, as if it were an icicle and not solid steel.

Patrick dropped the handle. "*You*, on the other hand, Ms. Carter . . ." He stepped forward, his boot crunching on the broken pieces of metal. Rae backed up a step, fear clouding everything. She'd thought she'd seen his true self the last time they'd fought, but now she realized he'd been holding back.

Not anymore.

He took another step toward her, moving slowly and deliberately, a panther on the prowl. "You, I have plans for."

Rae realized she'd backed away in the wrong direction; there was nothing behind her but a blank expanse of wall, her only exit blocked by Patrick's advancing form.

Alyssa shrieked and charged him from the side, blood streaming down her face. His eyes widened as she slammed into him, and he stumbled sideways a step. Recovering quickly, he reached down and grabbed a handful of her hair, yanking her off him, then swung her around and into her mom's pod. She hit the glass with a sickening thunk and slid to the ground, dazed.

"No!" Rae ran at him, but he casually backhanded her, the blow catching her in the jaw and sending her flying backward. Pain exploded inside her head, light dancing across her vision in broken, jagged pieces, and she clutched at the nearest pod for support as the world wobbled around her. Inside the pod, Doctor Anderson twirled around, his blue eyes seeming to stare accusingly at her.

Rae blinked away the pain just as Patrick kicked open the door to the nearest empty pod and tossed Alyssa inside.

"Don't!" Rae launched herself after Alyssa, but it was too late; Patrick slammed the door shut before she could reach her.

Rae scrabbled at the sides as red liquid gushed from the top and bottom of the glass case, thick and gelatinous. Alyssa opened her mouth to scream, her hands pressing against the glass, but no sound escaped; the moment the liquid touched her she gave a small shudder, then froze.

"Alyssa!" Rae met her friend's terrified gaze and knew Alyssa could still see her. Then the awareness faded from her wide blue eyes, and she was gone. Nothing but a body, suspended in time.

The pod filled completely with fluid, and Alyssa drifted away from the glass, her long hair a tangle behind her, hands still splayed as if she wanted to keep fighting.

"Let her go!" Rae turned on Patrick.

"Or you'll what?" He raised an eyebrow.

Rae could feel the fury burning through her veins, but he was right. She had no weapons, no plan, no way to beat him. Not this time.

"*She* doesn't have to do anything," a cold voice called from behind them.

Patrick turned, and Rae noticed the way his shoulders stiffened, his jaw tightening. He appeared almost nervous as Vivienne stalked toward them.

Rae bit back a gasp as her friend came fully into view. Vivienne's eyes resembled Patrick's now, the black of her pupils swallowing all the brown and expanding outward until only a hint of white remained. Her lips curled up in a small, savage smile. "I'll take care of you myself," she said, those eyes fixed on Patrick.

"Ah. I see the transformation is nearly complete."

Vivienne made a show of inspecting her nails, which were longer now, hooked and deadly. Talons. And her teeth, when she bared them, looked sharper. Pointier.

"Which means there's no reason for us to fight." Patrick splayed his hands out, as if to show he had nothing to hide. "We're on the same side, you and I."

Vivienne tilted her head, regarding him, considering. Then she looked past him at Alyssa floating soundlessly in the pod, and her face darkened. "I don't think so."

Rae felt something in her chest tighten. Even though Vivienne was clearly no longer the one in control of her body, her loyalty toward her friends remained.

As if sensing her thoughts, Vivienne locked eyes with Rae. "Stay out of the way," Vivienne ordered. "This is *my* fight." And then she sprinted at Patrick, moving so fast she was a blur. At the last second she turned abruptly and ran up the wall instead, then leapt at him from the side, her hands outstretched, fingers curved like claws.

She slashed him across the face before he managed to catch her around the waist and toss her from him. Twisting in midair like a cat, she ricocheted off the nearest pod and slammed back into him, all flashing teeth and tearing nails, her ferocity and speed a match for Patrick's strength.

Rae hovered nearby, wanting to help but knowing she'd just be in the way. All she could do was watch and hope Vivienne could defeat Patrick. And that afterward, there'd be enough left of her friend to bring back.

Patrick snarled as he slammed Vivienne into the wall, then reared back, crying out in pain as she sank sharp teeth into his forearm. For a second the fighting stopped as they both regarded each other, breathing hard.

They seemed almost evenly matched; Patrick's chest heaved, blood trickling down his face and arms and neck. Vivienne's shirt was soaked in her own blood, her lip split and one eye swollen.

"This is hardly dignified," Patrick panted. "For either of us."

"I don't care about your dignity."

"Maybe not. But I might have something you *do* care about."

"If you're referring to Vivienne's friends, save your breath. I don't care about them."

"Don't you?" Patrick asked, wiping at the blood trickling down his chin.

She shook her head. "I promised her I'd get revenge for her, and for them. It was part of our final deal."

Rae went cold at the words "final deal."

"No," she whispered, hands over her mouth.

"I'm not referring to her friends," Patrick said. "I'm referring to a chance for you to leave. You belong on this planet about as much as I do."

Rae stared at him. Was he really planning on taking her friend away to some other alien planet?

"And why would *I* want that?" Vivienne asked.

"Because surely you don't want to remain in that form forever. You could be so much more. Do so much more."

Vivienne shrugged, and for a second she almost looked like her old human self. "I think you're just stalling. It's time to end this."

"I'm hardly—" Patrick cut off as Vivienne flew at him again. This time the fight was almost too fast for Rae to see. Blood spattered, limbs flailed, and the two of them thrashed back and forth, slamming into walls and pods, bouncing off the walls and ceiling. And then, just as abruptly as it had begun, it ended.

With Patrick kneeling on top of Vivienne, crushing her small form into the ground. "I gave you a chance," he growled, one of his knees on her throat as she struggled beneath him. "You were too stubborn to take it."

Rae looked around frantically, searching for a weapon, something, *anything*, she could use. The only thing she saw was the handle of the machete, lying discarded to the side. She lunged for it, scooped it up, and ran at Patrick, knowing he would hear her coming and not caring.

She raised her arm, prepared to bring her makeshift weapon crashing over his head—

He made a small noise and toppled sideways.

Rae's steps slowed. She stared at him, confused, before she noticed the dart sticking out of his neck. "What the . . ." She turned.

A group of people wearing modified Green On! hazmat suits were clustered at the end of the long hallway, the man in front holding a large pipe propped against his shoulder.

Rae looked down at Patrick lying motionless, Vivienne sitting up beside him, and wanted to cry in relief. They were saved. "Thank you—" she began, just as the Green On! man brought the pipe to his mouth and blew.

A dart sailed past, hitting Vivienne in the shoulder. She gasped, then sank back to the ground, her eyes fluttering closed.

Rae frowned. "Wait, she's not—" she began, just as the man blew a third dart.

This one aimed right at her.

34.
CADEN

Caden wasn't sure how long he and Nate lay there, bathed in the steam of the vents, quietly roasting. It felt like hours but was probably closer to twenty minutes. He was glad Nate didn't ask any more questions because he couldn't have explained why it was so important for them to hide from other humans. All he had was an instinctual feeling that it would be very bad if they were discovered here.

Over the years, he'd learned to follow his Price family intuition. Still, as sweat trickled, and then poured down his face, he began to wonder if maybe just this once he was overreacting. He glanced at Nate, whose sweaty face had gone beet red, his glasses completely fogged over. "Maybe we—" Caden started.

Footsteps crunched through the dirt nearby.

He went silent immediately, listening to the stomp of heavy

boots over rocks and loose soil. He pressed himself harder into the ground, letting his awareness drift outward. Flashes of emotion brushed against him, but they were all tangled and chaotic. Purpose, and grim determination, and fear, and a deep, simmering anger. And beneath that, a surge of triumph. They'd accomplished whatever it was that had sent them onto the ship.

He started to withdraw when he noticed a very familiar energy signature, although it was subdued, as if something had muffled the normally vibrant colors. Still, there was no mistaking who it was.

He gasped.

"What?" Nate whispered, flailing. "Did they find us? Are we in trouble?" He wiped frantically at his glasses, but they just fogged right up again. "These things," he grumbled, giving up and just shoving them back onto his nose.

"Shh," Caden hissed. "They haven't spotted us. Yet," he added pointedly.

"Sorry," Nate whispered.

"They're leaving, actually."

"That's good, right?"

"No," Caden said softly. "No, it's not." He took a deep breath. "They have Rae with them."

35.
RAE

Rae woke slowly, her head pounding, her thoughts sluggish and scattered. She was desperately thirsty, her tongue a thick piece of leather in her dry, dry mouth. And her eyes felt gritty, as if she hadn't slept for days.

She groaned and sat up, rubbing her temples as she looked around.

Nothing made sense.

She was in a small, dark room, on a small, hard cot. No, not a room, she realized as she stared at the wall in front of her. A wall made of narrowly spaced metal bars. A cage.

Immediately the events of the past few hours slammed into her, and she scrambled to her feet.

The world spun and dipped, and she had to grab on to the nearest bar for support.

"You need to ease into it," a familiar voice said. "The drugs are still in your system. Go too fast and you'll just pass out again."

Rae blinked until her vision cleared, then turned—slowly—toward the voice. On the other side of the bars sat Patrick on his own identical cot, in his own identical cage. He looked quite peaceful, sitting cross-legged, his hands in his lap. For the first time ever, he wasn't wearing an expensive black suit. Instead, he was dressed in a bright green jumpsuit. It made him look younger, somehow. Less in control.

"What are you doing here?" Rae croaked.

"Me? I'm a dangerous creature. This is obviously where I belong. Waiting to be inspected and, eventually, dissected in the name of human scientific exploration." He flashed one of his big smiles, and it was so at odds with his words that Rae felt even more off-balance, as if she'd woken in the middle of a dream.

"I'm sorry," Rae said, meaning it. She thought of the photo her dad had taken of Patrick in his true form, wearing a Green On! tag, his eyes beseeching as he stared out from between the bars of a cage. Even though he was evil, this—being caged again, treated like some kind of animal—must be like something out of a nightmare for him.

"I am too."

Still thinking of that photo, Rae studied Patrick and the way his handsome face contrasted with those alien-black eyes. As if his true self were staring out from behind a human mask.

"Can you look like anyone?" she asked, suddenly curious.

"Technically yes, but it's much easier if it's someone I've spent a lot of time with. This form, for instance, belonged to a young CIA agent who was given the task of studying me." He smirked. "I returned the favor."

"What, um, happened to him?"

"He died."

Rae's eyes widened. "H-how?"

"How do you think?" He stared back at her with his black eyes, his face expressionless. He'd taken that CIA agent's identity, absorbing his life details and turning them into his own cover story. Of course he'd have had to kill him first, or he'd never have been able to get away with it.

Just like that, all of Rae's pity shriveled up. This man, this *alien*, was a murderer who had used her and her friends, sending them into a dangerous alternate dimension. He'd shoved Alyssa into a pod and dangled the possibility of a cure in front of Vivienne without ever intending to give her one. Not to mention how often he'd pretended he would help *her* find her dad. If anyone deserved to be trapped in a nightmare, it was Patrick.

"Why bother keeping that form now?" she demanded. "You're caught. They already know who"—she stopped, corrected herself—"*what* you are."

"Ah, but that is precisely why, Ms. Carter. If I revert to my true form, my *alien* form, I become simply a *what* to them. As long as I appear human, however, there's still a chance that they will think of me as a *who* and will treat me more fairly."

Rae winced, not liking the truth of that statement, or what it said about human nature.

Patrick's lips curled in a small smile as if he knew he'd just made her uncomfortable.

Scowling, Rae turned her back on him. "Where are we, anyhow?"

Patrick sighed. "Ms. Carter, I know most adults have a tendency to underestimate the abilities of children. But I selected you specially for my internship for a reason. Use that brain of yours to figure out the answers yourself."

Rae didn't appreciate his patronizing tone. Still, she glanced around, this time taking in more of the details of her surroundings. Her cage was only about five feet by five feet. Aside from her cot, she had a scratchy wool blanket, and a plastic bucket in the corner that she was afraid was meant to be the toilet. The back wall and the ceiling were both rough-hewn rock, while the sides and front were comprised of those narrowly spaced iron bars.

To either side she could see more cages like hers stretching in a line. As far as she could tell, only hers and Patrick's were occupied. Through the bars in front, she could just make out a long, narrow hallway that appeared to have been carved into the rock as well. A series of lights were set into the corners, casting a dim yellow glow over everything.

Rae walked carefully toward the back wall, her legs wobbly, head still spinning. But as she pressed her hands against that cool rock, she felt like her mind was finally clearing.

Wherever she was, it was deep underground; she could feel the pressure now of being beneath tons of dirt and rocks. It was enough to make her breath hitch and her heart race, and she dug her fingers into the wall, trying to push the panic back. Obviously this place had been built to last. It wasn't going to collapse on her.

She thought of the secret underground labs of Green On! with their abundance of cameras, the walls made of one-way glass. This place was different. It felt older, less high-tech. It must have been built first, before the labs. Maybe before the town itself, for all she knew.

So not Green On! then. But something related.

All at once she remembered the articles she'd read when she first came to Whispering Pines. She'd been researching missing people and had stumbled onto a rumor that there was an old abandoned military base nearby. When she'd asked her friends about it, they had all been skeptical about its existence. But as she stood here now, that was the only explanation that seemed to make sense.

"You're getting it, aren't you?" Patrick said. "I can see the wheels of that brain of yours turning."

"This is the secret military base," Rae said slowly, testing her theory.

"Well, more of a bunker really. But yes."

She'd been right; it *did* exist. She should have known since she'd experienced firsthand how easy it was to discredit the truth, especially if someone powerful had a vested interest in making sure others didn't believe it.

Someone, or some*thing*. Like an organization. One that essentially ran the whole town.

Rae tapped the rock wall, thinking of Doctor Anderson, her former therapist, and his suspicions about Green On!. After his wife's death, he'd been convinced they were up to something nefarious, and had started snooping around with a camera. Maybe *that* was the reason he'd been stuffed into a pod despite being innocent of the eye-snatching crimes that had originally landed him in Green On! custody.

"Did Doctor Anderson find out about this place?" Rae asked. "Is that why you locked him in a pod?"

"Goodness no!" Patrick laughed. "Only Green On! cares about keeping this place a secret. If Doctor Anderson had discovered it, they probably would have just killed him."

"That's awful!"

"Not as awful as what they would have done before killing him." Patrick sounded way too cheerful for someone hinting at torture. It was another reminder of how he was not human . . . but then again, the humans were the ones who would have been doing the torturing. So who was worse?

Rae decided not to follow that line of questioning. At least, not right now. "Why, then?" she asked instead.

"Why what?"

"Why put him in a pod?"

"Besides the fact that he was snooping where he wasn't wanted?" Patrick shrugged. "Because he was irritating."

Rae stared at him. "You're joking."

"Am I?"

"You can't just stick people in pods because they annoy you!"

"I think you'll find, Ms. Carter, that I can." Patrick grimaced. "Or, at least, I could."

Rae could hardly believe what she was hearing. Still, it made a certain kind of sense. Even Ms. Lockett, for all her threats, was probably only put in a pod because she was irritating Patrick, too.

Rae doubted the vice principal would have been any actual danger to him or his plans. He just didn't want to be hassled by her.

Rae leaned her head back against the wall, wishing she knew what was going on in the town above her. Were Ava and Blake okay in the woods? Was Caden looking for her? And Alyssa . . .

Well. *She* was safe, at least. Or as safe as someone trapped in a pod on an alien ship could be. But Vivienne had been drugged as well, and she wasn't down here.

Which meant Green On! must have taken her somewhere else.

Rae could feel the fear building in her chest again, tightening around her lungs. She wanted her inhaler, but a quick search of her pockets revealed that they'd taken everything from her when they shoved her in here. Not even a penny remained. At least she was still in her school clothes; the thought of a bunch of strangers stripping her down and putting her into a Green On! jumpsuit made her skin crawl.

"How did Green On! know we were on the ship?" Rae asked. It seemed awfully convenient for them to show up just after she, Vivienne, and Alyssa did.

"My fault. They must have rigged the door with some kind of alarm system. When I opened it for you and your friends, I'm assuming the good people here in this bunker were notified. And the rest is as you know."

"You didn't notice an alarm?"

"I'm sorry to disappoint you, but occasionally things escape even *my* observation. Especially as I am not an engineer. I may have a basic understanding of the different technologies, but it is limited.

It was why I relied on Doctor Nguyen. And why I hoped to acquire your father's assistance as well."

"For what?"

"Isn't there a more important question you should be asking right now, Ms. Carter?"

"Like what?"

"We both know why *I* am locked up in here. But why are *you*?"

Rae hated to admit that Patrick was right about anything, but that was a good question. Why *was* she there, locked away in a cage? The last thing she remembered seeing were the group of Green On! employees coming toward her on the spaceship. She'd thought they were there to save her. Now she didn't know what to think.

Rae took a slow, careful breath. She needed to be like her dad. To think things through methodically. She was locked in a cage beside Patrick in a secret military bunker somewhere below Green On!. What possible reason could there be?

And all at once it came to her. She stifled a gasp, the sudden realization shooting through her. "My dad." She turned to look at Patrick. "He's here, isn't he?"

Patrick smiled. "And?" he prompted.

She thought of the Green On! employees she'd run into in the yurt, and the things they'd told her about her dad. And about her role in this town. *Honey, you were brought to Whispering Pines for one reason and one reason only: you're a hostage.*

"And . . . they need me as leverage for him." Her head swam, and this time it wasn't the drugs.

"Clever girl," Patrick said. "I knew you'd get there eventually."

36.
CADEN

Caden guessed they only had moments to spare. This was no time for a moral debate.

"It's just, first the bikes, and now this?" Nate said.

"Yes, yes," Caden snapped. "I've set you on a life of crime. Now get dressed already. Someone's bound to come by any minute."

Nate sighed and pulled on the hazmat suit. It was too big for his scrawny frame, the arms and legs bagging almost comically around him. "There's no way this is going to work," he muttered, zipping himself up. When he was done, he held out his arms. The sleeves flapped over his hands.

Caden had to concede Nate had a point; he looked ridiculous. A small child playing dress-up in his father's clothes. But as long as no one looked too closely, Caden's magic could disguise it. He rubbed absently at the ring on his thumb, which had gone still and cold ever since he'd left the vents behind. A hunk of lifeless metal once again. "Ready?" he asked.

"What about you?" Nate asked.

"We'll just have to hope no one really notices me." There had only been the one hazmat suit, so Caden was wearing a stolen Green On! lab coat. With his abilities, he could—maybe—convince people not to really see him. People tended to focus on the uniform more than anything else anyhow.

As Nate reluctantly picked up his helmet, Caden glanced around the small room, making sure he hadn't missed anything. It looked like a tiny supply closet, with extra work gloves, boots, and socks carefully tucked away beside a shelf of cleaning supplies. Nate's hazmat suit had been hung in the corner, half-hidden behind a giant stash of single-ply toilet paper, and the lab coat had been folded neatly on top of a stack of bottled waters. There were no weapons, no useful tools, nothing he could see that would help them find and rescue Rae.

This whole operation felt way too seat-of-the-pants for Caden's liking. But when he'd seen Rae slung unconscious over the shoulder of one of the Green On! employees, it was as if his logical brain had just short-circuited, his need to save her overriding all other considerations. For once, he understood exactly how she must feel whenever she dove into trouble.

Without a word, he and Nate had followed the group away from the ship, past the elevator, and over to another entrance hidden behind a fake shell of rock. There they'd waited for a count of thirty before going in after them. By then, Rae was out of sight.

But Caden could feel her presence now and knew he'd be able to find her. That wasn't the problem. The problem was all the other people he could feel there too. All of them on edge, their energy swirling in sharp, panicky spikes. The people who'd taken Rae from the ship had weapons on them, and he was pretty sure most of the others in here would be armed as well. Armed, and clearly prepared for some kind of trouble.

It was a dangerous combination.

"I'm ready," Nate said, his voice muffled. Wearing the suit and helmet, he actually did almost pass for another Green On! worker. Almost.

Caden resisted the urge to check the time on his phone, already knowing it was rapidly running out. But with luck, they'd be in and out of here quickly. They just had to track down Rae and then figure out how to get her out. Easy, right?

He shook his head at himself, already knowing it would be anything but.

"Let's go." He opened the door of the closet and stepped out into the cramped hallway of the bunker beyond.

37.
RAE

Rae shifted on her cot, mulling over what Patrick had just told her. Or *not* told her, but rather led her to understand. Her dad was here—here!—in this same building. And Green On! needed him to do something he didn't want to do. Which was why they were keeping her prisoner.

"It's monstrous, isn't it?" Patrick said. "To use one's own child against them in such a fashion."

"I thought *you* were planning on using me against him," Rae pointed out. "Wasn't that why you were going to stick me in a pod?"

Patrick spread his fingers. "True. But my motive was merely self-preservation."

"How so?"

"How do you think?"

She racked her brain for everything she actually knew about him. His entire goal so far seemed to circle around the spaceship and the energy it would take to power it. Did he need it to escape? But then, why were there so many other aliens on it? Aliens that seemed able to transform their habitat into something more hospitable to them. Unless his "self-preservation" wasn't just for him . . .

"Green On! is working for self-preservation, too," she said at last. "They want to find a clean source of renewable energy. It's necessary for our future." She might not agree with all their motives, but that part of their mission, at least, she understood.

"Maybe that was their goal at first. But as companies get bigger, and their higher-ups get a taste of wealth, of power, those initial altruistic goals have a way of . . . changing."

"Into what?"

"Usually? Corporate greed."

Rae swallowed, her throat burning as if she'd been drinking shards of glass, the air suddenly too hot and so humid. She fanned her face.

"Oh, you poor dear," a woman said. "Are you thirsty?"

Rae looked up, startled to see a tall, slender woman in a Green On! lab coat standing outside the bars of her cage.

The woman smiled at her, her face warm and round-cheeked, her curly red hair pulled back into a bun loose enough to allow a few tendrils to escape. That, plus very large blue eyes and a smattering of freckles across her nose made her appear soft and kind-hearted. She could have passed for a favorite kindergarten teacher.

Rae mistrusted her immediately.

"You must be Rae Carter," the woman said warmly. *Too* warmly. It was definitely an act. "I'm Clara Thomas." She waited, but Rae said nothing. "I'm the CEO of Green On!," Clara continued. "But then, I'm sure you already knew that." She gave a self-deprecating laugh. "The price of fame in a small town."

Rae shrugged. "If you say so."

Clara blinked, obviously a little taken aback by that. "Okay," she said slowly. "Well." She cleared her throat. "Someone should be here shortly with fresh water for you and some food. We don't exactly have a gourmet kitchen down here, but our granola bar selection is pretty amazing."

Patrick shifted in his cell, but Clara kept her eyes glued to Rae as if she wanted to pretend they were the only two people there.

"Great," Rae said flatly.

Clara sighed. "I know you must be a little . . . confused, waking up in a place like this. But we've only placed you here as a precautionary measure. For your own safety, of course."

"So you'll let me out?"

"Of course!" Clara said, her warm smile back in place.

"When?"

"Well, that depends on you, Rae." Clara's expression shifted, turning cool and calculating before she covered it up again with another warm smile. "How would you like to see your father again?"

Rae froze. Instinctively she glanced over at Patrick. He was staring down at his lap, but his words from before echoed through her mind as if he were whispering them in her ear right now. *We both know why I am locked up in here. But why are you?*

Clara frowned. "Rae? Did you hear me?"

If Green On! really was keeping her locked up here so they could force her dad to do . . . something, then whatever it was must be terrible, or they wouldn't require a hostage. So if Clara wanted to bring her to him now, it must mean they were ready to make him do it.

Rae wanted to see her dad more than anything, but not if it meant she'd be used against him.

She looked up into Clara's face and felt a brief surge of panic. She didn't know what to do. And then she thought of how Patrick had also told her adults tended to underestimate children. Maybe she could use that to her advantage.

She widened her eyes. "I'm sorry," she said. "Did you say my father? He's *here*?"

Clara's frown smoothed out. "Oh, yes. He's been helping us for a while now. Very important work. So important he hasn't had time to be in touch with anyone outside the organization. But he's getting tired, and we believe seeing you now would help him to feel more . . . motivated."

Motivated. If Rae needed any proof that Patrick was right in his suspicions, this was it. Her insides churned, and she felt a sudden desire to smack this woman in the face. How naive did she think Rae was? Instead, Rae plastered on a fake smile, using it to hide all her other emotions.

Just like Patrick.

He'd hidden his true intentions by pretending to be something else entirely. And now she was going to do the same. It felt strange, like for the first time she almost understood him.

"I would love to see my dad again," Rae said, her voice breaking a little. And this time it wasn't an act.

"That's so good to hear. Oh, and look, here's water and food."

A short man in a Green On! lab coat walked over carrying a plastic tray. On it sat a glass of cloudy water, three granola bars, and a small apple. Rae stared at the liquid in the glass, her mouth watering at the idea of it. Cloudy or no, she would have killed for a sip.

"I'm going to unlock your door now," Clara continued, her voice low and soothing. "You can eat and drink, and then, when you're done, we'll go. Okay?"

Rae nodded, still staring at that tray. As thirsty as she was, she knew there was no way she could trust that water. Or anything else they gave her.

Clara pulled a large metal key ring from her pocket and fit one of the keys into the lock. Rae stood to the side, her hands at her sides. She tried to appear innocent. Just a kid, waiting eagerly to see her dad.

Clara pulled the door open wide enough for the other worker to step through with the tray. Rae reached for it.

And then, in one sudden motion, she shoved the tray up and into the man's face. He reared back, surprised, crashing into Clara, who slipped onto her butt, and Rae's way out was clear. She darted out of the cage, yanking the keys free and then sprinting down the hall while Clara yelled for her.

The last thing Rae heard before she turned a corner was the sound of Patrick laughing.

38.
CADEN

Caden glanced at Nate striding along beside him, his face obscured by his helmet, shoulders hunched.

"Stand taller," Caden said. "Act like you belong here."

"I *don't* belong here," Nate said, but he stood a little straighter. He also started swinging his arms, looking for all the world like a very enthusiastic chicken.

"Maybe less elbows? You're walking down a hall, not sashaying to a party."

Nate muttered something under his breath, but his stride evened out, his arm swing almost natural. "Better?"

"Much."

Caden tried to follow his own advice—confident stride, straight back, projecting the image that he was exactly where he was supposed to be. Just like Aiden would have done.

Caden frowned at that thought. He'd decided to stop comparing himself to his brother, but old habits were hard to break. And right now, Aiden was exactly who he needed to be. He could have strolled down these halls without a disguise, and no one would have looked twice at him.

Caden pictured a web of energy wrapping him and Nate in a cocoon that whispered *we belong here* to anyone who looked at them. When he was done, he felt strangely exhausted, as if he'd just tried keeping up with Rae on a run.

"You okay?" Nate asked, glancing at him.

Caden nodded. "Just . . . worn out. Let's keep moving." He managed to keep the spell up as he and Nate moved through the maze of the bunker. It seemed to be working; they passed a few other Green On! employees, as well as several people wearing faded army fatigues, and no one gave them more than a cursory glance, despite the fact that Nate flinched every time.

The bunker itself felt dark, the lights overhead dim and flickery. It gave the impression of being dirty, even though Caden had yet to see even a single cobweb. The hallways were crowded with both old and new technology, jammed into racks along the walls, and random doors led off to what Caden assumed were sleep quarters or possibly other offices.

The deeper they went, the more Caden could feel a strange building surge in the energy around him as everyone's emotions ran higher, fuller. Excitement and fear, so often tangled together, and beneath that a steely sense of purpose. It made him uneasy; something was about to happen. Something big. It also made it a lot harder for him to pinpoint Rae's energy signature—one small personality buried under an avalanche of strong emotions.

"Something's wrong," he whispered to Nate.

"Obviously," Nate said. "This whole place is clearly bracing for an attack."

Caden nodded. "That's exactly what it feels like." Then he looked closer at Nate. "How could you tell?"

Nate snorted. "Haven't you seen the way everyone is rushing around us? You don't need magic to know they're all running scared." He started to hunch his shoulders, then caught himself. "Do you think the monsters from outside can get in here?"

"Maybe, but I don't think so," Caden said. He and Nate had managed to slip inside before the entrance door was locked, but he'd noticed how thick it was, plus all the bolts on the inside. This place was a fortress, meant to hold.

Up ahead the hallway branched in two directions. Down one end, he could feel a large gathering of people. It felt like the heart of the whole place, throbbing and beating with purpose. Down the other, he sensed—

Caden froze, his whole body going rigid.

"What?" Nate said. "Is it the monsters? You were wrong, weren't you, and now they're all pouring in, and we're trapped in here and—"

Caden grabbed Nate's arm, his fingers clenching around his suit. "Shh," he hissed. "It's not that. It's Vivienne."

"What about her?"

Caden closed his eyes, double checking. Yes, it was definitely her. He opened his eyes and smiled. "She's here too."

"She is? Really? We found her?" Nate sounded excited and a little nervous. "I was afraid we wouldn't. Not before you had to . . . you know."

Caden nodded. "I was afraid of that, too."

"Well, where is she?"

"Down here." Caden led Nate toward Vivienne, trying to keep his pace brisk, but not *too* brisk. Nothing that would attract attention as they passed people all rushing in the opposite direction.

The hall seemed to stretch on forever, but finally Caden could see where it ended in a simple metal door. Two men dressed in army fatigues stood in front of it, both of them armed.

Caden's steps slowed, then stopped. He could try to use his powers on them, convince them to leave, but he wasn't sure it would work. In the past, he'd just nudged people along on a path they were already considering. Even Ava; part of her hadn't wanted to leave without Rae, but another part had known she needed to help Blake get to safety.

One of the soldiers eyed Caden and Nate, his jaw tightening. Caden could feel a cloud of suspicion growing around him. "What are you—" the soldier started, before a burst of static interrupted him. He scowled down at his walkie-talkie, then pulled it off his belt. "Yes?"

Another burst of static. Then a string of words. Caden could only catch a few of them. "Escaped," and "all hands," and "immediately."

"Both of us?" the soldier said, glancing at his companion.

The other soldier shrugged. "All hands means everyone. Let's go."

Caden and Nate stood to the side as the soldiers strode past them, leaving the door unguarded.

"Well, that was convenient," Nate said.

"Wasn't it, though?" Caden frowned. He didn't like it. Anything that was too easy was not to be trusted. Hesitantly, he walked toward the door, then reached for the doorknob. It turned, the door falling open. He exchanged a look with Nate before the two of them slipped inside, closing the door behind them.

Caden felt like he'd just stepped inside a cave, the air in here colder than out in the hall, and drier, somehow. The dim yellow lights of the rest of the bunker weren't present. Only a soft green glow coming from farther back in the room.

Caden walked toward it, drawn like a moth to a porch light even as his instincts shrieked at him to run, to turn, to go back. As he got closer, he saw that the glow came from a carved pillar nearly as wide as he was, and so tall it stretched almost to the ceiling. He squinted at it, trying to make out the shapes that had been etched into its surface, but they seemed to change and move as he looked. Faces—horrible and distorted—with long pointed teeth. And eyes everywhere. So many eyes. Watching him. Waiting for him. Wanting him to reach out and lay his hand against them. Craving the warmth of his skin.

He started to reach toward it.

Nate punched him in the shoulder.

"Ouch!" Caden dropped his arm. "What was that for?"

"You were about to touch a creepy unknown alien artifact! Have you seen any sci-fi horror movies at all? That is a Very. Bad. Idea."

Caden blinked, then looked back at the pillar, his skin crawling with the realization of how close he'd come. "I . . . didn't realize what I was doing. Thanks, Nate."

"You're welcome."

Caden glanced at Nate. "You weren't tempted to touch it?"

"Heck no!"

"You didn't feel it calling to you?"

"I keep a healthy dose of fear around me at all times. It protects me from foolish compulsions."

Caden smiled. "Well. Thanks again." He looked past the pillar, noticing now the glow of another behind it, and behind that as well. A line of pillars stretching back into the room. He shoved his hands deep into the pockets of his borrowed lab coat and gave the pillars a wide berth as he walked along, counting them. Eight in total.

No, he realized as he drew level with the eighth. There was a ninth pillar behind it. Only this one didn't glow, its surface dark and almost dusty-looking, as if it had started to crumble.

He heard a choked scream and looked up. "Nate?"

No response.

Caden frowned, turning to look back across the room. "Nate?" he tried again. Still no response.

Nate was gone.

39.
RAE

Rae felt as if she'd traveled back in time. Back to her personal nightmare, when she'd been running through a cabin in the woods, chased by a monster.

Ready or not . . . here I come.

She turned another corner, the lights dim around her, the halls cramped and claustrophobic. She could still hear shouting, but it was farther behind now. It wouldn't last; Clara would call for backup. They'd be able to catch her eventually. Her only real option was to hide.

As she ran, she could feel the weight of the stolen keys in her hand. Maybe they would be useful. But she didn't know the layout of this place, didn't know if she was running deeper into the middle, or out toward the edges. All she knew was that, somewhere nearby, her father was being held captive. And there was no way she'd be leaving until she found him.

She sprinted down yet another identical narrow hallway until movement at the other end sent her diving toward a cart full of green cloth parked against the wall. She jumped in headfirst, wriggling in until the material covered her. Immediately, the smell hit her. The metallic tang of old blood, acrid chemicals, and beneath those, sour, stinky body odor. This was a pile of dirty lab coats.

Rae tried breathing shallowly through her mouth and forced herself not to move as footsteps hurried past her hiding place. She waited until the sounds of people had faded, then counted silently to twenty before finally sitting up and pushing the coats away. Sucking in a lungful of clean air, she climbed out of the cart and continued down the hall.

She needed to find her dad, but the whole bunker was built like a labyrinth. It was almost as if every time they needed more space, the builders had just created a new hall or corridor. And most of those halls seemed cramped, with random equipment and the occasional cart stacked along the walls as stuff spilled out from rooms too small to hold it all.

Twice more Rae had to hide inside a cart or behind a stack of old computer monitors as she slowly made her way through the bunker, until finally she reached a hall that ended in a door guarded by three people, all wearing military fatigues and carrying weapons.

Rae ducked back around the corner, heart thumping, but no one yelled out for her. She took a deep breath, let it out, then peeked back.

The guards weren't even really looking at anything, just standing around talking. Even from here, Rae could tell they were nervous; one of them jiggled his foot, and another kept dropping her hand to her weapon as if seeking reassurance that it was still there. It made Rae wonder if they were bracing themselves for an invasion here, too. But then wasn't that the whole purpose of this group? To fight against invasions like this?

Rae eyed the door behind them. It looked like all the other doors she had passed on her way here, except that it was guarded. That was promising.

Her dad was probably being held somewhere under guard . . .

The door suddenly flew open. All three guards immediately stood at attention as Rae ducked back out of sight. She could hear a man speaking, and then a burst of static, followed by a woman's muffled voice. Then the sound of footsteps moving toward her.

Rae looked up and down the hall. There was nothing to hide behind here, but a few feet away stood another door. She rushed to it and turned the knob. Locked. Panicking, Rae spared one quick glance at the keys she'd stolen, but there were too many of them cluttering the ring; she'd never choose the right one in time. She sprinted to the next door instead. Heart hammering, she twisted the knob.

It opened.

Rae hurriedly slipped inside and shut the door quietly behind her, hardly daring to breathe as she waited. Seconds turned into minutes, and no one came after her.

"Whew," she muttered, glancing back at the room. It was piled with machinery, some of it beeping, others doing nothing at all that she could see. Turning her back on it, she slipped out of the room and crept back to the end of the hall. This time when she risked a glance around the corner, the next hall was empty, the door unguarded.

Rae hesitated for just a second, and then she ran to the door.

It was unlocked, the knob turning easily in her hand. Feeling a little like she was walking into a trap, she stepped inside.

The room was bigger than she expected, with a large operating table in the middle. She approached it, her apprehension battling with her curiosity. A body was splayed across the top. But not a human one.

Rae moved closer, unable to look away from the thing on the table. Its arms and legs were extended and held in place with straps, and its chest had been cut open, the skin peeled back, the organs removed. But its face . . .

Rae swallowed hard, staring into those flat, glossy eyes. Eyes that looked exactly like the eyes of the alien in her dad's photo. Like Patrick's real eyes.

She turned away, suddenly feeling sick. It was impossible to know how long ago this alien died. It might have been recently, or years ago, its body preserved for the right moment. Just as it was impossible to know what had killed it: Green On!, or something else. But she wondered if Patrick knew it was in here, being dissected. He'd said this was his eventual fate too.

Rae knew she shouldn't care, but, strangely, she did.

Clank!

She spun toward the noise.

Clank! Clank!

Along the wall a series of machines beeped, their monitors all lit up with charts and numbers beside other pieces of equipment flashing multi-colored lights. Rae drifted past them, peering into the farthest corner of the room, where something else moved, its body pale in the dim lighting.

She froze as the details filtered in past her shock.

A monster, humanoid, only with limbs too long and skinny, almost spiderlike, its torso and face covered in deep purple scars that wrapped around in bands as if a large tentacle had torn into them. And its eyes . . . where they should have been, there was nothing but smooth skin. Still, somehow it was able to look at her. To *recognize* her.

Just as she recognized it.

"Hello, Ivan," she whispered.

40.
CADEN

How could Nate be gone? There was nowhere to go! Caden's mind raced as he dashed around the pillars to the other side of the room.

Empty.

"Nate!" He was being louder than he should be, but panic robbed him of his caution. Nate was gone, and he was alone in a room full of creepy alien pillars, and—

Thunk!

He whipped around. A door Caden hadn't noticed was open on the side of the room. Nate popped his head out from behind it, his helmet off, hair messy and eyes wide. "She's in here," he gasped.

"What? Who? Where?"

"Vivienne! And . . . she's not alone."

Caden stared at his friend. "What do you mean?"

Nate's mouth formed a thin, grim line. "You'll have to see for yourself."

Caden hesitated, then walked over, sliding through the door and into the attached room. It resembled the room he'd just left—long and narrow, and full of shadows. But in place of glowing pillars, nine small square screens lit up the side of the room. He moved toward the closest screen. It was covered in numbers and beeped regularly, like a hospital monitor. And beside it—

"Vivienne," he gasped, staring at the small still figure. She looked more like a doll than a person, her body frozen, eyes closed. She was strapped upright to a metal board, her arms, legs, and torso covered in wires that connected to a slim metal canister set on the ground next to her.

He started to reach toward her, then stopped himself, unsure if touching her would be a good idea. Instead, he waved his hand in front of her face.

No response. Not even an eye flicker.

Frowning, he reluctantly tore his gaze from her, turning instead to the next screen. Beside it stood another kid, also strapped to a board, his arms and legs pinned in place. The glow of the screen cast eerie shadows across his oddly distorted face—the wide-open mouth, the flared nostrils, and the deep pits where eyes should have been.

Caden's heart beat faster as he studied that face, recognizing Jeremy Bentley, an eighth grader who used to go out with Alyssa, until Ivan the Unseeing had torn his eyes from his face and turned him into this zombified shell.

"Why are you here?" Caden whispered. The last he'd heard, all eight victims of the Unseeing were being held in one of Green On!'s underground labs. Then he pictured what those labs must look like now, overrun by aliens, and was grateful that someone had brought them all here.

Ever since Caden had brushed against their spirits while he was in the Other Place, he believed that he'd be able to cure them. Their eyes were gone forever, but their souls remained in reach.

Caden turned from Jeremy to study the next victim, a girl with long, matted dark hair and a gaunt face. Her jaw moved slowly back and forth as if she were chewing on something, and Caden wondered if she was aware of his presence. He couldn't tell; when he mentally tried to feel for her, there was nothing.

"Brandi Jensen," Nate said sadly. "Probably the kindest girl in our class."

Caden nodded. Brandi had been his neighbor and was one of the few kids in his school who had always been consistently nice to him, even after the rumors started. Looking into her mutilated face now, he remembered the horrible moment when she'd stumbled from the trees near his house, her eyes gone. How she'd pointed at Rae. *Lovely eyes . . .*

He and Rae had started spending more time together soon after that as they worked to solve the mystery of the serial eye-snatcher. Would they still have become friends if there were no Unseeing, no victims, no threats? Caden stared into the pits of Brandi's eyes and wasn't sure. Then he pictured Rae. Not her face, but her essence: smart, determined, curious. The kind of person who made up her own mind about things, who wouldn't have discounted him on hearsay alone, and he knew they would have found their way to each other eventually.

"I won't forget about you," he promised Brandi, resolving to help her and the others if he survived this night.

Caden started to turn away when he heard the raised voices of two women arguing in the room next door. He and Nate exchanged one quick, panicky glance, and then they both dove behind the last of the Unseeing victims, tucking themselves into the shadows in the corner of the room. Caden drew on his powers, wrapping a web of energy around them, a silent whisper that would tell anyone who looked this way not to see them.

"—promised me you'd help her if I delivered the hosts," someone was saying. "Do you have any idea what I went through to get them here?" With a start, Caden realized he recognized her. Mrs. Matsuoka.

"Why is this door ajar?" the other woman's voice demanded.

"How should I know?" Mrs. Matsuoka said. "Clearly I know nothing."

Caden shrank back into the shadows, listening to footsteps as Mrs. Matsuoka and her companion walked into their room. He tried breathing as quietly as possible, keeping his body still. Nate's own breathing seemed too loud next to him, the rustling of his hazmat suit advertising any slight movement. Caden had to hope his powers would be enough to disguise all that.

"Audrey," the mystery woman sighed. "I have every intention of making good on my promise."

"When?" Mrs. Matsuoka demanded.

Caden risked a glance up. Vivienne's mom looked terrible, nothing like the sophisticated, always-put-together woman he'd seen before. Her stern face was etched with more wrinkles than her lab coat, and there was no mistaking the blood spattered against the green of it or her limp as she walked over to gaze at her daughter.

"Just as soon as I can," the other woman said. Caden shifted his gaze to her, then froze, hit with another burst of recognition. This woman looked fresh, especially next to Mrs. Matsuoka, her lab coat mostly clean and unwrinkled, her face round-cheeked and healthy. Her red hair was pulled back into a loose bun, several strands escaping to curl around her face. A face that he'd seen mere hours earlier in their school's auditorium.

Clara Thomas. The CEO of Green On!.

The fact that Mrs. Matsuoka was talking to her so sharply would have been surprising in any other situation. But now, with her daughter held in some weird stasis and aliens taking over their town, Caden supposed that she no longer cared much about the future of her current job.

Just behind Clara stood two more Green On! employees, both of them wearing the same kind of hazmat suit that Nate was wearing, the only difference being that theirs actually fit them.

"And when will that be?" Mrs. Matsuoka asked, turning away from Vivienne to glare at her boss. "Because I am getting sick of false promises and no timelines."

"We need a ninth host—"

"Why the obsession with getting nine? There were only eight victims! As you well know."

"And if we want to transfer the one currently inhabiting your daughter, we'll need one more," Clara continued, talking over her. "I have the perfect host in mind, but unfortunately she's been temporarily . . . misplaced."

Caden felt Mrs. Matsuoka's guilt and alarm swirling around her. "Who?" she asked.

"Does it really matter? You want your daughter back. I suggest you not ask too many questions."

There was a shuffling noise and a burst of static. Caden glanced at Nate crouching beside him, his mouth hanging open, eyes wide, obviously listening intently as well.

"We need guards posted at Room 112B," Clara said. Another burst of static, and a garbled response. "Yes, I think it's time to start the transfer." Another pause, then, "Oh, I'll find her. Don't you worry about that. Over and out."

She dropped the walkie-talkie back into her pocket. "We'll begin with one at a time. This one, I think." She pointed at the boy next to Vivienne, and the two employees with her scurried forward to unhook Jeremy from his canister and wheel him away. They disappeared out of the room, the rattling of their cart echoing back through the walls.

"You're really going to do it, then," Mrs. Matsuoka said once they'd gone. "You're not going to try to save them?"

"They are beyond saving. We've tried everything we know of. But if this works, at least they'll still be useful."

"Useful? They're children."

"They're weapons. And they'll be worth a lot of money. Don't get soft on me now, Audrey. After all, we could never have gotten them here without your help. You are as much a part of this as any of us."

"I know," Mrs. Matsuoka said. "And I will carry that burden to my grave." There was so much sorrow in her voice that Caden didn't need any of his abilities to understand exactly how she was feeling. She was quiet a minute before she asked, "Will it hurt them?"

"No," Clara said, a little too quickly to be convincing. "They won't feel a thing." She patted Mrs. Matsuoka on the shoulder with false reassurance, then left.

Mrs. Matsuoka stayed behind for a few extra moments, staring at her daughter. Very carefully, she reached down and brushed a long strand of black hair off Vivienne's forehead, then turned to face the remaining kids. "I'm sorry," she said in a small voice. She took a breath like she wanted to say more, but no words came. Shaking her head, she turned and limped from the room.

Caden counted silently to ten before standing and stretching, relieving his aching back and trembling legs.

"What do you think they're planning on doing?" Nate whispered.

Caden looked at the remaining kids. They must be the hosts Clara was referring to. But hosts for what?

"I don't—" He stopped as a sudden memory came to him. Vivienne, telling him about how she'd been cursed after touching a pillar hidden deep underground. One covered in carvings. *There were faces with lots of teeth, long and gleaming. And eyes. So many eyes.*

He pictured the glowing pillars in the room next to them, and knew the truth: they weren't artifacts at all but alien embryos trapped behind rock.

And Green On! was planning on setting them free.

41.
RAE

Rae felt as if all the oxygen in the room had vanished. She couldn't breathe, couldn't move, could only stand there staring at the one who had first taught her that monsters—actual, literal, nightmarish creatures—were real.

"I *see* you're still afraid of me," Ivan said, his voice raspier than she remembered. His lips pulled back into a wide smile, displaying a mouth full of shattered teeth. "Thank you for that."

Rae stared at those teeth, the jagged edges of them, the holes where several had been knocked loose, and some of her fear lessened. She studied the scars again—thick purplish bands covering parts of his face, his neck, his torso, the edges ridged and painful-looking. He had been injured. Grievously so.

It made sense; the last time she'd seen Ivan had been when she'd kicked him into the rift, sending him back to the Other Place where things with tentacles had been waiting to feast on him. She remembered seeing them surround him, hearing him scream . . .

"How are you still alive?" she whispered.

"You can thank your friends here for that." He tapped something on his chest, and now Rae noticed the mass of wires attached to him, half-camouflaged by all the scar tissue. They connected to a slim metal canister set beside him, almost like something a scuba diver would wear on their back, only it also had a screen and a bunch of flashing, beeping lights and buttons.

"But *why* are they keeping you alive?" Rae asked.

"Because they do not understand." He made a sound, a sort of gasping wheeze. After a few seconds, Rae realized it was laughter. "They think they can control me. And through me, my progeny."

"Your . . . progeny?"

His lips pulled up again in that horrible smile, made worse by the broken teeth, the bleeding gums. "The children I left behind. The ones I created."

Rae thought of the Unseeing victims—the other kids who had lost their eyes to Ivan. Their eyes, and possibly their minds as well, all of them reduced to an almost zombified state of existence. "They brought you out of the Other Place because they thought you could heal your victims?"

Another laugh, this one more ragged. "To *heal*? I forgot how naive you were. Green On! expended a lot of effort to track me down and drag me out. Several of their own people died in the process. And you think they went through all that to help a bunch of worthless children?" He shook his head. "You poor girl. You have no idea who you're dealing with here. No, they want to use my 'victims,' turn them into weapons."

Rae frowned, not understanding. "Why?"

"For money, of course. Your government would pay a lot for the perfect assassins."

"But they're just children."

"Ah, they *were* just children. Now, thanks to me, they are perfect child-sized husks, ready to be filled."

"Filled with what?" Rae asked, dread curdling in her stomach.

Ivan's smile widened. "Stick around, and you'll find out. Because they still want a ninth host." His long fingers twitched. "And it was always meant to be you."

Rae had to get out of here. She turned and ran at the door, yanking it open and practically throwing herself out into the hall. She slammed the door behind her and turned to run—

And crashed right into a Green On! employee, his arm trapping hers at her sides, his other hand clamping over her mouth.

42.
CADEN

I t's me," Caden said quickly, feeling Rae's terror mounting.

Rae stopped struggling and gazed up at him, her eyes wide.

Carefully he removed his hand. "Sorry," he said. "I didn't want you to scream—oof!"

Rae threw her arms around him, hugging him so tightly his lungs ached. He wrapped his arms around her, too. She smelled like dirt and blood, and he didn't care at all. He was just so relieved to have found her again.

"Hey, feeling a little left out here," Nate said.

Rae pulled away from Caden and held out an arm to Nate, pulling him into their hug, his bony shoulders digging into Caden, making the whole experience slightly less pleasant.

"Better?" Rae asked, her voice muffled.

"Not really," Nate wheezed. "Now I'm feeling a little suffocated."

Rae let them both go. "You are hard to please, you know that?" She looked at them, her eyes glistening. "I don't know how you're here right now, and I don't even care. I'm just . . . I'm so glad."

"We can tell you everything on the way out," Caden said, glancing nervously down the hall. "But we need to hurry."

"Way out?" Rae shook her head. "I'm not leaving yet."

Caden frowned. "We have to go."

"There's still Vivienne," Nate said. "And the others."

"I know," Caden said. "And I'm hoping they'll be safe enough here, inside the bunker. It should protect anyone within its walls from the blast. After we've cleared the woods, we can figure out how to help them. But right now, we really have to leave."

"The blast? The woods?" Rae looked between them. "What is going on?"

"Caden needs to blow up the forest in order to save the town," Nate said. "It's much more technical than that, which usually I'm all about, but right now I'd actually rather skip the details and just get out of here. This place is creeping me out."

"I can't leave," Rae said again.

"Why not?" Caden asked.

Rae's brown eyes were serious, her jaw set. "They're holding my dad captive somewhere in this place. And I'm not going anywhere until I find him."

"Your dad is here?" Caden said. "You're sure?"

She nodded. And just like that, Caden knew they were stuck here. He couldn't even argue; he'd promised her that he'd help her find her dad. Now it was time to pay up.

"Where?" Nate asked.

Rae chewed her lip, suddenly looking uncertain. "I don't know," she admitted. "But they have something they need him to do right now, so I'm assuming he'll be wherever the action is. Is there a command center here? Some kind of central gathering point?"

"I believe so," Caden said, remembering the sense he'd gotten of a large gathering of people down the hall from where they were keeping Vivienne. Rae's face filled with hope, and he sighed and scrubbed a hand through his hair. They really, really didn't have time for this.

Caden looked at Rae, and then at Nate beside her. Aiden had told him that Nate would be safe from the blast as long as he was touching Caden when it happened. If he were telling the truth, then Rae should be safe enough with him, too. Caden wanted to trust his brother. But . . . he couldn't. He knew Aiden too well.

If Caden wanted to make sure his friends were safe, he needed to get them out of the woods first before he destroyed the vent. Which meant they had to leave. Now.

"Do you think you could find it?" Rae asked, staring at him with those big brown eyes. He could feel her hope vibrating around her, as fragile as a moth's wings, and below it a certainty that if anyone could help her, it would be him.

And despite his better judgment, he nodded. "I think so."

Rae gave him a big smile. The kind that lit up her entire face and made his chest ache. And even though he knew this whole thing was a bad idea, he suddenly felt better about agreeing to it.

"I'm assuming this place will be crawling with Green On!

employees and soldiers," Nate said. "So . . . how are we going to free your dad? We can't just waltz in there and escort him out."

Rae's smile vanished, replaced by a look Caden knew all too well. A look he didn't like at all. "Can't we, though?" she murmured.

"You have a plan, don't you?" he said.

"I do." She tugged on the end of her ponytail, a flicker of unease rippling through her. "But I don't think you'll like it."

43.
RAE

Rae was more nervous than she thought she'd be as she was marched toward the command center, Nate and Caden walking on either side of her like a pair of prison guards.

This plan was a terrible idea.

Not since she'd broken into Doctor Anderson's house had she attempted something so daring with so little forethought. Only this time, there was much more at stake.

"Almost there," her companion said from behind her in a disturbingly familiar voice.

Rae couldn't help a quick glance back, shuddering slightly. "I wish you didn't look like that."

"Feels like you're traveling with a ghost, doesn't it?"

Rae didn't want to think too hard about that, so she just nodded.

"It's weird for me, too. Ready to go in?"

"No," Rae said. But it didn't matter, because the hallway opened up, and there was the main room.

Rae got the impression of it being both huge and cramped at the same time. Its ceiling hung low, covered in fluorescent lighting that cast weird shadows. Machines lined all the walls, many of them filled with flickering screens and flashing buttons that reminded Rae of the room she'd seen with the dissected alien. Only here, at least a dozen people in Green On! lab coats hovered around all the equipment like flies at a picnic, furiously scribbling notes and checking tablets. She was so distracted by all the beeping, flashing, note-scribbling action that it took her a few seconds to notice the mostly cleared table in the middle of the room.

And the bearded, bespectacled man sitting at it.

Her breath caught as she looked at him. And the past year melted away . . .

The memory surrounded her. Her dad standing in her bedroom doorway, his expression uncertain in a way it never used to be. Not with her. *"Hey there, sugar cube. Got time for your old man?"*

She'd been furious with him, she remembered. So angry that she had pretended not to hear him, instead flipping through a book.

"Rae. I'm sorry. Really."

She'd sighed and looked up. And he'd looked so tired, his face drawn with bags under his eyes, that some of her anger vanished. *"You promised we'd go hiking today."* She knew she sounded pouty and childish, but she couldn't help it. Ever since her dad had begun working on Project Gray Bird, she barely saw him. He left for work before the sun came up and didn't get home most evenings until long after dark. Now he was working weekends, too. It felt like she was losing her dad, and she hated it.

"*I know. I did promise. But I had to work. It was last minute, but important.*" He'd walked into her room, then sat on the bed beside her. "*Where do you want to hike next time?*"

"*You mean when you're not busy?*"

He'd managed a small smile. "*I won't be busy forever. It only feels that way. But things are finally starting to wrap up on my project. It'll be done soon, and then we'll have plenty of time for hiking.*"

"*Really?*"

"*Really. A couple more weeks, tops.*"

Rae had closed her book, releasing the rest of her anger. She could never stay mad at her dad for long. "*I want to go someplace new. And challenging. Lots of vert.*"

"*Vert, huh?*" he'd laughed. "*Okay, little mountain goat. I'm sure we can find something that fits those requirements.*"

And as he gave her a small, sideways hug, she'd been confident that, in a couple more weeks, there would be no more long work nights. No more waiting around for him only to have him no-show. No more broken promises.

She would have her dad back again.

Instead, a few weeks later, he vanished.

Rae blinked away the memory, staring now at the man in front of her. He didn't match the one she remembered. That man had been large and robust, with thick, dark hair and a quick smile. This man was a shadow, his hair gray, his beard patchy and white, his face lined like old paper. His shoulders had gone thin, almost birdlike, and they slumped inward, and his hands, as he turned something in them, trembled.

Still, the expression on his face was so achingly familiar, his thick eyebrows drawn together in his classic look of concerned concentration. The one he wore when he was so deep in thought that the rest of the world vanished around him. Her mom used to joke that the house could be on fire and he wouldn't notice when he was in that mode.

Her dad. Sitting here, in this place.

Rae squeezed her eyes shut, but the tears still leaked through, hot and furious. She'd found him again. Part of her had thought it would never happen. That maybe he was dead. Despite all her protests, her determination to keep looking, she'd almost resigned herself to never seeing him again.

And now he was here.

She wanted to spring up and run to him, and it took all her willpower to stay still. To wait. Because he wasn't alone. Soldiers surrounded him, stationed near the table and around the room. And hovering over him like an impatient vulture was Clara.

Rae watched her mouth move as she said something to him, but over the sounds of the other scientists, the buzzing machines, and the clinking of metal, Rae couldn't hear her.

"What's this?" a soldier asked, finally noticing them.

"A prisoner, obviously," Rae's companion said.

The soldier's eyes widened.

Rae knew it wasn't going to work, but then a strange look

crossed the woman's face, and she nodded, her eyes going slightly vague as she waved them through.

Rae shifted uneasily. Caden had said he would use his powers to help as much as he could. Was this his doing? Could he control a person's thoughts now? A spark of fear burst inside her, but she did her best to smother it. For all she knew, he'd be able to feel that, too. To feel it, and then remove it, changing her.

No. She trusted him. He wouldn't do that. Not to her.

Then they were behind her dad, close enough to hear without being in his or Clara's direct line of sight, and all of Rae's other concerns fell away.

"—need you to cooperate one final time," Clara was saying. "This is the last thing we will ask of you."

Her dad snorted. "As if I believe that."

"This is what we've been working toward this whole time! What *you've* been working toward. All your research has led to this moment. Don't you want to see what it would look like? To test your knowledge?"

"Not really."

Rae almost stepped back in shock. Her dad had always been about following a thread all the way through to the end. She couldn't imagine him not wanting to see what his research would lead to. This strange lack of curiosity was worse than his changed physical appearance; it made Rae worry that something inside him had been broken.

"And why not?" Clara demanded furiously. "This could change everything!"

"Like I keep telling you, it isn't safe. If I succeed in powering that ship up, it could trigger an explosion that would take out the entire town. *And* all the people in it."

The ship? Rae froze. It made sense; her dad had been part of Operation Gray Bird back in California where he'd studied a spaceship. His job had been to attempt to reverse-engineer the fuel source. Maybe he'd succeeded in that before he'd tried to leave the program.

Before he'd been kidnapped.

"It didn't before," Clara said. "That *friend* of yours powered up the ship, and nothing happened."

"Because *he* knew what he was doing; he didn't bring it to full power. That was just a taste."

"And look what it did!" Clara spread her arms, indicating the machines all around them. "All these devices lit up. The knowledge we've gained from that brief moment could keep us learning for a hundred years."

"Then be satisfied with that!" Rae's dad slammed the metal box he'd been studying down on the table with a sharp crack that made Clara wince. "Be satisfied," he continued in a softer voice, "and leave me in peace. There's nothing you can do to me to make me change my mind. I won't risk the people of this town. I won't risk my family."

"Your family," Clara said, her own voice equally soft. "And how safe do you think they are?"

Rae saw her dad stiffen. "Is that a threat?"

"I didn't want to have to resort to this, but . . . we have a special guest here with us today. Your youngest child. Rae."

He shook his head. "I don't believe you. If she were here, you'd have dragged her out already."

Clara put a hand on his shoulder, her knuckles white. "Perhaps I've just been waiting for the right time." She let him go, then took a step back, then another, moving close enough that Rae caught a glimpse of her face, twisted in determined fury, before the woman turned and strode from the room.

Rae watched her dad massaging his shoulder. He sighed and dropped his hand, his fingers resting on the tabletop, his back hunching. He looked old and defeated.

"Now, I think."

Rae glanced at her companion: a short, slender woman, her black hair hanging loose around her shoulders, her lab coat spotless.

Doctor Nguyen smiled back at her. "It's showtime."

44.
CADEN

Caden hovered just behind Rae. No one looked twice at him. They were all too focused on their work, and on a woman's too-loud conversation with a man who must be Rae's dad in the middle of the room. It didn't hurt that Caden was using his powers, gently nudging everyone to look elsewhere, to ignore him and the rest of his group.

Rae's dad leapt to his feet. "No! No!" He shook his head violently.

"Yes," the woman beside Rae said, tossing her black hair back over her shoulders, her face so familiar. Doctor Nguyen's face. Even knowing it was a lie, Caden couldn't detect a difference between this woman and the one he'd known.

"Dad." Rae's voice broke, her eyes full of tears.

Her dad stopped shaking his head and looked at her, and

Caden was hit with a wave of emotion—love, fierce and protective. An overwhelming joy at seeing his daughter again. And beneath all of that, a deep, dark despair, wrapped around the knowledge that he would have to make a terrible choice. One that could cost him everything.

Caden managed to pull his awareness free, but he was gasping, his insides raw as if they had been scraped clean. A nearby soldier glanced at him, frowning slightly.

Don't notice me, Caden thought at him, but it wasn't as effective as it should have been. The soldier did turn away eventually, but with a look that said Caden hadn't been forgotten.

Caden sagged against the wall behind him, feeling suddenly exhausted. How much magic had he been using this whole time, first in the forest and then in this bunker? More than he'd thought, he realized. He was dangerously close to being drained.

"How could you?" Rae's dad demanded of Doctor Nguyen. "You promised me you'd keep my family safe! You promised . . ."

"I'm sorry, Chris," she said. "I had no choice."

"There's always a choice. You've just made the wrong one. Again." He shook his head, his lip curling. "I thought you'd learned, but you've always been their creature, haven't you?"

Doctor Nguyen shrugged. "Maybe so. Now, *you* have a choice to make. Will you come with me now, or—"

"I'm not going anywhere! You know as well as I do that the energy source on those ships is unreliable at best. And this one . . . I believe powering it up would trigger—"

"Yes, yes, an explosion that could take out the town. I've heard all this. But I've also spent a lot of time on that ship, and I believe you are mistaken. Working together, we should be able to power it up safely."

Chris shook his head. "I can't take that chance."

"Perhaps you don't fully understand what it is I'm saying here. We have your daughter." She gripped Rae's shoulder, and Rae flinched, playing the part of the hostage, even though Caden knew the ropes binding her were loose enough that she could easily pull free. "There's a *chance* that you might trigger an explosion that could harm the town and the people in it, if you cooperate with us." Doctor Nguyen paused, leaning in. "But there's a *certainty* that your daughter won't live to see her thirteenth birthday if you don't."

"I couldn't have said it better myself," Clara said.

Caden gasped; he hadn't noticed her returning to the room, but now she stood just behind them. She smiled at Doctor Nguyen, a wide, unfriendly smile that made the hairs on the back of Caden's neck stand on end. Something was definitely wrong.

"I'm so glad you were able to find Rae," Clara said, her eyes never leaving Doctor Nguyen's face. "How . . . convenient."

Caden and Rae exchanged worried glances.

"Now," Clara said, speaking into a walkie-talkie.

The doors to the room flew open, and a half dozen soldiers poured into the room, surrounding Caden and his friends.

45.
RAE

For the briefest of moments, Rae had thought that every-thing was going to be okay. That their plan—*her* plan—was working.

Until it wasn't.

"Grab them," Clara ordered, and the soldiers sprang into action, one of them dragging Doctor Nguyen's arms behind her back, a second tackling Caden to the ground. Rae saw Nate attempt to bolt, but he ran straight into a guard, his too-big helmet flying off him, just as another man put her dad in a headlock.

"Let him go!" she shrieked, wriggling free of her ropes and lunging at the guard holding her dad. She drove her head into his stomach, and he grunted, his grip on her dad loosening. But by then another soldier was there, grabbing Rae's arms and yanking them back so hard tears sprang into her eyes. She blinked them away and realized it was all over.

They were trapped.

Clara stood in front of them, looking furious and much less like a favorite elementary school teacher. "Nice try," she said, staring hard at Doctor Nguyen. "But I know you're not Hahn; I saw her body myself." Her lip curled. "What was left of it."

Doctor Nguyen smiled, her features blurring, shifting, until Patrick stood there instead. "I was afraid choosing her face might have been a mistake."

"Why did you, then?" Clara asked.

He shrugged. "Call it a tribute, if you will. Her death was . . . regrettable. I thought she might appreciate playing some sort of role in freeing her friend."

Rae's dad made a small, choked noise.

Rae couldn't bring herself to look at him, her own sorrow building inside her until she was afraid it might burst. She didn't like Doctor Nguyen, exactly; the woman had let Patrick use her and her friends like pawns in some alien chess match. But she'd also saved Rae from an underground Green On! lab, and then again rescued her from the ship.

She wondered if Patrick really did regret Doctor Nguyen's death. She met his eyes, his *real* eyes—beetle-black and gleaming—and thought of how he'd been smiling when she showed up at his cell with her stolen keys. Like he'd known she'd be back all along.

If I free you, will you help us? she'd asked.

I will.

Do you promise?

Cross my heart, Ms. Carter.

This is a terrible idea, Nate had spluttered. *Caden, talk some sense into her!*

Rae had turned to Caden, who had been watching the whole thing, weighing it all silently in that way of his. And she'd known that, if he told her not to do this, she'd listen to him.

Are you sure? was all he asked.

And she wasn't. Not at all. But this wasn't like her usual impulsive decisions, either. She wasn't throwing herself into danger headlong without thinking about it. She'd thought, and weighed her options, and realized that Patrick was her best chance at freeing her dad. Her only chance, really. She had to take it and hope for the best.

So much for that, Rae thought now. Her best hadn't been good enough. Despite everything she'd gone through, she wasn't able to free her dad. Instead, she'd made things worse for him because now she would be used against him.

A wave of remorse crashed through her, and she wondered if this feeling here was what had motivated Patrick to try to help her. After all, he could have just fled tonight, but instead he'd been true to his word; he'd stayed and tried to help her free her dad, just like he'd promised. Maybe he really did regret Doctor Nguyen's death. He might have regretted a lot of things.

Not that it mattered. Regret or no, there was nothing they could do now.

Clara smiled, a small, sly expression. "As you can see, Chris, we do have your little Rae here with us."

Little Rae. That comment cut through Rae's fear, igniting a spark of annoyance inside her. "I might be little, but I still got away from you."

Clara's eyebrows drew together. "True. For a time. But not again, I think."

"Look, Clara, I'll cooperate," Rae's dad said quickly. "So there's no need to . . ." He stopped, as if he couldn't bring himself to say the words.

"To what?" Clara cocked her head to the side, still watching Rae intently. "To harm your precious offspring?"

He winced. "Exactly."

Clara's eyes narrowed, and Rae felt as if she were staring into her soul. "Oh, I don't know," Clara said at last. "I think you could use a little demonstration." Her eyes swept over the group. "All of you."

Rae heard footsteps and looked past Clara to see a soldier wheeling Ivan out, his thin body still strapped to a board and wrapped in wires. In the brighter light of the command center, his scars looked worse, the ridged edges red and raw. His arms hung limply at his sides, fingers curled inward, hiding his palms. Rae remembered how those had opened to reveal deep dark pits. No, not pits, exactly. More like black holes, with the power to suck the eyeballs right from a person's head.

But no matter how terrible Ivan was, Clara was ten times worse. Ivan might not be able to help his nature, but Clara and Green On! could.

"Jeremy," Nate gasped, and Rae saw that Ivan wasn't the only one who'd been wheeled out. Jeremy Bentley, Alyssa's former boyfriend-turned-zombified-Unseeing-victim, was strapped to his own board. His hair hung in limp strands across his forehead, straggling into the place where his eyes should have been. His mouth opened and closed as if he were trying to say something, his nostrils flaring.

Behind Jeremy came two more soldiers carefully wheeling out some kind of strange stone pillar, its surface a bright green. No, Rae realized, it was actually a deep glossy black, like onyx. The green came from within, a sort of glow that highlighted the carvings on the sides. Carvings of faces with teeth that hung past their chins and glowing eyes that all seemed to be watching Rae.

"What are you doing?" Patrick asked, and he almost sounded worried. *That* scared Rae more than anything.

"An experiment," Clara said. "Set that down here," she ordered the soldiers with the carved pillar, pointing to a spot right in front of Jeremy. "You, unstrap him." She pointed at another soldier, who began gently peeling back Jeremy's restraints.

"This is a terrible idea," Patrick said. "Truly, astoundingly awful. You have no idea what you're about to unleash."

"I have it perfectly under control," Clara said.

Patrick shifted, his body tensing.

"If he moves again, shoot him," Clara ordered. "Our weapons might not be as effective on his kind, but I doubt even he would survive a direct shot to the head."

"Clara, maybe you should listen—" Rae's dad began.

"Listen?" Clara snapped. "To *him*? Like *you* did? And how did that work out for you, Chris?" She shook her head. "I am through listening. We are running out of time. We need action. Now, put the boy's hands on the column," she told the soldier who had unstrapped Jeremy.

The soldier was young, barely older than Ava, Rae noticed, her eyes wide beneath the rim of her cap, her lips trembling. Still, she obeyed her orders, guiding Jeremy over to the column.

He was as docile as a toy at first, but as he got closer, he began to make a soft keening noise in the back of his throat, his limbs thrashing as he tried to back away. The soldier struggled to hold him, and finally Clara sighed and marched over, grabbing Jeremy's hand by the wrist and slapping it to the column herself.

Jeremy froze, his whole body going stiff. A tremor ran through him, like water rippling in a high wind.

"Fools," Patrick muttered.

"Why?" Rae whispered. "What's going to happen to him?"

"You'll see soon enough." Patrick raised his voice. "All of you will. Too bad it'll be the *last* thing you see."

"Oh, stop," Clara said. "As long as I have his master," she pointed at Ivan, "he's perfectly under control."

"His *master*?" Patrick laughed. "The Unseeing are parasites, not puppet masters."

Clara frowned, a hint of uncertainty crossing her face. Then it cleared. "You're lying."

"Am I?" Patrick gazed at her with his pitch-black eyes. She was the first to look away, staring instead at Jeremy.

He was shaking harder and harder, the glow of the column oozing into his hand and up his arm, filling his body until he shone like a small green sun, the light bursting from his empty eye sockets and streaming from his gaping mouth. Rae squinted, unable to stare directly at him. Even Clara flinched back. But seconds later the glow faded, then winked out.

The room looked suddenly much darker.

Jeremy stood with his back to them, his shoulders rising and falling as he took deep, even breaths.

"Now what?" Rae said.

"Now, your father is going to do *exactly* what I ask of him," Clara said. "No errors, no tricks." She looked at Rae's dad. "My new weapon here will accompany you to the spaceship . . . to make sure you get there safely." She smiled.

"And what about my daughter?" he asked.

"Oh, she'll stay right here with me. As long as you cooperate, she will be quite safe as well. If you don't, well, I hear she and this creature," she pointed at Ivan, "have some unfinished business."

Rae flinched, but it wasn't Ivan that scared her. Not anymore.

"Fine," Rae's dad said, his jaw set. "Let's get this over with."

Clara smiled, her face softening. "That's the spirit. Jeremy, are you ready?"

Jeremy didn't move.

"Jeremy?" she said again.

No response.

"Nudge him, would you?" she said to the young soldier standing beside him.

The soldier hesitated, then put a hand on Jeremy's arm.

It was the wrong move; Jeremy spun, one hand lashing out at

the soldier. She screamed and fell back, clutching at her arm as blood spurted everywhere.

Something landed at Rae's feet with a wet *thwap*. She stared down at it, her mind going numb as she took in the details: four fingers, a thumb, the creases on the palm. And the clean white flash of bone jutting out from the severed wrist.

"What the—" Nate breathed.

The thing that had once been Jeremy smiled at them all, his lips drawing back to reveal sharp fangs, his eyes an all-encompassing black.

46.
CADEN

Jeremy spun slowly, studying everyone's faces. The soldiers around Caden and his friends drew back, hands reaching for weapons, while the wounded soldier leaned heavily against the now-dark pillar. She clutched her arm to her chest, her face bone-white, as blood soaked the front of her uniform and pooled on the floor at her feet. No one moved to help her.

Jeremy lifted his face, sniffing, and Caden remembered how Vivienne had done the same when the smell of blood began affecting her.

"What is he do—" Clara began, just as Jeremy darted forward, sinking his teeth into the throat of the injured soldier. She didn't even have time to scream before it was over.

Jeremy stood, wiping his mouth. He locked eyes with Caden and grinned, his teeth stained red, his chin dripping.

"Control him!" Clara told Ivan.

Ivan spread his arms as wide as the straps holding him would allow. "I can't. Not tied up like this."

Clara hesitated for just a fraction of a second, and then she fumbled with the straps, undoing them.

"No!" Rae shouted, but it was too late; Ivan was free.

Caden reached for his powers . . . and nothing happened. It was like groping in the dark for a light switch you knew was there and coming up against a blank wall. He tried again, digging deep inside himself, but it didn't help; his powers were gone.

Magical burnout. It had happened to him once before and had taken days to recover from.

Use me, the ring whispered, soft and insistent. *Borrow* my *power*.

It was a terrible idea. Use the power of a demon? That always came at a cost.

Ivan leapt down, mouth stretched in a wide grin to display all his jagged, broken teeth. He took a step toward Rae, then turned and lunged at Clara instead, knocking her to the ground.

Clara screamed and thrashed as he pinned her to the floor, using his knees to keep her down while his palms came up over her eyes.

Caden froze, stunned. The soldiers around them aimed but didn't shoot, unable to hit Ivan without risking Clara. The only one who reacted swiftly was Rae.

She grabbed the fallen soldier's rifle and swung it at Ivan like a baseball bat, smacking him across the side of the face. He toppled sideways, crumpling to the ground beside Clara. Rae raised the rifle over him again, her eyes hard, jaw set. Then she stopped and slowly lowered it. "Not worth it," she whispered.

Clara sat up, looking dazed. She blinked rapidly a few times, then scrambled away from Ivan, who lay there twitching and moaning. "Kill it!" she shrieked, pointing at him. "Kill it now!"

"Wait a second," Rae began, backing up a step as the soldiers lifted their weapons. "Shouldn't you—"

Movement exploded from behind the soldiers. A tornado of teeth and claws tore into them as they turned, too slowly. Caden saw blood spurting, limbs flying, and then Patrick was grabbing him by the arm, yanking him away.

"We need to run. Now!"

Patrick shoved Rae forward as the soldiers around them erupted into chaos. Shots rang out, loud and terrifying, and Rae and the others took off for the exit.

Caden caught one last glimpse of Jeremy—of the thing that now wore Jeremy's skin—covered in gore and advancing on Clara, before he turned and sprinted after the others.

"Don't look back," Patrick warned as terrible sounds followed them. Screams and choked gurgles and worse.

Caden didn't need the warning; he already had enough nightmares. Instead, he ran. And for once, he felt like he was actually moving pretty fast.

An alarm sounded overhead, the lights flashing brighter. More soldiers ran past, most of them not even bothering to glance at Caden or the others except to shove them out of the way. Caden noticed a few scientists leaving rooms on the sides as well, looking anxious.

"What's happening?" a woman asked, grabbing Caden by the sleeve and jerking him to a halt.

"There's a loose alien," Caden said. "In the command center. It's . . . it's a slaughter."

The woman's face went pale. "Oh," she breathed.

Caden hesitated, then added, "We're leaving the bunker. Come with us if you want."

"Caden!" Rae yelled from up ahead. "Hurry!"

"And go where?" the woman asked. "We already fled from Green On!. It's full of monsters. Where can we go?"

"Trust me, better to take your chances with the monsters out there than the one in here." Caden pulled his arm free.

The woman let him go, her eyes wide. "There are others," she said.

"Tell them to come too. But we can't wait."

She nodded, and Caden turned and ran after his friends, wondering if any of the remaining scientists would really follow. He could imagine the creature that had been Jeremy as it stalked through the halls of the bunker, slaughtering any human it passed.

Vivienne was still here. Would she be safe?

"Wait!" he yelled, sprinting after the others. "We have to go back for Vivienne."

"Vivienne is here?" Rae asked, stopping abruptly.

"To go back is to die," Patrick said, nudging Rae forward.

Rae dug in her heels.

"Rae," her dad said, his face pale. "Please, honey, we have to keep moving." He looked terrible, his face ashen, sweat soaking his brow. Caden got the sense he'd been kept deep underground for most of the past year, and it had certainly taken its toll. For once, Caden wasn't the one struggling the most to keep up.

"Dad, she's my friend. I can't leave her."

"She's not your friend anymore," Patrick said. "You saw what happened with Mr. Bentley back there."

"That's different. Jeremy was already gone. Vivienne is still in there."

Patrick frowned. "There's a reason we kept that particular alien species encased in stone for this journey. A reason why we only brought them as embryos and not as fully-fledged creatures. They have one mission once they have matured: to eradicate the dominant species on the planet." He paused, looking around at the rest of them. "Don't you understand? Their entire purpose is to bring about your extinction."

Extinction. Caden felt the terror that word evoked deep in his bones.

"It's why I was instructed to only employ them if absolutely necessary," Patrick said.

"Instructed?" Rae's dad said. "By whom?"

"Mr. Carter, this is hardly the time to discuss my origin story, wouldn't you agree? Not when your daughter's life is at risk. Because once the former Mr. Bentley has finished with the unfortunates in the command center, he will hunt you down too. Your only hope is to get out quickly and seal the door shut behind you. And pray it's enough to hold him."

"But Vivienne—" Rae began.

"Should be fine. I expect she's woken up by now; whatever they used to knock her out won't be effective for long. She can hold her own against the other. *We* cannot."

Rae hesitated. "Caden?" she said.

Caden didn't want to be the one to make this call. Vivienne was his friend too, and he had precious few of them. But he had a job he needed to do. If he died here, all of Whispering Pines died with him. "We need to go," he said at last. "There's something I have to do."

"And what's that?" Rae asked.

Caden glanced over his shoulder. The bunker felt quieter now, despite the alarm still blaring in the distance. It was too easy to imagine Jeremy stalking them through the mazelike passages. "Let's keep running, and I'll tell you."

47.
RAE

" . . . need to destroy the vents below the spaceship," Caden finished explaining as they wound their way toward the bunker exit. "It's the only way to save everyone."

"Wait, so there's some sort of magical doorway below the ship?" Rae said. "*That's* why Whispering Pines is so weird?"

"It's a spiritual vortex," Caden said.

"Sounds like a magical doorway to me," Rae muttered, shaking her head. She'd seen so many things that should have been impossible—monsters and aliens and alternate dimensions—and she'd watched Caden perform literal magic spells. But still this was hard to believe. She glanced at her dad's skeptical expression and knew he wasn't buying it either.

But then, he didn't know Caden like she did. Caden wouldn't lie about something like this.

"So let me get this straight," her dad said. "You need to some-how destroy the geothermal vents and thus trigger an explosion that will wipe out everything in the forest. Only, the rest of the town will be safe because, luckily, your family has set up some sort of magical force shield around the Watchful Woods that will contain the blast. But only if you trigger it within the next hour."

"More like two hours, but otherwise yes," Caden said.

Rae's dad snorted. "Of all the unbelievable stories I've—"

"He's right, Dad," Rae said. "I can personally vouch for the force shield—"

"Protective wall," Caden corrected.

She glanced at him. "You've been spending too much time with Nate lately, haven't you?"

"Hey! I've barely corrected anyone lately," Nate said. "I've been too busy trying not to die."

"A worthy goal, to be sure," Rae's dad said. He stopped jogging and looked at Rae, his eyes intense, searching, like she was a puzzle he wasn't quite sure how to solve.

Rae shifted, uncomfortable with that kind of scrutiny. Her dad had never looked at her that way before. He'd always been the one who really saw her and understood her. Only, a lot could change in a year. She knew *she* definitely had. Her father must have changed too. She stared back at him and wondered how much she even knew him anymore.

She swallowed down the sudden lump in her throat. It might feel like there was a lot of distance between them, but it would pass.

All they needed was time. Time they would only get to share if Caden's plan worked.

"The *protective wall*," she emphasized, "closed around me and Ava when we were trying to get to Green On!. It trapped us inside the woods. It's why I'm here, actually."

"And Ava?" he asked, his eyes widening. "Is she . . ."

"She's safe," Caden said quickly. "Nate and I met her and Blake in the woods on the way in. She should be outside the barrier by now."

"How would she have gotten out? If this so-called shield is as sealed as you claim."

Rae frowned, stung by her dad's condescending tone.

Caden hesitated. "I, um, gave her a spelled stone to guide her to my brother." He managed a sheepish grin, his hand sliding through his thick, spiky hair in embarrassment. "I know it's hard to believe—"

"Not at all," Rae's dad said. "A magic stone? Why not?" He threw up his hands.

"Dad," Rae said, her voice trembling. "I told you, it's true. Don't you believe me?"

He glanced at her, and there was that look in his eyes again. The look of a stranger. "I just . . . this is all a bit much."

"You've been held in secret in an underground bunker, forced to work on alien technology," Nate pointed out. "Many people wouldn't believe that, either."

Rae saw her dad mulling over the truth of that. "Okay, okay," he said at last. "Fine. I'm suspending disbelief. For the moment. But I have one question: if we destroy those vents and the ensuing explosion takes out everything in the forest, then doesn't that mean all of us would be caught in it as well?"

Rae flinched. It was a good point. She glanced at Caden. Instead of answering the question, he spun a ring on his thumb. A very familiar ring. One she'd last seen on his brother . . .

"Why do you have that?" she asked.

A sudden banging echoed behind them.

"Dying in a fiery explosion will become the least of our worries in a second here," Patrick said. "Keep moving. We're almost out."

Rae picked up her pace, mentally urging her dad along as more noises echoed behind them. Shouts and footsteps. Screams, long and terrible. A few smatterings of gunshots. And beneath it all, her dad wheezing as if he were the one with asthma.

"Here," Patrick said, taking a sudden turn down another branching hallway. "Just ahead." He pointed, and Rae saw the tall metal doors set into the side of the rock wall. Rae wanted to sprint, but she made herself go slower, staying right behind her dad, mentally urging him on.

Finally, they reached the doors, only to find that they'd been sealed shut with a dozen thick bolts. Without a word, all of them set to throwing the bolts back, moving as quickly as they could.

The noises from behind them had grown quiet. All except for one: the sound of fast-moving footsteps, headed in their direction.

Rae's fingers ached as she worked another bolt open, sliding it painstakingly back before moving onto the next one. And the next. One more bolt to go. She reached for it.

Caden gasped, and Rae glanced back.

Jeremy stood at the other end of the hall, his hair soaked, his face smeared with blood. His new black eyes seemed to drink in the shadows as he took a step toward them, slow and deliberate. Unbidden, Patrick's words sprang through her mind.

Their entire purpose is to bring about your extinction.

They'd wasted too much time arguing about plans, and now none of them would matter.

48.
CADEN

Jeremy took another slow step toward them, his face bathed in the light still flashing overhead. He no longer resembled the boy Caden had known. Underneath the blood that spattered him, the planes of his very skull had shifted, making him appear older, his face gaunt and hungry, the jaw too long to accommodate the growing teeth. And those eyes, the way they gleamed with the shiny blackness of a beetle's wings, hard and uncaring . . .

Caden had thought that maybe he could eventually save the victims of the Unseeing. But looking at Jeremy now, he knew *he*, at least, was gone forever. Erased and replaced.

"Almost . . . there," Rae grunted, working at the last bolt. It slid with agonizing slowness before finally clicking open. "Help me with the door!"

Her dad leapt in, tugging at the thick metal plate as Jeremy sprinted toward them, mouth opening, fangs glittering. Instinctively, Caden reached for the power of the ring—

Triumph surged through him, and his mind's eye filled with the image of the demon. Not as it had first appeared in the Other Place, hidden inside the body of a harmless old woman. But the *real* entity. The thing that had stared out at him once that prison of flesh had rotted away.

It wasn't so much a physical shape as a presence. Something as cold and vast as the void of space. And *hungry*. So hungry, it longed to devour the world.

As that entity swelled beneath Caden like a rising tide, he had a sudden flash of insight: if he allowed it to feed on the energy of the vortex in order to stop the aliens from pouring forth, what would he be unleashing in their stead?

Wham!

Another shape crashed into Jeremy, sending him tumbling into the wall.

Caden blinked, pulling back from the ring and from his thoughts, the present snapping into focus. Vivienne stood there, her long black hair swirling around her shoulders.

"You need to run," she said, glancing at Rae, then Nate, and finally Caden. "Now."

"We can't leave without you," Rae said.

"You have to." She flashed a smile, and for a second she looked like the old Vivienne. The one Caden had grown up with. "I'll be fine."

Jeremy groaned and pushed away from the wall, his eyes wide and dark, like two pits of tar. He focused them on Vivienne. "What are you doing?"

"Stopping you," Vivienne said, widening her stance.

"But . . . why? These are prey. They're for eating."

"Not these ones."

Jeremy's nostrils flared as he sniffed the air. "You're tainted." His upper lip curled in disgust. "You stink of them."

"Come on!" Patrick snapped, pushing the door open wide enough for them to slip out.

Jeremy rushed forward. He feinted to the left, then lunged to the right. Vivienne matched him speed for speed, blocking him with her body and throwing him to the ground. He sprang to his feet and slashed at her with one curled hand, leaving a spray of blood.

Rae gasped, but Vivienne didn't seem fazed. She caught Jeremy's next swing and used his momentum to yank him around and back into the wall.

Crack!

Bits of stone flaked off the wall where Jeremy had hit. He staggered back, dazed, then shook it off, turning to face Vivienne, his stance widening.

"Rae, we need to move." Rae's dad took her arm. "Please, honey. I just found you again. I can't lose you." His voice broke on the last word. Apparently that was enough to make Rae follow him. Nate tossed one last glance at Vivienne over his shoulder before darting through as well.

Caden hesitated in the doorway. He hated to leave Vivienne like this. "Vivi!" he yelled. She didn't answer, but her head tilted in his direction. "When you win this fight, don't leave the bunker. It won't be safe outside until tomorrow."

She nodded once, and then Jeremy was on her again, all wild punches and snarling teeth.

When you win, Caden repeated silently, putting all his hope into those three words. And then he slipped outside, pulling the heavy door shut behind him.

"Should we lock it?" Nate asked, uncertain.

"Absolutely," Patrick said. "We do not want anything following us."

"But Vivi—" Rae started.

"We don't want her following us either," Patrick said firmly, moving forward to lock the door.

Before he could reach it, it lurched open. Instinctively, the others all shoved back, pushing the door closed.

Shouts echoed from the other side, and someone pounded at the metal door.

"Wait!" Caden said. "There are people in there!"

Quickly Rae's dad hauled the door open, and a handful of men and women in Green On! lab coats spilled out. "Shut it! Shut it!" a tall, athletic-looking woman shouted, and the door was slammed shut again behind them. Patrick locked the door, and this time no one stopped him.

Caden looked at the motley group. There were five of them: two women, including the one he'd run into in the hall, and three men, one with glasses thicker than Nate's, another who looked like he was old enough to be someone's grandfather, and a third who towered over all of them, his lab coat straining around his shoulders, an equally massive weapon held in his hands. "Is this everyone?" Caden asked.

The woman he'd first met nodded. "Everyone willing to come." Her eyes were red-rimmed and swollen, like she'd been crying. Like there'd been someone specific she had tried to convince, only to fail.

Or maybe whoever that person was, they were already dead.

Caden turned away from her grief. "I guess we'd better get moving."

Caden rubbed at the ring on his thumb as he ran with the others down the tunnel. His brother had claimed he'd banished the demon, but now that Caden had brushed against the power inside the ring, he was sure that wasn't true. He could still feel its presence lurking in the back of his mind. A spider, waiting for a nice, juicy fly.

Maybe *he* was the fly. Or maybe it was all of Whispering Pines. Or the world itself.

The demon had told him that Prudence—the original Prudence, the one who had been his ancestor—had feared it so much she'd sent her own daughter away to protect her from it. But when monsters had threatened her town, she'd become desperate enough to strike a deal.

What kind of deal? Caden had asked.

Oh, the usual. Her body and soul in exchange for the power to seal away the monsters residing in her town. The demon had said it so casually, as if a body and soul were nothing.

Caden had almost promised his *own* body and soul to the thing, back when he hadn't understood what he was dealing with. He was only free now because Aiden had agreed to take his place. He remembered that moment clearly. Especially the disturbingly eager way his brother had looked at the demon, as if it held the answer to his deepest, darkest desires.

Are you certain this is what you want? the demon had asked Aiden.

I want power, Aiden had said. *And I know you can give it to me.*

And the price?

Take me and not my brother, and I will pay your price.

Caden wanted to shake those memories away, but he couldn't. And as the spaceship came into view now, he couldn't help wondering if this plan of Aiden's was somehow part of that bargain. Maybe the demon hadn't been banished at all. Maybe this—the vortex, the energy—was Aiden's price. Something the demon would want more than his body or soul.

Caden's steps slowed, then stopped. He stared up at the shimmering blue-green disc ahead, then dropped his gaze to the vents beneath.

"What is it?" Nate asked, stopping beside him.

"I can't do it."

"Can't do what?" Rae asked, doubling back toward them.

"I can't use Aiden's ring to destroy the vortex."

"Why not?" Nate asked.

"Because . . ." Caden wasn't sure how much to explain, so he settled on, "I don't trust my brother."

Rae and Nate exchanged a look. "Yeah," Rae said slowly. "Neither do we."

Caden ran a hand through his hair in frustration. "But I can't just leave the vortex there. I need to destroy it before the shield spell fails, or—"

"All of Whispering Pines is toast," Nate finished for him. "Yes, we're well aware of that."

"What's the holdup?" one of the scientists demanded. The big one with the weapon.

"Yeah, I thought you were leading us out of here?" the oldest one said. He glanced over at the spaceship, then deliberately turned his back on it, as if he'd had enough of alien technology for one lifetime.

"There's something I have to do first," Caden said.

"Then do it already," the scientist with the weapon snapped, his eyes darting around the cavern. Now that Caden was looking too, he noticed that this place was actually riddled with tunnels. It suddenly felt very unsafe to remain here for long.

He glanced up and caught Rae's dad watching him. Beside him Patrick stood staring up at the ship, his head cocked to the side. Caden turned and saw that all five of the scientists were now staring at him, too.

The clock is ticking, little brother.

With all those impatient eyes on him, Caden couldn't think. But he would have to make a choice. Which would be worse: aliens or a demon? He found himself reaching for his pendant—the one he'd given to Vivienne. His hand closed on nothing, and he let it drop again.

"What if there was another way to destroy the vortex?" Nate asked quietly.

"Like what?" Caden said.

Nate glanced at Rae, then away again quickly, his cheeks going pink. "The spaceship."

Rae was the first to catch on. "What? No. My dad said—" She stopped. "He said powering it up might make it explode," she finished, understanding.

"Exactly. And an explosion on top of the vents might destroy them."

"That's a lot of *mights*," Caden said.

"I don't like the uncertainty any more than you do, but what choice do we have?" Nate glanced over at the ship, the light from it bouncing off his glasses. He hunched his shoulders, shooting Rae another quick, guilty look. Caden couldn't understand why.

And then it hit him. "Mr. Carter is the only one who knows how to power it up."

Rae's eyes widened, then narrowed. "No," she said flatly. "Absolutely not."

Nate shuffled his feet, his face flushed, but he made himself look at her. "I'm sorry, Rae. Really. But everyone we love is in that town, and—"

"And we are *not* risking my father's life! Not when I just got him back."

"Not even to save your mom? Your sister? Not to mention everyone else's families?" He held her gaze, and she was the first to look away.

"Aren't you forgetting someone?" Patrick said.

The three of them spun to face him.

"*I* can power up the ship." He crossed his arms over his stolen lab coat.

"Why would you help us?" Caden demanded.

"Help you? Mr. Price, I assure you, I would be doing this for myself."

"Somehow that doesn't make me feel any better," Caden muttered.

"I heard something down there," the bespectacled scientist said. He pointed down a nearby tunnel, and everyone froze for a moment, listening.

Caden heard the soft pitter-patter of many tiny little feet before it faded again.

Patrick sighed. "Let me be frank since we are rapidly running out of time here. I have no intention of allowing this ship to explode. Instead, I want to power it up so I can fly it out of here. Fortunately for you all, that alone should still be enough to destroy the vents beneath it. *Unfortunately* for you, I will require assistance."

"What kind of assistance?" Rae asked.

"The mechanical kind." Patrick glanced at her dad.

"No," Rae said firmly, crossing her own arms. "Do it yourself."

"I can't, Ms. Carter. The engine needs to be repaired, and I can't fix it myself. I've tried. There's only one person who has the knowledge and abilities to help me." Patrick smiled. "So, the choice is yours, Chris. Help me power up the ship, or take your chances with Mr. Price and his magic ring."

Caden felt his face go hot and knew Patrick was using Mr. Carter's skepticism to manipulate him. At the same time, it *did* seem like the best option, so he kept his mouth shut.

Rae's dad looked from Patrick to his daughter, and then back at the ship. He shook his head and laughed. "It looks like Clara will get her wish after all. Fine, I'll help you. It will probably take us some time, though. Enough for the rest of you to get out of the tunnels and through the woods to safety."

"What about you, Dad?" Rae asked. "How will *you* get to safety?"

"I'll be safe enough on the ship."

"The one that's going to explode?" Rae said skeptically.

"I told you, it won't explode," Patrick said. "Not if we do it correctly."

The "if" made Caden nervous. And he could tell by Rae's face that she didn't like the idea either.

Caden felt a sudden strange lurch, as if the ground had turned to liquid beneath him. He stumbled, putting a hand to the wall.

"Are you okay?" one of the scientists asked him.

"Aiden's spell," he gasped. "It's weakening." He looked at Rae. "If we're going to make it, we have to leave now."

"That tunnel there is the quickest way out." Patrick pointed to a small crevice half-hidden in the shadows behind the ship. "It should take the rest of you close to the edge of the forest." He turned to Rae's dad. "Come along, Chris."

Patrick took a step away, but Mr. Carter ignored him, focusing instead on his daughter. "So. I guess this is where we split up."

Rae bit her lip, her eyes glistening. "Dad . . ."

"You go with your friends here. And I . . . I'll see you real soon, okay?" He didn't sound very convincing. But before Rae could argue, he pulled her into a crushing embrace, kissed the top of her head, and let her go. And then he turned and walked away, Patrick falling into step beside him.

"I'd say that's our cue," the scientist with the weapon said. "I'll take the lead." He strode confidently toward the crevice in the wall and disappeared inside.

"Mason, wait up!" one of the other scientists yelled as they all hurried to catch up with him.

"Coming?" Nate said.

"We're right behind you," Caden told him.

Nate nodded and followed the scientists, and then it was just Caden and Rae standing alone.

"Are *you* coming?" Caden asked Rae, already knowing the answer.

She tore her gaze away from her dad's retreating back to look at him. "I'm sorry," she whispered. "I can't let him go alone."

"He has Patrick."

She made a face. "As if that's better."

Caden managed a small smile, but it wilted quickly. Because he knew if she went with her dad now, he might never see her again . . .

They stared at each other, and Caden thought of all the things he could say to try to convince her to come with him. But he knew words wouldn't work. Not on someone like Rae. She'd made up her mind, and there would be no changing it.

Unless he used magic.

He felt the ring on his thumb buzzing, the metal practically vibrating with eagerness. It would be easy to draw on it, to wrap his will around Rae's and make her change her mind. He knew it wasn't a good idea to use its power, but this would be such a small thing. It wouldn't be like he'd be unleashing it. And, really, he'd be doing Rae a favor. They both knew there was a strong chance her dad wouldn't come back from this. But he was a grown man, free to make that choice. She was only twelve and still had so much life ahead of her. Wouldn't it be for the best if he made her come with him to safety?

He ran his finger over the ring. And then he made his choice, already knowing he might never forgive himself for this. But that didn't matter now.

Only Rae mattered.

49.
RAE

Rae felt strange, as if she were running in a dream, her body moving without her. Maybe it was because part of her knew she was going in the wrong direction.

But she'd made her choice. She refused to question it now, to think of everything she was about to lose . . .

She approached the spaceship, still awed by the reality of it, her eyes drawn to the rippling of its surface. Her dad and Patrick had already vanished inside, but the door remained open, looming there like the mouth of some deep, dark tunnel.

Rae hesitated just outside, thinking of Caden's last words to her.

You're my best friend, he'd said, his voice trembling. *I was alone before you came here.*

Instinctively, she'd put her arms around him in a quick, tight hug. *You're not alone anymore. Even without me, you wouldn't be alone.*

His own arms had tightened around her, holding her close. So close she could hear the pounding of his heart, could smell him— sweat and dirt and, beneath that, the faint scent of some kind of peppermint soap. And for a moment she'd let herself feel comforted by his closeness, her fear fading into the background. Somehow with Caden, she always felt just a little safer. *Still,* he'd whispered into her hair. *Don't die out there, okay?*

I'll try not to.

She'd stepped back, his arms dropping to his sides as he let her go. She could feel his eyes on hers, could feel the weight of more words he wanted to say. She'd braced herself, knowing in her heart she wouldn't be ready to hear them. And maybe he'd understood that because he'd just nodded.

And so she'd turned and sprinted away from him.

Now that she was here, she wondered if she should have said more to him, too.

Hopefully she'd still get the chance.

50.
CADEN

oward, coward, coward. Caden chanted the word as he hiked along the tunnel after the others. He should have said more to Rae, should have told her . . . what, exactly? That he liked her? He could tell she knew that already. Just as he could tell she didn't feel the same way about him.

Or maybe she did. Maybe he was misreading her. Without his powers, he couldn't be sure. And now he'd never know because he hadn't been brave enough to ask. But at least he'd been brave enough to let her make up her own mind. He hadn't tried to force her to do what *he* thought was best.

For the first time, he truly knew he would never be like Aiden. And that thought was almost enough to make up for the rest of his self-doubt and uncertainty.

The tunnel ended abruptly in a wooden door.

"Huh," Nate said, looking at it. "That looks . . . promising."

Caden glanced at the five scientists with them.

"Want to take the lead again, Mason?" the scientist Caden had first run into said, nudging the man with the weapon.

"Ladies first, Rebecca," Mason said, his tone mocking.

"I'll do it." Caden stepped forward and pushed. The door swung open, revealing the Watchful Woods.

Or what had once *been* the Watchful Woods.

Caden stepped outside, his jaw hanging open. Everything was different. The whole area must have undergone a rapid transformation while he and Nate had been underground.

Every tree seemed to have mutated, turning into twisting masses of tentacles that waved dreamlike through the eerie green of the atmosphere, the trunks all covered in glowing, pulsing fungi. Some of those tentacles looked different, and Caden wondered if they were all plants, or if some of them were really aliens lurking below ground, ready to eat them. The soil felt spongy beneath his shoes, like the ground of the Other Place, as if he were walking on very thick, slightly damp carpet. Mist rose from it in expanding swirls, making it impossible to see very far into the distance. Still, Caden had the sense of eyes watching them from all around.

He listened. All was quiet. As if the things in this part of the woods had been startled into silence by their arrival. It made the hair on the back of his neck stand on end.

"It doesn't even look like our planet anymore," Nate whispered beside him. He took a deep breath, then wrinkled his nose. "The smell is familiar, though. Like the school cafeteria on mystery meat Monday."

"This," Mason said, "is impossible."

"I think you mean improbable," the tall scientist corrected, her expression smug.

"Whatever it is, it's super weird," Rebecca added. She glanced at Caden. "Still think we can get through this safely?"

"I . . . hope so," Caden said. "At this point, we don't really have any other choice, right?"

No one looked happy about that, but it was the truth. Huddling together, the seven of them shuffled away from the tunnel and into the alien jungle.

"Wait," Caden hissed, holding out his hand as he caught movement up ahead. A giant centipede at least six feet long crawled up the side of one of the trees, dragging a body with it into the canopy. Caden couldn't tell if it was human or alien and decided he'd rather not know.

"Well, that's a creepy sight I could have lived without," Nate muttered. "How far away are we from your brother?"

Caden watched the bug until he could no longer see it. He thought he could still hear the clicking of its many feet against the wood of the tree. "Close," he said. Even without his powers, he could feel his brother like a beacon, beckoning him out of the woods.

"Close is not really an exact distance." Nate's voice held an edge to it, like he was on the verge of hysteria. Caden understood; they'd been through a lot that day. But this—seeing their world completely transformed—was somehow the hardest thing to deal with.

It was too easy to imagine this spreading and taking over the planet.

"The whole place, it has more oxygen," the scientist with the glasses muttered, staring down at a tablet. "That's probably what some of the new plant life is supposed to do . . ."

Nate gasped.

"What?" Caden asked him.

"Oh, nothing." Nate pushed his glasses up. "Just that more oxygen means a bigger explosion. That's all. How strong is your brother's protective barrier?"

"Strong enough," Caden said, hoping it was true. "But not for much longer." He glanced back at the scientists, who were now clustered around the tablet, examining the readings on it as if they were safely in one of their labs. "There's no time for that," Caden said. "We need to move, and fast. And whatever you do, avoid the tentacled plants."

"Why?" the bespectacled scientist asked.

"They'll eat you," Caden said. "Let's get out of here." He started forward, leading them through the alien world that was once the Watchful Woods.

51.
RAE

Rae found her dad and Patrick in the heart of the spaceship, both of them deep in conversation in the engine room, surrounded by tangled wires and beeping machinery.

"Dad!" she yelled.

He looked up, his eyebrows raising as she raced toward him. "Rae? What are you—" He stopped, his mouth working for a moment as if words had failed him. "You were supposed to leave with your friends!"

"I wanted to stay with you."

"This, what we're about to do, isn't safe," he said, his shock turning to anger. "You need to go."

Rae faltered, surprised by his fury. Then she recovered. "Go where? I wouldn't be able to catch up with the others now. So it would just be me alone, running through a monster-infested forest."

He threw up his hands in frustration. "Can't you see I did all this to keep you safe? Everything I went through. And you're throwing that away!"

Rae took a deep breath so she wouldn't yell back, then said, as calmly as she could, "Nothing around here is safe, and nothing anywhere will be safe unless we stop the invasion."

She took a step forward, willing her dad to see her. To see the Rae she'd become. The one who had endured cruel taunts at school and not been swayed by them. Instead, she'd doubled down on her research into missing people and government cover-ups. She'd learned how to see the truth beneath the story, how to follow facts, no matter where they led. All tools that had helped her when she moved to Whispering Pines. It had always been about finding her dad again. All of it, everything she'd gone through.

And if she had walked away now, leaving him when he needed her the most? Well, it would have all been for nothing. "You promised me new hikes," she whispered. "I just want to make sure you'll still be there to keep that promise."

He sighed. "Rae, things change—"

"Whether you wanted her with you or not, your daughter is here now," Patrick cut in. "Might as well make the best of it." He smiled, his eerily black eyes staring at her as if he'd known all along she'd come. As if he'd planned on it.

Rae frowned, suddenly uneasy. She might have freed Patrick, and he might have been helping them now, but she didn't trust him. There was no way he wasn't up to something.

"Rae," her dad said, and then he stopped and rubbed the bridge of his nose. "Never mind. Patrick's right; you're here now. There's nothing I can do to change that. Just . . . stay out of the way, would you?"

Rae flinched. She hadn't expected her dad to be happy, exactly, that she'd gone against his wishes. But she'd thought he might at least be . . . well. Something more than resigned. "I'm sorry," she started, and then she stopped herself. "Actually, no, I'm not. I never gave up looking for you. Not once in this past year. Even when people told me I was insane, to let it go, that you'd just run off. I *knew* you'd been taken. And I was *right*."

If she'd been expecting her dad to apologize, or be impressed, or anything, really, she was disappointed. His expression never changed—cold, disappointed, his eyes those of a stranger—as he went back to the wiring tangled around him. Rae's heart sank.

"I can help," she whispered, but he just shook his head, muttering to himself as he worked.

She turned away from her dad, blinking rapidly. She was *not* going to cry, not now. She would prove she could be useful. She made herself focus on the large room around her.

Several screens were up and running. One of them showed the entrance to the ship. Rae stared at it, understanding now how Patrick had known when she, Vivienne, and Alyssa had arrived here. Other screens showed snippets of news from around the world, while still more had maps of places she'd never heard of, and diagrams of planets, and charts that made no sense at all.

Rae tore her gaze from them, noticing now the energy reader she'd retrieved from the Other Place. It sat in the very center of the room, connected to the rest of the ship by a series of wires.

"Why are you helping us move your ship?" she asked Patrick.

"This isn't actually *my* ship," Patrick said. "Mine is in northern California." He started flicking levers and pressing buttons. "And I've realized, Ms. Carter, that this technology needs to be removed from human hands. Your species cannot be trusted. You claim to want clean energy but actually only want better weapons. Something to give you an edge over your enemies." He shook his head. "Left to your own devices, you would use the things you learn from this ship to destroy yourselves."

"That's not fair," Rae said. "Most humans would rather have something that would help save the Earth than any kind of weapon."

He smiled at her like she was a naive child. "And this, here, is exactly why I prefer to work with children. And why I'll help you now. I've decided that I don't want to see the extinction of the human race. Some of you have . . . potential. Maybe in a couple hundred years, you'll actually start to live up to it."

Rae glanced at her dad, but he was completely enthralled in his work, oblivious to the rest of the conversation. This was his element. Despite his initial reluctance to come here, she could tell he was very excited about getting to see and do everything in person. And even though she was still hurt by the casual way he'd dismissed her, she found herself smiling. *This* was the dad she knew. Perhaps more of him was still in there than she thought.

"Ms. Carter," Patrick said. "I need you to watch this screen for me and let me know when the power is up to about seventy-five percent." He swung a screen around that had been hooked up to the energy reader.

"Why? What happens at seventy-five?" Rae asked, settling down in front of the screen.

"That's when we'll have enough energy to fly." He flashed her a smile. "Don't worry, I'll drop you and your dad off before heading into space. Unless you want to come with me . . ."

Rae stared at him. "Space? You're leaving?"

"Of course. The main reason I've been trying to power up this ship is so I can finally get off this planet."

"I thought . . . the invasion . . ."

"Yes, yes, but it was never meant to be *here*. We landed here by mistake. Your planet is not the best suited for us. And, like I said, I don't want to cause your species' extinction. I've seen too much of that kind of thing on my own planet." His smile fell away, and for the first time, Rae thought she detected sadness on his borrowed face.

"Your planet—"

"We can discuss all this some other time, perhaps. But I'm pretty sure the Price spell isn't going to hold much longer. In fact . . ." He made a show of checking his watch. "It looks like we've got less than an hour."

"Oh."

Then Patrick turned to Rae's dad. "Mr. Carter, if you will just follow me for a moment, I need your expertise elsewhere. And Ms. Carter?"

"Hmm?"

"Keep watching that screen. Sometimes there's a surge in energy. If that happens, I'll need you to yell for me."

Rae nodded. And as Patrick led her dad out of the engine room, she couldn't help the burst of pride she felt at the knowledge that her dad knew more about fixing the fuel converter on an alien ship than an actual alien.

But as she watched the numbers on her screen slowly climb, something about it all began to bother her. And then she realized . . . This is what Patrick wanted the whole time!

He'd acted as if he were helping *them*, but really it was the other way around. He'd needed her dad's assistance from the beginning, and so he'd managed to somehow manipulate the entire situation. Which meant what? Rae wasn't sure, except for one thing.

She'd been a fool to trust him, even a little.

A sudden sinking feeling of dread took hold of her. She glanced one more time at the screen, noticing that the percentage had barely risen, before she slipped out of the room to find her dad. She had gone through way too much to lose him now.

As she passed rows and rows of empty pods, her anxiety rose higher, turning into fear; by the time she reached the pods containing Alyssa and the other humans, she was running. There was Ms. Lockett, and Doctor Anderson, and several other Green On! workers who must have irritated Patrick in some way. And then—

Rae stopped abruptly, her hand going to her mouth. "No," she whispered. "No, no, no!"

In the final pod floated her dad. His eyes were closed, his expression almost peaceful as he drifted in that deep red liquid.

"I was wondering how long it would take you to come find us."

Rae turned, but not fast enough; Patrick grabbed her from behind and stabbed something into the side of her neck.

"How . . . could . . . you . . ." she managed as her limbs went heavy, her eyelids fluttering. She could feel the pull of unconsciousness and fought it off with every fiber of her being, knowing that to give in now was to die. But her whole body felt like it had turned to sand, her mouth gritty, her vision fading.

"Just returning the favor from before." Patrick picked her up like she weighed less than a paperback novel.

She could hear the wheezing of her breaths, and the beating of her heart as it slowed way down. She tried to flail against Patrick, but barely managed to do more than twitch as he gently placed her inside another empty pod, propping her against the cool glass.

"Don't . . ." she whispered through numb lips.

"I am sorry, Ms. Carter. But it was always going to come to this." He stepped back, and the door to the pod slid silently shut.

Rae should have known better than to trust that conniving, sneaky creature. She *had* known better. And still she'd let him trap her. And as liquid bubbled up from the bottom and began dripping down on her from the top, she watched Patrick turn and walk away, leaving her alone.

Get up, she told herself. *Fight. At least* try *to escape!* But all she could do was sit there as fluid oozed around her, as warm and sluggish as blood. It should have been horrifying, but it was somehow very relaxing, and as it rose higher and higher, covering her chest, and then her face, sliding inside her nose and mouth and over her eyes, she found herself drifting off.

Her last thought was that at least she'd found her dad. Maybe that was always meant to be the end of her story, just like Patrick had said.

Her consciousness slipped away, and everything went black.

52.
CADEN

Caden took the lead, since he was the only one who knew where to go, sprinting around twisted trees and over jagged underbrush, ducking tentacles and veering away from anything that moved. He'd hoped the extra oxygen in the air would help him, but after a few minutes he felt worse than usual, winded and light-headed, his temples throbbing. It was all the fog swirling everywhere, making it impossible to focus, hurting his eyes.

"Faster, boy," Mason growled from right behind him, his giant weapon slung under one arm. "Do you *want* to get us all killed?"

Caden bit back his retort; he didn't have the energy for it anyhow. Besides, he knew the man was just terrified. People were always at their worst when they were scared.

Someone screamed, and Caden whipped around. A scientist flailed as a tentacle wrapped itself around her body, lifting her off the ground. Other tentacles joined the first, snagging her arms, her legs, her neck.

Caden stood frozen, unable to use his magic to help. *Keep running,* he told himself, but his feet wouldn't move. Even knowing he could do nothing to save her, he wasn't able to just run away.

The ground nearby trembled and cracked as the thing attached to the tentacles began to surge upward—

Blam! Blam!

Mason shot the tentacles, his aim surprisingly good. They writhed, then withdrew, dropping their prey to the ground. She clawed her way to her hands and knees, coughing and retching, her coat torn, blood oozing from several places where the mouths on the tentacles had begun to feed.

The ground settled as the creature hidden below decided to wait for easier prey. Still, Caden knew the woman's blood would attract more things. "We need to keep moving," he said as the grandfatherly scientist helped the woman back to her feet. "Everyone okay?"

"Yeah, just great," the woman snarled, wiping a trickle of blood from her neck.

All around them the plants shivered and then began to sway rhythmically in a breeze that only they felt. That had to be a bad sign.

Caden began running again, his legs slow and clumsy.

"I thought . . . more oxygen . . . would be a good thing," Nate gasped behind him.

"It can be," Rebecca answered, sounding much less tired than him. "There's a reason why we are trying to plant more forests. But this level here is not good for us."

"It's all about the ratios of the gases," the grandfatherly scientist added. Even *he* sounded less winded than Caden felt, despite the fact that he had to be pushing seventy. "There needs to be a balance. I fear for the future of the Earth if this spreads across the globe. It could mean extinction. And not just for humanity."

"Plus, there is such a thing as oxygen toxicity," Mason piped in. His own dark skin had a chalky, unhealthy glow to it, as if to emphasize his words.

Oxygen toxicity. Caden wondered if that was what he was feeling, or just the effects of not enough running training before this point. The trees at the edge of his vision seemed to be blurring and growing darker, and his head wouldn't stop pounding.

Just ahead he could see the glow of the barrier. They were almost there. Just a little farther.

"We're going to make it," the bespectacled scientist said, sounding almost surprised.

The ground began vibrating beneath Caden's feet as all around them the forest filled with the sound of rumbling, as if a lot of water were rushing past. The hairs on Caden's arms stood on end, and he felt the surge of energy, of things ready to burst.

"Run!" he screamed, moving faster.

The soil split around them like rotten fruit as aliens sprang up, tentacles protruding from their heads, whipping around to snatch at their small group.

Mason turned and took aim, but he only got off one shot before a tentacle grabbed him from behind and yanked him straight into a large, gaping mouth. It snapped shut before anyone could react, and he was gone.

"No," the tall scientist whispered, her hands over her mouth. Then louder. "No! Mason!" She started in that direction, but Caden shoved her back, not caring that she was an adult.

"He's gone! Keep running!" He pushed Nate next, trying to get the group moving again. "They can't get us past the wall."

Rebecca tripped as a tentacle reached for her leg. Nate stopped, crouching to help her, but it was already too late; another tentacle snagged her other foot and dragged her backwards, her hands leaving clawed divots in the soil. She barely had time to scream before it was over.

A tentacle lashed out toward Nate next, but Caden smacked it with both hands, and it recoiled. He shoved Nate forward, the two of them sprinting. Caden hoped the other scientists were there too, but he couldn't look for them, couldn't focus on more than just Nate in front of him and the line of stone up ahead.

Twenty feet away. Then ten. So close.

Another scream, followed by the awful crunching sounds of bones breaking. Caden barely flinched. Five feet.

"Here!" Aiden yelled. "Right here!"

There was the narrow gap in the wall, a dark space against all that pulsing light. Caden threw himself through it, then staggered to his feet, staring wildly at the other survivors. Besides him and Nate, only two of the five scientists had made it: the old man and the tall woman. The others . . .

"The ring," Aiden gasped. His skin seemed almost translucent, his eyes way too big and dark. They reminded Caden of Patrick's eyes. As if whatever looked out from them wasn't entirely human. "You were supposed to . . ." And then his eyes shut and he crumpled to the ground.

"Aiden?" Caden lurched toward him, fear gripping his heart. His brother didn't answer. "Aiden!"

KABOOM!

Caden looked up in time to see a blazing wall of fire tearing through the woods toward them. For a moment it seemed to pause at the wall. Then Caden felt the shield collapse, and a hot, invisible force slammed into him. The last thing he saw was the ground rushing at him.

53.
CADEN

Everything hurt. Caden blinked, and that was painful too, as if his eyelids were made of broken glass. All of him felt like that: fragile and shattered.

Someone groaned.

"Nate?" Caden croaked, his throat as raw as the rest of him.

"At least I know we're not dead," Nate rasped. "It would hurt less."

"Are you sure about that?"

A pause. "Good point," Nate conceded.

Caden pushed himself up to sitting and looked around. For a second, he wasn't really sure *what* he was looking at. He could see the stone wall, its surface as black as Patrick's eyes, and as glossy, as if all of the moss had been scraped clean and replaced by polish. And beyond it . . .

"It's gone," Nate breathed. "All of it."

The entire Watchful Woods had vanished. The trees, the aliens, the ground itself. Gone. In its place was a giant crater.

Caden staggered to his feet, still staring. "Gone," he repeated.

"Do you think . . . Rae—"

"She's fine," Caden said automatically, hoping it was true. If anyone could survive all that, it was Rae.

Nate nodded, but his expression was doubtful. "I'm going to go check on the other survivors."

"Wait, Nate?" Caden called.

Nate paused.

"Thank you. For coming with me, and everything. You're a lot braver than you think."

Nate managed a smile. "Tell that to Vivienne when you see her." His smile faltered. "Do you think—"

"She's fine too," Caden said, more firmly than he felt. "That bunker was built to last."

Nate nodded, then limped off.

"That is the biggest sinkhole I've ever seen," Aiden said.

Caden whipped around.

Aiden sat a few feet away, his chin resting on his knees. Deep shadows lined his eyes, and the corners of his mouth were pinched like an old man's, but he'd looked worse in the past.

"You're okay!" A strange light-headedness washed over Caden. It took him a moment to understand what it was: relief.

"I've been better. But I'll live." Aiden smiled. "And so will everyone else. Thanks to me, I might add."

"So you managed to hold the spell after all," Caden said.

"I did. No thanks to you."

Caden frowned. "What do you mean?"

"You didn't follow the plan, little brother. Remember the plan? The one I painstakingly outlined for you?"

"You mean the one where I was supposed to feed your pet demon a bunch of magical energy?" Caden said.

Aiden's eyes widened, and then he started chuckling. "You figured it out. I see you've grown less trusting. Good."

Caden felt his irritation rising. His brother was the reason he'd grown less trusting. Well, his brother, and Caden's own recent experiences with that same demon in the Other Place. "What exactly *is* your deal with the demon? You told me before that you banished it, but that's obviously not true." Caden waited, but his brother didn't say anything. Just watched him with an annoyingly amused expression on his face.

Caden decided to just ask the question already. "Do you still owe it a price? For the powers it granted you?"

Aiden sighed. "It's . . . complicated."

Caden made a show of sitting down and getting comfortable. He raised his eyebrows at his brother, waiting.

"Fine. The short answer is yes. I still owe it. But thanks to Vivienne's sealing stone, I don't have to pay up until I die, and by then I'm sure I'll have found something else it wants more than my soul. In the meantime, I control it and its power."

"So if I had dropped the ring into the vents—"

"It would have satisfied the demon's price, and my mortal soul would no longer be in jeopardy. But alas." Aiden shrugged. "Thanks a lot, little brother."

Caden refused to feel guilty. "Wouldn't it also have given the demon a lot of power?"

"Oh, to be sure. Possibly enough to break free of my control, even."

"And you didn't think *that* would be a problem?"

"Ah, but you see, *I* would have gotten a lot of power too. I could have handled the demon."

Caden opened his mouth, then shut it again and shook his head. It wasn't even worth arguing about. Aiden might have been changed by his experiences this past year, but in this, at least, he was the same as he'd always been, still sure he could handle anything. It was actually kind of reassuring; in an ever-shifting world, it was nice to have something remain constant. Especially since Caden himself had changed so much over the course of this last month.

He stared out at the sinkhole that had once been the Watchful Woods and felt a certain kinship with it. Before Rae showed up, he'd been lost in himself, consumed by loneliness and guilt over his brother. He didn't have any friends, and he'd convinced himself he didn't want any. The only thing he wanted was to get out of Whispering Pines as fast as possible, and away from the family business.

But now he realized he wanted to stay, to eventually take over Paranormal Price and protect the town of Whispering Pines from the supernatural.

Only, most of the danger had been from things spilling out of the Other Place, and now there *was* no Other Place. So where did that leave him? Where did that leave his whole family?

"You know," Aiden said, "things are going to be a lot different around here now that the spiritual vortex is gone."

It was as if his brother had read his mind. Caden twisted to look back at him. Aiden was watching him carefully, a calculating look to his eyes that Caden really didn't like. "Different how?"

"Well, there will still be the usual hauntings and visitations, the occasional minor spell gone awry. But that's about it. No alternate dimension. No aliens. No monsters. In short, it'll be boring. But there are other vortexes. Hotbeds of paranormal activity. We could take Paranormal Price on the road, go visit some of them." Aiden grinned. "See what trouble we can get into."

"I don't know, I could use a little bit of boring for a while."

"For a while. But eventually you'll get tired of it."

Caden wanted to argue. But he was afraid that his brother might be right.

Their mom had promised Caden that *he* was the successor to Paranormal Price, but he knew Aiden wanted it too. He thought of his brother's words from the other day. *I've realized that I don't want to do it alone. We'll be a team, you and me. We'll take over together.*

"I don't think I could do it," Caden said at last.

"Do what? Leave Whispering Pines?"

Caden shook his head. "I don't think I could work with you."

Aiden's eyes widened. "You don't mean that."

"I do." Despite everything, Caden knew he would always love his brother. But it was time for him to strike out on his own. To see who he was without the shadow of Aiden hanging over him.

"What if—" Aiden began, when running footsteps cut him off.

"Caden!" Ava sprinted toward him, her expression wild. "Where's Rae? You found her, right?"

"I . . ." Caden stopped, unsure of what to say. "I did," he finished at last. He should have known Ava would still be here by the wall, waiting for her sister, should have prepared for this moment.

"Okay," Ava said slowly. "Then where is she?"

Caden swallowed, suddenly wishing the sinkhole had taken him with it. He could tell her about her dad . . . but what if *he* hadn't survived? Would it be better or worse for Ava to know Rae had found him? He stared into Ava's wide, hopeful eyes.

I'm trusting you. Don't let me down.

So much for *that* promise. Caden took a deep breath. "She's, um—"

Bzzt! Bzzt! Bzzt!

Ava jumped, her hand flying to her pocket. "Oh!" She pulled out her cell phone, staring at it as if she'd never seen it before.

"Cell service must be back," Aiden said, watching them.

Ava shot him a dark look.

"Aren't you going to answer it?" he asked.

"Who is it?" Caden asked.

"It's the hospital," Ava said. She chewed her bottom lip, then answered it. "Hello?" A pause, then, "Yes, this is Ava Carter."

The voice on the other end was too quiet for Caden to make out the words, but Ava's face went white. "I see," she breathed.

Immediately Caden thought of Blake, and his stomach sank. It just seemed so unfair for him to have survived a giant centipede attack, a race through an alien-infested forest, and an Unseeing, only to die now.

Ava hung up the phone, her eyes wide and unfocused.

"What is it?" Caden asked. "Is it Blake? Is he . . ." He couldn't bring himself to finish that question, but Ava was already shaking her head.

"It's not Blake." She looked up at him. "It's Rae."

54.
RAE

Rae woke slowly, her mind groggy, her entire body aching. It felt like she was lying on a cement block.

"Where am I?" she tried to ask, but her words came out a jumbled mess, like she was speaking through a mouthful of cotton balls.

Then the memory of what happened hit her—Patrick, the pod, the feeling of breathing in liquid—and she sat up, her eyes flying open. Even though everything hurt, the pain seemed a minor inconvenience to the possibility of waking up in a distant future on some unknown planet.

Machines beeped and squawked and hummed around her, and there were wires in her arms and tubes up her nose. Panicking, Rae tore the tubes out and ripped the wires from her arm, frantic to get away.

"Easy, easy," someone cried out, grabbing at her arms, holding her down. She fought harder, thrashing wildly.

"Rae, seriously, knock it off!" another voice snapped.

Rae stopped struggling, the familiarity of that voice cutting through her terror. She blinked, her vision blurry, but slowly the shape beside her sharpened into Alyssa, her face pinched and anxious. And next to her stood Caden.

Behind them, the rest of the details of the room came into focus. The white walls and ceiling, the guardrail beside her, the electric lighting above. She was in a hospital room. She recognized the sharp, antiseptic smell of the place.

A *hospital*.

Relief coursed through her, and she sagged back against the pillows.

"How are you feeling?" Caden asked.

"Never better," she croaked.

He grinned. "So, terrible, huh?"

"Pretty much." She managed her own weak smile back. "How am I here?" The last thing she remembered seeing was Patrick's face through the glass as the liquid bubbled up around her. *I am sorry, Ms. Carter. But it was always going to come to this.* She'd thought that might be the last thing she saw *ever*.

"How are *you* here?" she added, frowning at Alyssa. She'd been in a pod too.

"No one knows," Alyssa said. "The orderly on duty said he didn't see what happened. Just that he looked up, and there we all were, laid out unconscious on the floor of the ER."

"Just you and me?"

"Everyone from the pods." Alyssa grinned. "My mom is *so* angry. If Patrick ever shows his face again . . . well, let's just say he'd be getting a lot worse than a detention."

"Yeah, your mom is extra scary right now," Caden said.

Alyssa looked a little proud.

"And . . ." Rae was almost afraid to ask, but she had to know. "My dad?"

"He's just fine," Alyssa said. "He woke up when I did and has been pacing nonstop since then. Everyone else in the pods is out and awake, in fact. Only you didn't regain consciousness."

"Why?"

Alyssa shrugged and tossed her ponytail back. "I guess you had other drugs in your system?"

Rae rubbed her neck, thinking of the needle Patrick had stabbed her with. She'd felt so betrayed by him in that moment. And now . . . now she didn't know what to think. He must have released all of the humans before leaving.

Why? Why had he done that?

She remembered again that moment in the bunker when he'd claimed to regret Doctor Nguyen's death. He'd seemed almost human there. Perhaps all that time he'd spent among people, pretending to be one of them, had rubbed off on him.

Alyssa glanced from Rae to Caden and back again, then straightened. "Well. I guess I'd better go let everyone know you're awake." She gave Caden one last very meaningful look, then left the two of them alone.

"What was that about?" Rae asked.

"Oh, um, nothing, really." Caden coughed. "She apologized to me, did you know that? And here I thought today couldn't get any weirder."

Rae smiled. "I'm glad." She waited, but Caden had gone strangely silent. "Was there anything else?" She wanted to go find her dad, to see with her own eyes that he was okay.

Caden looked away, his ears going pink. "Uh, yeah," he started. "Look, Rae . . . I thought I lost you, and . . ." He rubbed the back of his neck, still not looking at her. "I just, I never told you how I felt . . ." He trailed off again.

Rae could feel her own face flushing. *Please no,* she thought. She wasn't ready for whatever this was. Maybe someday she would be. Weeks, or months, or possibly years from now, after her dad had settled back in with her family and her life had become quiet and predictable again. But not now. "You didn't lose me," she managed. "I'm still here. I'm not going anywhere."

Finally his eyes met hers. Those familiar eyes, warm and brown and full of an emotion so strong it scared her more than any monster. "I really like you, Rae."

Rae hesitated, then took his hand, folding her fingers around his. "I really like you, too," she began.

"But . . . not the same way," Caden finished for her. He sounded resigned but not surprised.

Rae shook her head. "I'm sorry. You're one of my best friends, and I can't imagine my life without you in it. But right now I need to focus on my dad. I found him again, but I don't know him anymore. He doesn't know me, either." She swallowed hard. "I'm not ready for any other kind of relationship yet."

Caden nodded. "I understand."

"Are we still good?"

He smiled and squeezed her fingers. "We are."

"Friends?"

"Hopefully always."

Someone coughed at the entrance, and they both glanced up to see her dad waiting there, obviously listening in. Rae could feel her face burning hotter than ever as she hastily drew her hand back from Caden's.

"I'll see you in a bit," Caden whispered, standing abruptly.

"Caden?" Rae called out to him before he could leave the room.

He paused.

"Thank you." It seemed so inadequate. "For helping me, for believing in me, for . . . well. For everything." Because it was true; she couldn't imagine a life without Caden in it. Not anymore.

"Anytime," he said, and slipped away.

Rae's dad watched him leave. "He seems like a good kid. A bit strange, but good."

"Everybody here is a bit strange," Rae laughed. "I think it's why I've gotten along with them so well."

"You're not strange, sugar cube."

Rae just gave him a flat stare.

"Okay, *I* don't think you're strange," he amended, and sat down on a chair next to her bed.

"Thanks, Dad. Glad my own father doesn't think I'm strange."

He grinned and brushed a strand of hair from her face, then grew serious. "Rae, I wanted to apologize for how I acted on the ship. You were very brave, and I am proud of you."

Tears stung Rae's eyes, and she blinked rapidly to clear them. She hadn't realized how much she'd needed to hear those words from her dad again.

He cleared his throat. "And I know that we've all changed a lot in this past year, but I'm looking forward to getting to know the young woman that you have grown into."

Rae smiled at him. "Thank you, Dad." She sniffed. "I'm just glad to have you back."

He hugged her, and while it was more tentative than the all-encompassing, protective hugs she remembered, she still wouldn't have traded it for anything. And she knew she was looking forward to getting to know this new version of her dad as well.

The door to her hospital room opened, and Ava poked her head in. "You're awake!" She turned and yelled, "Mom! Come quick!"

Rae's mom came running into the room, her hair flying, face flushed, nurse's scrubs askew. She froze at the sight of Rae and her dad, and it was as if all of time itself stood still.

This was the moment Rae had been dreaming of all year. When she finally found her dad again, and they would all be together. A family, just the way they'd been before.

But as Ava and her mother rushed forward to throw their arms around her and her dad, Rae realized that it wasn't exactly the way she'd pictured it. Something was different. *They* were different.

"You're smothering me," Rae laughed, and finally, reluctantly, her parents and her sister let her go.

"I still can't believe you found him," her mom said, her fingers clutching her dad's hand so tightly it had to be painful.

"I told you I would."

"I never doubted you," Ava said.

Rae grinned at her sister. "I know. And I couldn't have done it without you."

And then they were all hugging again, and this time Rae didn't complain. Instead, she closed her eyes and tried to soak in this moment, to let it replace the one from her fantasies. And she understood now that they could never go back to how it had been before; all of them had changed too much. All they could do was move forward and embrace their new reality. Together.

55.
CADEN

Caden found his brother waiting for him down the hall.

"What are you doing here?" he asked.

"Waiting for you. Why is your face so red?"

"It's not." Caden looked away, glad his brother didn't have the same gifts for reading emotions as he did.

"Even your ears are red." Aiden peered closer at him. "Hmm," he said, his lips twitching into a knowing smile.

"Hmm, what?"

"You talked to Rae, didn't you? Professed your undying love?"

Caden could feel his face—and his ears, dang it—growing even hotter.

"You did!" Aiden crowed. "And how did that go for you?"

Caden shrugged. "It went."

"Oh." Aiden's amusement slid away. "That bad, huh?"

"It was okay. Kind of the way I expected." Caden had known the moment he opened his mouth that Rae didn't feel the same way he did. Despite his current lack of powers, it was obvious, her discomfort stamped all over her face. Still, he was glad he'd said something. And maybe someday her feelings for him would change. If not, well, she was still the best friend he'd ever had. He could be content with that. "Why are you waiting for me?"

"I need your help."

Caden froze.

Aiden laughed. "Don't make that face, little brother. It's not for me. It's for Audrey Matsuoka. She asked if I'd do something for her."

"When? Just now?" Caden asked excitedly. "Is she okay? Is Vivienne? Are they . . . is the bunker—"

"Slow down there." Aiden held up his hands. "I don't have all the details, but yes, she's okay. Or she seemed okay enough when I spoke with her. Before you ask, no, you can't see her now. She's in surgery. And Vivienne is . . . well." He paused. "Alive," he said at last.

Alive.

There was a lot of potential meaning in that word. Caden swallowed, not sure if he wanted to ask any follow-up questions. He remembered Vivienne as she'd been in the bunker, all gleaming black eyes and sharp flashing teeth. And then he thought of the girl he'd known. The one who had been with him in the Other Place, and a wave of sorrow washed over him.

Aiden watched him, expressionless. "She'll be okay too," he said quietly. "She won't be the same person, but she's like you. Strong, in here." He tapped Caden on the chest, right above the heart.

Caden blinked, surprised. His brother had never believed in the importance of emotional strength before. He must have changed more than Caden had thought.

"As for the bunker," Aiden continued, "it's still standing. More or less. And so is at least one of the tunnels leading from it to the surface."

"That's surprising," Caden said, thinking of the sinkhole, and how complete it had looked from above. It made him wonder what else might have survived, deep below ground . . .

"Since I do owe Mrs. Matsuoka a favor, I agreed to help her. But I'll need you."

Caden nodded, even though the words "favor" and "help" coming from Aiden made him extremely nervous. "I don't have any magic right now," he warned.

"That's okay. I just need you to act as my focus. The power can come from me."

That made Caden even more nervous, but he followed his brother down the hall and out of the hospital anyhow.

Caden sagged back against the wall, feeling more exhausted than he'd thought possible. Still, they'd done it. He and Aiden, working together, had managed to call back the souls of the seven remaining Unseeing victims.

He stared down the row of their unconscious bodies, splayed out across the cellar floor, each of them on their backs with their palms up. It would be hours before they woke from their magically induced slumber. By then they'd have been transported to the hospital where they could get the physical care they needed. They would never be able to see, and Caden knew there would be other changes. But at least they were no longer caught in that in-between space. They could be reunited with their families. And they'd have a chance at a normal enough life.

Caden turned away from them to look at his brother. Aiden leaned against the wall next to him, looking almost as tired as Caden felt.

"What?" Aiden asked, not bothering to open his eyes.

"Nothing."

"I can feel you staring at me. Just say it already."

"It's just . . . you helped them."

"Yes, so?" Aiden cracked open an eye. "I can help people some-times."

"You can, but you don't. Not usually. Not unless there's some-thing in it for you."

Aiden opened the other eye and stared back at Caden. "Maybe I've changed."

Caden wanted to believe it. But . . . . "Or?" he asked.

And Aiden grinned, an expression so Aiden it was impossible not to appreciate it. "Or maybe I wanted you to see how well we work together on things like this. You and me, Caden. You might not want to admit it, but we do make a great team."

And for the first time, Caden found himself picturing what it would be like to run Paranormal Price with Aiden, cleaning up supernatural messes and saving lives together. Maybe they really could make it work . . .

"Caden?" their mom called. "Aiden? Are you both down here—oh!" She stopped halfway down the stairs, her eyes widening as she took in the row of sleeping kids. "You did it."

"They did what?" their dad asked, walking down behind her. Then he stared too. "By golly," he whispered. The two of them exchanged a look heavy with meaning.

Caden's mouth went dry as they turned that look on him. "W-what?"

His mom walked down the remaining stairs, her steps slow. Caden noticed that her hair was more white than black now, and as she got closer, the harsh bulb overhead cast her features into sharp, unflattering relief.

It was as if she'd aged twenty years in a day.

His dad wasn't much better, his hair sticking up in patches, the wrinkles lining his eyes and mouth forming deep, dark crevices.

Blinking back sudden tears, Caden rushed forward to hug them. His dad first—the one who had always been there for him. A never-ending source of comfort and stability. And then his mom. The person he'd always looked up to, always wanted to please most.

"We're okay, Caden. We're okay," she murmured into his hair, releasing him. She took a step back, reaching into one of the wide pockets of her skirt and pulling out a very familiar, very battered leather-bound book.

Her Book of Shadows.

Immediately Aiden went still, his breath catching. Caden glanced at him, then back at his mom.

She looked between the two of them for a long moment. "It's time," she said simply, holding the book out.

To Caden.

He stared at it, frozen in shock. She'd claimed he was her choice, her heir to the family business, and, more importantly, to its secrets. But still, part of him had never believed it, had always assumed when the time came, she'd pick Aiden.

"Take it," she said. "It's yours now."

Caden could feel his brother's eyes on him as he reached forward and took the book, remembering the first time he'd touched it. How it had fought him. Now, it felt welcome in his hands, as if it belonged to him.

Because it did.

"I . . . I don't know what to say," he managed, looking up into her dark eyes. They were full of a quiet pride he'd never seen directed at him before, and he saw the same look reflected in his dad's wide smile. He turned.

Aiden was not smiling. But he also didn't look surprised. He reminded Caden of himself, after Rae had asked to remain just friends. Like he'd known this was coming all along, and he might not like it, but at least he understood it.

"Nothing has to change yet," his dad said quickly. "After all, you're still in middle school. Your mom and I will still run the business."

"You'll just be taking a larger part in it," his mom added. "When you're ready."

And as Caden looked down at the Book of Shadows—his Book

of Shadows—he knew it wasn't true. This changed everything. He smiled up at his parents. "I'm ready."

Aiden cleared his throat.

Caden laughed. "We'll see, older brother. Keep proving to me that you've changed, and maybe."

Aiden grinned triumphantly.

"I haven't promised anything," Caden said quickly.

"Maybe not yet," Aiden said, sounding confident that, once again, he'd get his way.

"Let's go back upstairs," their mom said. "I want to make sure an ambulance is on the way for your friends here. Plus, we still have a lot of work to do before Doctor Anderson comes home."

Caden spared one last look at the seven figures lying on the cellar floor of Doctor Anderson's house. The place where it all began . . . and now where it ended. Then he turned and followed his family up the stairs, ready for the next chapter and whatever else it might bring.

EPILOGUE

{ ONE MONTH LATER . . . }

A re you sure you're ready for this?" Vivienne's mom asked her.

Vivienne nodded, even though she wasn't sure. Not by a long shot.

"I'll be back to pick you up at nine. But you can always call me if you want to leave earlier, okay? There's no shame in—"

"It's fine, Mom. Really," Vivienne said, cutting her off. She made herself smile, wanting to reassure her.

The baring of teeth. Always a reassuring sight.

Quiet, you, Vivienne told the voice whispering in the back of her mind. Still, she was a little proud of it; she'd recently explained the concept of sarcasm, and it was really starting to get it.

"Okay. If you're sure." Her mom reached out, resting a hand against Vivienne's cheek, her palm cool. She did that a lot lately, touching her as if to make sure she were really there. "You have your inhaler?"

Vivienne laughed. "Yes, Mom. Always." She opened her car door and slid out. "I'll call you if there are any problems. I promise. Otherwise, see you in a few hours." She started to shut the door, then stopped. "Mom?"

"Yes?"

"Thank you for letting me do this."

Her mom nodded. This was the first time she'd agreed to let Vivienne out of her sight since the moment she'd been released from the hospital.

"I love you," Vivienne said.

"I love you, too," her mom said. She managed a smile. Small and shaky, but there. "Have fun."

"I will!" Vivienne closed the door and walked the remaining few feet to Caden's house. Squaring her shoulders, she knocked.

Caden opened the door. "You made it!"

"I made it." Vivienne grinned at him. "You thought I was going to bail, didn't you?"

"Of course not," he said. "Nate did, though."

"Hey!" Nate called from somewhere behind him. "I did not. I told everyone there was at least a seventy-percent chance that you would come."

"Wow, you gave me a thirty-percent chance of skipping out?" Vivienne walked inside, pausing to kick her shoes off by the door. "Thanks for that vote of confidence."

"Just being realistic." Nate pushed his glasses up higher on his nose, looking her over, his eyes lingering on hers. "You look . . . like you."

The last time she'd seen him, her eyes had been all alien-black and scary. "Try not to sound so disappointed," she said.

Nate laughed. "I'll get over it. Come on in. Pizza's already here. I waited to eat mine so you'd have a chance to mock me as usual."

"Oh, good." Vivienne glanced at Caden, who was watching her carefully.

"You're really okay?" he asked quietly as he followed her into the living room.

She touched the pendant he'd given her and nodded. "I think I really am."

"Vivi!" Rae yelled.

"Rae-Rae!" Vivienne yelled back. She braced herself as Rae charged her, wrapping her in a hug. Alyssa was close behind, throwing her arms around her too, and something inside Vivienne relaxed; she'd been worried all her friends would secretly be a little afraid of her, but they acted as if she were normal. As if she belonged.

"We missed you," Alyssa said, letting her go. She and Rae stepped back, and suddenly Vivienne was face to face with Becka, holding a can of soda and looking less than pleased.

"Um," Vivienne began, shifting awkwardly. "I'm sorry I tried to drink your blood."

Becka shrugged. "I can't say it was my favorite moment."

"Are you okay?"

Becka nodded. "I'm fine. Except for this." She touched the side of her neck, and the slightly raised ridge of a scar.

Vivienne winced. "I really am sorry."

"I know." Becka dropped her hand. "Honestly, it's a great conversation starter. I tell people I survived a vampire attack, and they're all very impressed."

A vampire? The voice in Vivienne's head sounded offended. *I am an advanced race, nothing like one of those abominations.*

Wait, are they real? Vivienne thought back at it.

No answer.

Are they?

This is one of those facts I'm supposed to keep to myself.

"Vivienne?" Becka asked.

Vivienne blinked, tearing her mind away from the idea of actual, real vampires. "Sorry. Lost in guilt-ridden thoughts."

Becka put a hand on her shoulder. "I forgive you. This time." She squeezed a little harder than was friendly before letting her go. Vivienne didn't complain; she understood. It was fairer than she deserved.

Vivienne accepted a can of soda from Matt, then nodded at Blake sitting on the sofa next to Alyssa. He looked like he'd recovered, although his eyes were still a little haunted. Vivienne doubted he'd ever lose that look.

"A toast!" Nate announced abruptly. "Not only is this a welcome-back-to-humanity party for Vivienne, but it's also a true celebration of survival. This time with no ulterior motives." He shot Rae a sharp look.

Rae bit her lip and glanced away.

"Rae-Rae?" Vivienne asked, suddenly intrigued. "Is there another reason you wanted everyone to gather tonight?"

"Oh no," Nate muttered. "I should have known."

"It's just . . . I can't help noticing that no one has found the spaceship yet," Rae said slowly.

"Because it left our planet," Matt said, a touch too quickly.

Rae shook her head. "My dad doesn't think so." Her dad was working on starting up a new energy company in Whispering Pines. One that—according to Rae—would be purely for the good.

Vivienne used to believe that companies could be purely for the good. But after her recent experiences, she'd come to realize that even the ones that began with the best of intentions could inevitably change as they got larger, eventually becoming more about their own success and survival than about their cause. It was why her mom had refused to join Mr. Carter when he'd offered her a position.

"What are you suggesting?" Caden asked.

"I think Patrick is still around here somewhere."

They all looked at one another, an uneasy silence building in the room.

"You know what I think?" Vivienne asked abruptly. Everyone turned toward her. "I think you, Rae-Rae, have been a girl on a quest for too long. You were looking for your dad all year. Now you've found him. And while I know you're happy about it, you can't help feeling like something is missing. Right?"

Rae frowned. "That's not it."

"Are you sure? You're not just looking for some other quest to fill that hole?"

Rae started to shake her head, then stopped. "Well, maybe that's a little true."

Vivienne laughed. "That's you. Always on a mission to save someone."

Rae smiled a little at that.

"I'm sure there will be plenty of opportunities for future quests," Vivienne continued. "This is still Whispering Pines, after all. But for tonight, I think we should all celebrate something even more surprising than the fact that we survived the world's worst internship and saved everyone from extinction."

"Oh, yeah?" Becka said. "And what's that?"

Vivienne grinned. "Caden Price, *the* Caden Price, is throwing a party."

"I guess that *is* pretty surprising," Alyssa said.

"Hey!" Caden objected.

"I mean, can you imagine if I told you a few months ago that we'd all be partying at the Price house?" Vivienne shook her head.

"Things do change," Caden said. "Even here."

"Yes, they do," Vivienne said quietly.

"I'll toast to that," Nate said quickly, raising his can again. "To Caden Price, thrower of parties!"

"To Caden!" everyone cheered.

Vivienne glanced at Rae, who had been a catalyst for that change, and then at Caden, who looked embarrassed but happy as people continued cheering and clapping him on the back. Her gaze swept over Alyssa, her oldest friend, and then lingered on the others in the room. All people she cared for deeply. They'd gone through something together, and none of them would be the same again.

But they would get to move on with their lives, the events of the past few months fading until one day it all felt like a dream. That was why she wanted to distract them now. To turn them away from Rae's line of questioning.

And you? the voice in her mind whispered.

Vivienne drifted toward the window. Outside the stars gleamed, calling to her. She had made her peace with the alien inside her, the two of them sharing this one body. Thanks to the newly devised "inhaler" she'd been given—full of a diluted mixture of the same drugs Doctor Nguyen had crafted for her special EpiPen—Vivienne was able to keep the alien consciousness suppressed. But it wasn't gone. It would never be gone.

It was now as much a part of her as her lungs or her heart. A little voice in the back of her mind. Strange, often disturbing impulses. Occasional flashes of deep, uncontrollable hunger. Those all belonged to her now too.

She watched as one of the stars seemed to burn a little brighter than the others. If she squinted, she could tell it was moving swiftly across the sky. Not a star at all. She grinned and raised her can in its direction in her own private toast.

Watch out, Patrick, Vivienne thought. *Because someday I'll find you again.*

Oh, he's counting on it, the whisper in her mind crooned.

Vivienne took a sip of her soda, letting the too-sweet taste fill her mouth and wash away the apprehension those words caused.

She glanced behind her at the others. Rae caught her eye and smiled, and Vivienne felt a burst of warmth in her chest. And she knew, no matter what she tried, Rae would still be there with her anyhow. Ready for that next adventure.

Vivienne might not know what the future held for her. But at least, whatever it was, it wouldn't be boring. And she wouldn't be facing it alone.

Acknowledgments

Thank you to all our readers for staying with Rae and Caden until the end. We appreciate you more than you can know.

Thank you as well to our editor Sarah McCabe. You are a plot wizard, and we're grateful we got to have your magic on our side once again.

We appreciate each and every person who helped make this story into a book, including Justin Chanda, Karen Wojtyla, Anne Zafian, Eugene Lee, Elizabeth Blake-Lin, Tiara Iandioro, Caitlin Sweeny, Alissa Nigro, Lisa Quach, Perla Gil, Remi Moon, Ashley Mitchell, Yasleen Trinidad, Saleena Nival, Kate Bouchard, Nadia Almahdi, Lisa Moraleda, Nicole Russo, Christina Pecorale and her sales team, and Michelle Leo and her education/library team.

Xavier Collette, thank you for another beautifully creepy cover.

We wouldn't be here without the hard work of our agent, Jennifer Azantian, who has championed us from the beginning, and the rest of her team, including Ben Baxter. We're so glad we have a place in ALA.

Thank you to Tara Creel, who was once again willing to wade through the opening of our messy first draft and help us find our way to the right ending. Also, to the rest of Kidliterati: Suzi Guina, Katie Nelson, Jennifer Camiccia, Kaitlin Hundscheid, Liz Edelbrock, Taylor Gardner, and Alexandra Alessandri for all your brainstorming help and enthusiastic support, on this and every other project.

Both of us got to experience the joys of juggling writing deadlines and new babies, so first, welcome to the world Eoin and Juniper. And second, thank you to everyone who helped make that juggle possible, including older sisters Evelyn and Ember, our husbands Sean Lang and Nick Chen, our aunt/neighbor Kitty English, and our in-laws and parents Lyn and Bruce Lang, and Rose and Rich Bartkowski. Thank you as well to the rest of our families, including our siblings Rosi and Ed Reed, and Jesse and Ashley Lang.

And finally, thank you to *The X-Files* for scaring the daylights out of us when we were kids and thus inspiring this whole series.